Forgotten Dreams

Doris Leadbetter

Other titles published by transita

Elissa's Castle by Juliet Greenwood
Scuba Dancing by Nicola Slade
The Waiting Time by Sara Banerji
Turning Point by Bowering Sivers
Uphill All the Way by Sue Moorcroft

transita

Transita books reflect the lives of mature women.
Contemporary women with rich and interesting stories to
tell, stories that explore the truths and desires that colour
their lives.

To find out more about transita, our books and our authors
visit **www.transita.co.uk**

Forgotten Dreams

Doris Leadbetter

transita

Published by Transita
3 Newtec Place, Magdalen Road,
Oxford OX4 1RE. United Kingdom.
Tel: (01865) 204393. Fax: (01865) 248780.
email: info@transita.co.uk
http://www.transita.co.uk

British Library Cataloguing in Publication Data
A catalogue record for this book is available from the British Library

Cover design by Baseline Arts Ltd, Oxford
Produced for Transita by Deer Park Productions, Tavistock
Typeset by PDQ Typesetting, Newcastle-under-Lyme
Printed and bound by Bookmarque, Croydon

ABOUT THE AUTHOR

Doris Leadbetter was born and raised in Bradford, Yorkshire. She was a member of the Bradford Theatre School and worked both as a director and backstage. While there she wrote children's plays, several of which were performed on BBC TV and ITV.

She moved to Australia with her mother and two children in 1963 and married her second husband, Richard, in 1969. She worked for 12 years for the CSIRO (Commonwealth Scientific and Industrial Research Organisation), in Western Australia. During this time she visited the Simpson Desert, fell in love with its landscape and formed the initial idea for *Forgotten Dreams*. Doris retired from the CSIRO in 1985 and she and Richard moved to Bendigo. She began writing again and published a number of books, including educational materials, poetry and a weekly newspaper column.

In 1994 she moved to the outskirts of Melbourne where for ten years she taught Professional Writing and Editing courses in a number of academic institutions. She completed two books of poetry, three novels and was commencing work on another when she was diagnosed with secondary bone cancer in July 2004. Doris died on 27 November 2004, aged 76.

Doris was a life long sceptic, rationalist and constant seeker after the truth, and a woman very like Helen in

Forgotten Dreams. Doris will long be remembered for her writing and for the many students she encouraged and inspired to become better writers.

For more information about Doris and her work visit www.transita.co.uk

DEDICATION

For Richard, Vicki and Dominic who made her long life
worth living.
28-12-27 – 27-11-04

PROLOGUE

For a young man, this new land – this ancient land – is mysterious, exciting and perhaps dangerous.

John Craven thinks about the possibilities as he lies in the narrow bed. He thinks, too, about home. He comes from an old family, set in its ways and trusting to them. Nothing much has changed in Yorkshire since the first Craven ran away from a marauding Anglo-Saxon band and lived long enough to buy the land around the place where the battle had been fought. Well, that is what the family tradition says. The Cravens are wealthy – 'comfortable', as his father prefers to say – and their only son has been free to follow his dreams.

'Craven by name, but not cowardly'. Not much of a family motto, but it serves well enough. John, like most of his ancestors, is a stalwart, stubborn man.

Now John is here, at last. In the country he has longed to see, preparing for the adventures he dreamed of as a child.

This is Italy. This is Rome. This is the Year of Our Lord 1540 and the Catholic Church is John's safe harbour as he waits for his pilgrimage to begin.

The sounds of the street rouse John. In truth, he has been awake for an hour or more taking in the unfamiliar smells and sounds, the strangely heavy, wine-drowsy air of the city.

Two men go past the house, one shouting at the other that he has been cheated by a merchant who bought good oil and sold it disguised as better oil. John's knowledge of Italian is adequate to understanding the story, and the man's anger, but the calm explanation by the other man is too subtle for John. He likes his stories to be straightforward, to the point, like John himself.

He gets out of bed, pulls on his robe, washes his hands and face in the rough terracotta basin on the table by the window. With a deliberate gesture, he welcomes the day by flinging open the heavy wooden shutter across the window. The sun is rising fast in the East, and the two men's argument blows away in a dusty spiral as they walk slowly towards the far end of the Piazza.

Their gestures – argument – conciliation – acceptance of defeat – entertain John as he watches. Englishmen are too reluctant to show their feelings, he thinks. The Pilgrim is often exasperated with John when a simple nod is the only response to a deliberately provocative request. John smiles as he remembers the last time a nod led to three days of hard physical work in the hospice.

Now that the two men have gone, the street is empty. The bright colours which will flood it with excitement and brilliance are subdued now. As though, John thinks, there is a greyness over the city at this hour, as though it is the time for quietness, for sombre thoughts, for fears rather than hopes.

Fears. John wonders whether he should feel any fear for his future. The Pilgrim does not discuss his plans for John but there is a certainty that something is being planned for him, as for the others in the Company.

What would John like to do with his life? What a question! Travel, of course. Teach, of course. Learn – oh yes, he would like that. John has already learned so much – to speak languages other than his mother tongue, to understand people so different from himself, to be a man apart from others and yet one of them too.

Maybe today he will find out how he is to spend his life.

Maybe today.

CHAPTER 1

HELEN BECAME AWARE OF THE MOVEMENT, a sinuous undulation on the periphery of her vision as she turned her head to read the right-hand page of the book.

She knew she must not move. She tried to slow her breathing as her body struggled to pump adrenalin to muscles already tightening ready for flight.

She must not move.

The snake paused, swayed its head from side to side as its tongue tested the air: as if it knew there was a difference here. Helen wondered if it could smell her skin or her fear.

She sat still, her eyes on the snake's head. Was a snake like a dog and did not like eye contact? Should she look away? Could she look away? She was wearing Blundstone boots but she wished that her socks were longer. The skin of her ankle was vulnerable and so close to where the snake lay almost as still as she was.

To calm herself, Helen tried to be scientific about it; to watch this close contact with another species. To admire its glossy skin, its length. *God! The creature must be nearly two metres long!* The trail it had made in the red sandy soil looked like the track of a finger drawn through spilt sugar.

Helen thought calm thoughts. She tried to be still. A nerve twitched in her face and she wondered if the snake could hear it, see it, sense it.

It was still very cool and at this early hour cold-blooded animals are lethargic. Until the heat of the sun gave it energy, the snake would probably do no more than move slowly around, sensing what was new or different in its familiar territory.

It seemed to have finished checking Helen out; with a slow swirl in the sand it turned away and glided through the red sugar to another rock, several metres away. Helen watched it go behind the rock and stayed perfectly still until she saw it emerge from the other side and continue its journey down the slight slope of the scree. When she could see it no more, she breathed deeply, and stretched out one leg at a time until her muscles relaxed and she could stand up.

This was her territory too and Helen should not have been taken by surprise by the snake. She had been coming to the north west of Western Australia for several years and was used to animals coming close. She always enjoyed the curiosity of kangaroos and wallabies, the ponderous emus, and birds so brilliant that they sometimes glittered like jewels on the naked branches of parched gum trees. Helen loved everything this isolated corner of the world could offer – and still she could forget to be wary of snakes. Especially King Brown snakes – the deadliest in Australia.

She picked up the book and went – very cautiously – down the scree and into the tent. She checked it carefully; no snakes, thank Heaven.

Somehow the book had lost its appeal. A thriller – a murder story – which had been her bedtime and early morning reading for a couple of weeks. Now its excitement had palled. *You can't beat an encounter with a snake for excitement.* She put the book away in the metal-cornered wooden box where Jack had packed their chess set, a few other books and her working papers.

If she wasn't going to read, maybe she should write to someone – it wouldn't be put in the post for a while but it would be welcome when it arrived. She would let Teresa know that everything was going well, even if they hadn't found the cave. Helen fished a postcard out of the box and sat on the camp bed to write. The postcard was a photograph of Montana; she looked at it for a moment, remembering when she had spent a sabbatical there. Her mind drifted back to Teresa and the last time they had been together.

The planned farewell party had been low-key, at Helen's insistence and much against Teresa Vandenburg's exuberant suggestions.

It came at the end of a year that Helen enjoyed but, since making up her mind to retire, the time seemed to pass slowly. She was asked to reconsider her decision to leave the job. However, now there was a reason to leave so compelling that she could no longer ignore it.

She was still young enough at sixty-two, and fit enough, for a few more trips to the desert. The Western Australian climate was hot and very hard on people. Temperatures could be below freezing in winter and over fifty degrees Centigrade in summer. In the north, far away from the State's few cities and country towns, people never bothered to talk about drought. What was there to say? It was almost always bone dry. There was an occasional flurry of rain; every few years, there might be enough to say it was raining.

Helen was accustomed to the outback's excesses, and so was her husband, Jack. Sometimes they combined her professional interests with trips to less demanding places, but most of their holidays were spent on the inhospitable fringe of the desert.

Now was the time to prove that her guess was right. Guess? How she resisted that word – 'informed guess' was the closest she allowed.

After ten years at the Fremantle laboratory of the Commonwealth Scientific and Industrial Research Organisation, her job provided a fascinating conclusion to her career.

The advent of remote sensing using satellite imagery added a dimension beyond her earlier research experience. She left a comfortable university teaching post for CSIRO when she was promised access to the latest equipment and the time to follow her own 'line of inquiry'.

For the last couple of years one small discovery – if it was a discovery – had grown into a powerful belief, an irresistible urge.

Perhaps her boss, Rod Ackroyd, the Chief of the Division of Land and Soil Investigations, smiled a little when she talked of finding an ancient water course in the heart of the desert, but the idea was intriguing and not totally beyond possibility. So Helen was given the job with the mapping team and enjoyed it until she was almost sixty-three.

For Helen's last day at Fremantle, Teresa organized a low-key, minimalistic, almost invisible, farewell lunch (the adjectives were Teresa's litany of disappointment) and the Chief had invited Jack to join them.

They ate in the canteen. People drifted in to sit four at a table, with cold roast chicken, ham and salad provided by the canteen manager. The centre piece was a huge fruit salad barely contained in the hollowed halves of a watermelon. The fruit salad was the gift – and the creation – of Teresa, who loved Helen dearly. Teresa was American and somewhat self-indulgent when it came to people and fruit salad.

Helen became aware during the last couple of weeks that there was real affection in the relationships she enjoyed at the research centre. She was surprised to find herself reluctant to close down her end of the laboratory, to say goodbye to the two scientists who shared the space.

At the farewell lunch, Charlie Lennard made a graceful speech, teasing her as he often had for poaching on his end of the lab, which he now intended to take back. Rob Woods made virtually the same comments.

Collusion, the Chief called it. 'A rare case of genuine collaboration,' he said in his speech.

Then it was Teresa's turn to say something.

'I am so happy that you all came to say goodbye to Helen. I can't say that I understand exactly what she does in the lab... '

'It's called "work", Teresa,' the Chief said.

'Yeah, well. What I do understand is that Helen is – well, great. She explains Australia to foreigners like me really well. I mean, up there is just like Arizona, she says. But different, right? She was telling me yesterday that everything up there has changed, that once there may have been a sort of Garden of Eden – '

Helen squirmed as most of the people in the canteen looked at her with amusement.

'Garden of *Where*?' A colleague said as he offered to fill Helen's glass, an offer which she refused.

'Anyway, I think her ideas about what the deserts of Australia might have been like are poetic, exciting and – very interesting. Yes.'

When Helen stood to say her farewells, she allowed herself a little sentiment, thanks to Teresa's coaching. Helen had meant simply to thank the Chief and her colleagues for their support, say how much she had enjoyed her time with CSIRO,

5

and that now she intended to work even harder in her retirement. Brief, grateful, amusing. Just the ticket.

As she looked around the friendly people she had known little about, so preoccupied had she been with her work, she felt a need to express some of these thoughts. Teresa had offered to write something for her, but Helen had her own ideas and was glad she had turned down the offer.

'I don't know about a Garden of Eden, Teresa. I think I was a bit carried away there.' She smiled at Teresa, who was eating another bowl of fruit salad.

'The geography has changed, of course; and I do think there might have been more water around within the last few hundred years – more recently than has been believed. I hope to find out about that in the next few weeks.' Helen took a sip of wine, glanced at Jack, who nodded.

'I have a very supportive husband – thank you Jack – who has been the stronger partner in my life. I tend to be very single-minded. What I want I usually try to get without fuss. Jack understands that and organises me accordingly. It's the same here at work. I do my job and hope that other people won't mind if I seem to take little interest in them or their work, their lives. I do care, but work has always been too exciting to ignore. I am grateful for everything you have given me; professional support, trust, friendship. I leave the lab with – well, affection for all of you.'

In the rest of her speech, Helen reflected on the years she had spent studying the structures and idiosyncrasies of landforms, and how much her work owed to Landsat imagery, the photographs taken by cameras mounted on distant satellites.

'Once I was able to study the wider perspective of landforms, through the use of satellite mapping, my work advanced by leaps and bounds. What we know about Australia's historical geography leapt ahead too, especially as so much of the country is still untouched, not buried beneath cities and agricultural change.

'I want to thank all of you for your friendship and support.'

Helen's speech was more gracious, more personal than she had intended.

She sat down. Jack passed her a glass of wine. Helen thanked him with a brief smile. Her husband knew she wouldn't want to show too much emotion in front of her colleagues.

Conversations started up: football, the weather, funding for research (never enough), Helen's work and where it had ended.

Rod Ackroyd walked over to Helen and sat down at the table across from her. 'We shall miss Dr Lytton.' He smiled at Jack as he spoke.

'I shall miss all of you,' Helen said. 'I'm a bit surprised by that. I mean – you know.'

'When are you setting off on the field trip, then?'

'Tomorrow. We'd be off today if Helen had her way.'

Jack reached across to the next table and helped himself to a wineglass which was still upside down. He filled it from the bottle of dry white wine in front of him and passed it to Ackroyd, who took a couple of sips.

Helen was looking off across the canteen, watching her former laboratory mates tease a young woman, an assistant in the Divisional Library. It had been like that for her when she was in her first job.

'They have to be more careful now, don't they?' She brought her attention back to Jack and Rod. 'I'm sorry – I was just thinking that girls aren't fair game any more, are they? And a damn good thing they aren't.'

'If you're under forty the rules don't seem too difficult. It's the old blokes like me and Jack that have to watch ourselves.' Rod finished his drink quickly and stood up.

'I must go. Good luck, Helen. Keep us posted. And don't forget to pack your bathers.' He grinned, to make the point that he was teasing her.

Helen smiled and shook her head.

A shriek of laughter erupted from the girl Rob and Charlie were tormenting. As she backed away from him, Rob held his hands to his head like antlers and moved in mock threat towards her.

'Some young women don't know the rules, either. Let's go, Jack.'

Jack picked up the gifts and the graceful sheaf of wild flowers which had been presented to his wife.

Teresa saw them stand up and came hurrying across. She was almost as thin as Helen, but dressed in such a way that she seemed larger, more sensuous. She was thirty years younger, but they had been as close as Helen's reserve had allowed.

'Don't leave yet! I haven't had a chance to talk to you!'

Helen gave Teresa's arm a squeeze, but didn't pause in loading Jack with packages.

They left the canteen with smiles and good wishes on all sides.

Teresa opened the door of the old Commodore and helped Jack put the flowers on the back seat. Helen got into the front seat. Teresa stuck her head in and gave Helen a kiss on the cheek.

'I'll be waiting for a call. If you're right, it's going to be great news.'

8

She stood back as Jack started the engine and slowly drove the car out into Kerferd Street. Teresa waved, Helen waved. In the rear view mirror, Jack saw Teresa watching the car as it left the laboratory grounds, and vanished from her sight around the corner.

Inside the car, Helen was already talking about getting an early start the next day.

Everything was packed, of course. Packed and set out on the lounge room floor in apple-pie order. They didn't really need a list after so many field trips over the years, but practice made perfect and Jack rather enjoyed going over everything and ticking items off the list. *'Shorts: Jack 6. Shorts: Helen 6. Underpants: Jack 4. Underpants: Helen 4. Bras: Helen 2. Shirts, assorted: Jack 6 ... '*

After checking, he would load the LandCruiser and the trailer, never an easy task when they were going off for several weeks.

He occasionally reminded Helen that when he was a young civil engineer, working for a bridge-building company, this had been his first allotted responsibility and he had never left anything essential behind. Now it was a matter of pride that he would forget nothing, nor overlook anything. Helen could, and did, leave it to him.

They were going a long way this time; on a journey that had started almost a year ago.

By the time she made the decision to retire, Helen had been studying the Landsat images for five hours at a stretch, for some months. She had compared this with that, like with like, unlike with unlike. She had matched artificially-enhanced colours, contours, shapes and shadows. She had made allowances for discrepancies, time, mechanical twitches – everything she could think of. And still, at the corner of the tiniest portion of the least significant and most minute area of the high-resolution images, almost on the edge of the desert, there was – this blip. This infinitesimal slip, this nudge. Helen had asked her colleagues to have a look for it, and neither Rob nor Charlie could find anything disconcerting. Rod Ackroyd had been asked to look, and he couldn't see anything either. No matter how carefully Helen enlarged the image with the computer, definition was soon lost. Only on the small image was the hint of a structural change visible. Visible only to Helen.

Even when she pointed out exactly where she could see it, and what she could see, the other scientists were blind to it. They fetched in other eyes, younger eyes, eyes used to looking through microscopes. Nobody but Helen could see the almost invisible – or quite invisible – mark, the equivalent of a stroke of a butterfly's antenna. Helen was quite sure it existed. She studied it over and over again, using the differing angles of the satellite's passage through the sky to provide her with subtle changes in the image. It was not always there; just sometimes. But those 'some times' were enough to persuade her that in a remote part of Western Australia, not deep into the desert but far enough to discourage people from going, there was a rock formation forming a cave. And in that cave was a black, shallow pit.

The pit did not contain the red sand of the desert. The blackness she could see in the images was the blackness of long-rotted vegetation, now solid like peat. Helen believed she had discovered the remnant of an unknown and ancient waterhole in an area where any rivers had dried up centuries ago, where no flood had ever been recorded.

Beneath that rock, Helen was convinced, inside the cave whose darkness was penetrated only when the satellite flew low in the sky and the sun was just right, lay a dry marsh. A bog. This was evidence that water had covered even this arid corner of a long-dry continent, and more recently than had ever been imagined by scientists.

Now they were off to prove it.

They got off with a minimum of delay early the next morning. Jack checked the LandCruiser, the trailer, the tyres. He walked around the house checking that all the windows and doors were secure then, with a satisfied nod, he got in beside Helen and started the engine.

'Well, we're off, dear,' he said.

'Yes, we're off.'

After two overnight breaks at motels, the tired travellers came in sight of their first destination, the small town of Barwick. Jack had looked it up in the Royal Automobile Club's book and they were not at all surprised to find that there were few buildings other than the Primary School, which consisted of a transportable classroom alongside a fibreboard house. A toilet block was tucked around the side under some scrubby trees.

'That must be him: David Collins.' Helen pointed to the man squatting on the concrete steps outside the classroom. As they drew near, he stood up and raised a hand in greeting. He wore shorts and long socks and his boots were as dusty as the school steps. Over a thin, faded shirt, he wore a sleeveless sweater, rather to Helen's surprise. It was already hotter than she found really comfortable.

The cloud of red dust that had swirled behind them since they turned off the highway subsided when they stopped, settling over their hair and clothes as they walked over to David. Helen tried to smile without opening her mouth wide so as to keep the sand out. It worked until she was almost within a handshake's reach of David, when a willy-willy whisked through the schoolyard, spinning the sand into a choking spiral.

'Damn!' Jack had reached David and was shaking his hand as the willy-willy went by. 'I hate these things!'

'Get used to them up here,' David said. 'Early mornings, regular as sun up.'

David invited them inside for a drink, but they chose to stay outside, standing under the solitary tree by the gate, stretching tired muscles while they drank a tin of beer, cold from the fridge. Behind the exchange of names and civilities, Helen was aware that they were sizing each other up.

'Get many visitors up here, do you?' Jack said.

'Not many. A few holiday makers: they stop for a break – use the toilet block if the gate's open, as it usually is. Japanese tourists sometimes find their way through Barwick. Can't think how. Nothing here.'

The cold tin felt good in the early heat of the day. Helen sipped the beer and held the tin between her hands. A couple of times Jack rolled his tin across his forehead.

'The Japanese don't know what to make of me. I reckon I'm the first aboriginal they have spoken to. Even when they speak English, they seem surprised that I do. Sometimes one of them will try to talk to me in a sort of Pidgin English.' David laughed, a loud, infectious kind of laugh that made Helen and Jack smile with him.

'Maybe it was Pidgin Japanese?'

Helen enjoyed David's story; he told it well, with gestures that seemed to sum up a Japanese being abundantly courteous but baffled.

'Whatever it was, they went away smiling.'

'Do you speak – anything else?' There were so many indigenous languages and Helen had no idea what was the local one.

'A bit. Not much.'

There was companionable silence for a while as they drank their beer and enjoyed the cold condensation on the tins. The quiet pleased Helen; she had never liked the social pressure to make conversation.

'Had some African-Americans through a year back,' David said. 'Family of them; a couple of kids, Mum, Dad, Grandpa. The kids were obviously dying to ask about me – about being black like them – but their parents were very circumspect. They were careful not to ask anything to do with race. Too careful, really. You know?'

Jack nodded.

'The youngest kid – she'd be about four – kept putting a finger on my arm. Just checking.' The memory clearly amused David; he grinned at Helen and shook his head. 'Just checking, eh?'

'Have you lived here long?' Jack's voice was tired, polite.

'Few years now. Came to teach here when I graduated. Back home, I suppose. Came from these parts.'

'You're the only teacher here?' Helen said.

'With seventeen kids in town, Barwick Primary School rates no more than one.'

They lapsed again into silence. Jack leant against the gate post while David squatted down on one haunch with a leg stuck straight out in front of him. They always do this, Helen thought, in films about Australia. Squatting down like that is a mark of 'typical' Australian behaviour. And it was comfortable. Not that she could quite manage it now. Not after a long drive.

Another willy-willy started up in the far corner of the schoolyard, spinning across on a random path, scattering scraps of dried grass as the swirl of dusty sand rose after it.

'Going to be a hot one today,' David said. 'Probably going to hit a century again.'

When the willy-willy had passed, Helen went over to the schoolhouse steps and sat down.

'Tell us about Barwick,' she said. A nice, long rest was a good way to get her muscles working again. And Jack's.

'Not much to tell.' David looked around. 'The State government built the houses thirty years ago when the railway line went through. Basic stuff; two bedroom transportables, cyclone fencing round them, no grass of course. Not much anyway. Too hot. There were a few bigger houses for the bosses and some farmers retired here so their wives would be nearer to shops and facilities.'

'Facilities?' There were none in sight, that Helen could see.

'Well, there used to be a shop here. Before they built better roads and closed the railway line. Now there's just the garage round the back here. Barney sells petrol and diesel, of course, and flies his old Cessna to Meekatharra a couple of times a week for the papers, frozen milk, bread – stuff like that. Eggs – cigarettes. Brings fresh veggies and fruit with him; sometimes the odd passenger going to and from the doctor.'

'That it?' Jack finished his beer with the same finality as his question.

'That's it. Barwick.' With a flourish worthy of an actor, David swept his arm around. It seemed to Helen like a good finale to their 'getting to know you' scene. She stood up, gave David the empty tin and dusted off her hands.

David led Jack inside the schoolhouse to see the shopping he had done on their behalf: fresh food for a few days and provisions for a trip that could last five weeks. Everything was packed into margarine boxes, which the two started carrying out to the trailer, leaving the fresh food for last. There were plastic drums of water and steel jerrycans full of petrol; small gas cylinders for the cooking stove, lamps carefully packed into a case. Helen and Jack had brought with them all the canned and packaged food they would need.

'You've done well,' Jack said. He accepted another cold beer, and Helen did the same.

David smiled – a little tightly, Helen thought. She hoped he hadn't thought Jack's remark patronising. Jack always gave praise where he thought it due.

As though he sensed Helen's disquiet, David opened the classroom door and indicated an invitation for the Lyttons to go in.

'Have a look round?' he said. The memories of paint on doors and window frames on the outside of the building were blistered by the heat, and flaked at a touch.

'Thank you, yes.' Helen led the way in, amused to see how much like any other classroom this was. Even the chalky smell was familiar. There was a blackboard, there were desks, chairs, pictures on the walls. A bigger desk was on a platform at one end of the room. Four large fans hung from the ceiling. The big windows were flywired and had blinds halfway covering them.

'Seventeen children, David?' she said.

'On a good day, yes. Two of them are four years old; the rest are between six and fourteen. Then they have to go to the other school to finish off. Boarding school, of course. Too far to travel every day.'

'Seventeen,' Jack said. 'Not many, is it.'

'It's enough.' David shrugged.

'They'll benefit from all the extra attention you can give them,' Helen said. She was looking at the paintings by the children, hung up in a row along the back wall of the classroom. They were pictures of an imagined city: cars, trains, tall buildings eight stories high, and a traffic light figured in most of them.

'You must be glad of a break.' Jack spoke from the doorway, where he was looking along the unpaved, unmarked street. 'You don't mind spending the time working with us?'

'Of course not! You're scientists, right? Should be an interesting change for me, now the kids are on holiday.'

'I'm the scientist,' Helen said. 'Jack's the planner, organiser – '

'And general factotum,' said Jack.

Even to Helen, it sounded like a well-rehearsed exchange. Which it was.

'I'll be glad to get away for a while.' David pointed across the schoolyard to a gap in the peppermint trees. 'A bit sick of the scenery here.'

Children and dogs were playing on the dusty spaces between the houses and the school. The houses were a uniform grey; they had lost whatever colour they used to have.

'What's that, then?' Jack pointed down the road to a small, brightly-painted building.

'Oh, the Uniting Church used to be pretty strong here in its manifestation as the Methodists. It's their Hall. They have services there every fortnight, and the Catholic priest from Meeka comes over and says Mass once a month, on a Thursday night. There's a noticeboard outside with a sign on it: "Ring this number for pastoral care in any denomination." I've always liked that.'

Helen stood up and joined Jack at the door. Such grass as the residents of Barwick had tried to grow had dried up to a brittle, yellow stubble. A few pot plants added a splash of brave colour in pots outside front doors. They were mostly geraniums and a few natives. Helen noticed the flowers were red, all of them.

'Best be making tracks, then,' said Jack, offering his empty tin to David.

Helen gave her tin to David as he held out his hand for it.

David didn't head off back to the schoolhouse; for a moment he leaned against the doorframe of the schoolroom, the empty tins clicking together in one hand.

'Sounds like an interesting trip, Dr Lytton.' He didn't sound at all interested, Helen thought with some amusement. Australian men seemed to think it inappropriate to sound enthused or curious. Laid-back, that was what Teresa called it, and it sometimes exasperated Teresa almost beyond endurance.

'I think it will be, David. I'm glad you're going to be with us.'

He nodded and went down the steps.

Helen was pleased with David. He was in his late twenties, she thought – a short and square man, with closely-cut hair, and with short stubby fingers. A practical man. He was dressed much like Jack. Like both Helen and Jack, he carried a broad-brimmed hat. Nobody up here took risks with the sun.

Loading the LandCruiser took little time as Jack had left space for David's contributions. Helen was relieved to see that the men approved of each other; that David seemed to recognise that Jack knew what he was doing. Jack clearly liked the way David had done exactly what he had been asked to do, and the way he had given Jack the invoices without fuss.

Helen watched the loading, her mind elsewhere. She looked around the township; nobody was on the street. If you could call it a street.

Two children came around the corner, chasing a tennis ball. One was an aboriginal child with a cluster of surprisingly blonde curls; the other child had the olive skin and thick black hair that suggested a Mediterranean origin. There had been a lot of Italian and Greek migrants up here, Helen remembered. The kids looked at the visitors with curiosity but when Helen smiled at them, they scampered off and started to play cricket with the tennis ball and a stick.

'May I use your bathroom, David?' she said.

'Second on the left,' he said, pointing.

The building was prefabricated and had probably been transported to Barwick on the back of a couple of trucks, like the school itself. These buildings were designed to be moved from site to site, and had separable halves which workmen could fasten together in a few hours. Helen had seen a lot of them on her travels around the outback.

Through the bathroom window, Helen could see that a septic tank was buried off to one side under a load of imported gravel, with a vent pipe sticking up through the gravel. There was a water storage tank on a high platform beyond it; no doubt a water carrier came to refill it when the tank started to sound hollow if it was rapped with a knuckle. The house was a basic design with four rooms, and a verandah on three sides. She had noticed from the outside that, like the classroom, the paintwork was scraped almost to the colour of the sand by the abrasive action of wind and willy-willy.

The inside was painted a faded grey, not at all conducive to decorative touches. There were a couple of pictures on the wall of the living room, through which Helen had to go to reach the bathroom. They were reproductions of familiar bush scenes by nineteenth century artists.

David Collins seemed to use only one of the two chairs which matched the brown leather sofa; there was a footstool in front of it, with a pile of magazines and a couple of books on a small table at its side. Pristine and plump, the cushions on the other chair and the sofa carried scenes of mediaeval jousting in faded colours. There were orange curtains, of a kind which Helen had seen before; they were like the curtains in the government flat she had lived in while working for three months in Canberra. Somebody must have bought a few kilometres of the stuff for the government. The curtains were pulled across the windows. They would keep the room cooler while David was away.

As she washed her hands, Helen looked at herself in the mirror over the washbasin. She saw the familiar thin face, hair which was a mixture of sandy ginger and white, and eyebrows too bristly now to lie down. For a fleeting moment, she was reminded of her father. She combed her hair back and flipped the rubber band around the short pigtail at the back.

After two nights in motels on the way up here, it would be good to sleep in a sleeping bag again, maybe under the stars if the tent were too hot. The bathroom was neat and clean, she noticed. One towel, no clutter. Good, they would have little time for niceties on the trip. A man living alone could be much more messy than this and make camping out uncomfortable.

She walked slowly through the hallway to the front door, glancing around. The house was scattered with books, but nothing else.

Just like home, she thought. A reasonable degree of mess.

Helen paused in the doorway and watched Jack and David for a moment, fanning herself with her straw hat. Her husband was only a little taller than David, and a mite overweight now. He was almost the same age as Helen and, like her, was reasonably fit although there was a bit of a scare last year when his heart developed a murmur, whatever that was. Their doctor said that Jack should take life a bit more easily, so he had given up golf.

Now he was engrossed in studying a map with this man who was to be their guide for a few weeks. David certainly looked all right, Helen thought. That was one uncertainty resolved. Now she could forget about it and get on with the other uncertainties.

She walked across to the men, who had spread a couple of maps along the bonnet of the LandCruiser.

When they had planned the field trip, Jack had pointed out that although the Landsat map seemed sharply detailed, the scale was so large that in fact they could be wandering around in circles for days unless a local guide could understand the shapes and shadows of landforms well enough to identify the details exactly. That was why David was here.

They had waited for the school holidays, so that David would be available, although it would mean travelling in the hottest season. January and February in this part of the world were always hot.

As Helen reached them, the men turned one of the maps sideways so that she could read it with them. Jack had already unrolled the Landsat map that most nearly matched the scale of the road map, but of course they looked totally different. For half an hour Helen explained about landforms, shadows, shapes and the absence of tracks. At last David said he had a pretty good idea where they should look for the rock formation, but it might take some days to find. If it existed. Helen didn't mention that she was looking for signs of an old water system; she didn't want David to be dulled with scepticism like her colleagues at the laboratory. David's job was to locate the structure which was something like a cave. Her job was to find out what was in it.

'You don't actually know it, then?' Helen had entertained little hope, but there had been just a small hope, that David would know this part of the desert well enough to identify the place straight away.

'No; but if it's there, we'll find it.'

'You know this country very well, we were told.' Jack sounded a little too bright and optimistic, Helen thought; maybe he wasn't all that confident.

David smiled. 'Like the back of my hand. Well, nearly. It's Arundijilaba country; my family. My uncle's uncle took me through this country all the time; taught me its history, our history. I know the place pretty well.'

'You're an Arundi – ; I'm sorry, what was it?' Helen made a gesture of apology.

'Arundijilaba, yes. Hardly any of us left now. A family or two in Perth, some moved to country towns and married local people. We've all left the traditional ways behind, of course.'

'Well, that should make it easier to find what we're looking for, shouldn't it? You being so familiar with the place?'

He nodded, smiling.

Helen was not entirely sanguine about it; she had done enough field trips into the desert in pursuit of particular landforms to know that it could take weeks to narrow down a search for the cave.

David locked up the house and put the key under a flowerpot by the front door. It seemed rather too obvious a hiding place to Helen as the pot, and there was only one, held no plant. David must feel secure up here, so far from the city.

Within a few moments they were on their way.

They drove on the highway for a few kilometres. The road was well constructed because heavy rigs came through Barwick on the way to the far North, where the mining companies had built their own towns. There were no kerbs, no cambers. Just a straight black line vanishing to a point in both directions. About six kilometres out of Barwick, David pointed to the right and Jack turned the LandCruiser off the road.

The desert they were driving across was not like the sand dune deserts of other parts of the country. The ground was flinty, red soil with little vegetation. Rain was scarce, measured not in centimetres but in months, even years, between falls. A lot of rocks were scattered about; over time the rocks exploded shards in the heat, making it tricky to walk about unless you were sure-footed. You could not afford a ricked ankle out here.

There were a lot of small hillocks, scree-sided hills up to twenty metres high, with larger slabs of rock flung across the tops during ancient upheavals of the earth, slabs now scraped smooth by centuries of abrasive sand-laden wind. This kind of desert was rough and red, the rocky sand seemed to go on for ever with little plant life, and hundreds of rocky outcrops fooled the eye into seeing shapes that vanished as you drew close to them.

There were no tracks; vehicles had to make their own way and as soon as the dust settled behind them, there was no trace of their passage.

The LandCruiser was tough in design and famously good at coping with this kind of landscape. Jack drove slowly, not stopping while they ate the ham and cheese sandwiches the last motel had made for their lunch, and David's, but stopping frequently to take their bearings. Helen used a compass and

David seemed to be marking off certain landforms in his mind, as though he carried a memory of what he was seeing.

They had reached a small billabong when dusk came, suddenly as always in the desert, and briefly. Jack and David put up the tents alongside the LandCruiser, first sweeping the ground free of sharp rock fragments. The tents were bright green, to ensure visibility from a distance.

David said he would use his sleeping bag, but sleep outside the tent. 'Make more room for the provisions,' he said.

The men anchored the guy-ropes with heavy rocks, in case of willy willies. Helen threw a couple of sleeping bags onto the camp beds Jack had set up in the tent she and Jack shared.

While Jack assembled the camp stove, David lit a fire, not always necessary at night but a pleasant place to sit around and chat. Helen fetched the three fold-up chairs, made from aluminium and canvas, from the LandCruiser and set them up around the fire.

Jack cooked steak kept cool in the fridge plugged into the LandCruiser, and they ate salad with it – the last salad they would have as it was too bulky to make space for in the fridge; out of the fridge in the desert heat it would be limp and lifeless in no time at all. A bottle of white burgundy was shared among three plastic cups.

David fetched a spade from the LandCruiser and dug a small depression in the ground for the bones and other remnants of the meal. There were no cans as yet to pack into plastic bags to take back with them.

He covered the remains neatly with the removed earth, and put a few stones on top. He picked up his cup and sipped the wine.

'This is a really great trip for me. I'm a single man, you know? So I had planned nothing for the school holidays except, perhaps, a trip to Perth to see Allan Broadley – you talked to him – and maybe a couple of other old school friends.' He sat down, poking the ash in the fire under the kettle.

Jack asked him gently prodding questions; David admitted that he would probably not have gone south – somehow the attraction of the city faded when the time came to pack up and go. He would probably have done exactly what he was about to do, but alone and with no particular objective.

'I would have gone bush, probably. When I was wondering what to do in the holidays – stay in Barwick, or go to the city – Allan rang from the Aboriginal Centre in Perth. This scientist was looking for someone to help find a particular spot in the desert within a couple of hundred kilometres of Barwick. Would I like the job? Yeah, OK, I would, I told him. So here I am, acting as a sort of guide. Allan said the scientist was bringing her husband along, and they would share the cooking. I made sure of that; I wasn't going to be perceived as a black servant, not me.'

He must be feeling comfortable with us to say that, Helen thought. Comfortable with us and the wine.

In the near-dark, Helen saw David's broad smile as a double row of white teeth. She smiled back; they were all feeling relaxed, thank goodness.

The evening was very warm. Insects swarmed around the lamp. The billabong was still; the stars reflected in it made Helen feel as if she was floating with them, stars above and below.

They drank Nescafé and enjoyed the silence.

Helen was thinking about the problems a man like David would have; a primary school teacher, an aboriginal, unmarried and living alone. Bluntly, so bluntly that Jack shifted his position abruptly and she knew he was embarrassed, Helen asked David if being black and living in a remote country township created problems for him. David poked again at the ash.

Sometimes, he told them, he wondered if he would marry – there were few educated black women up here in the country and he had experienced enough racist attacks, many of them physical, to shy clear of white women.

Still, it was his country, and he loved living here. He would spend the school holiday in the bush with Helen and Jack, and get back that feeling of belonging. His grandfather had been right about that; the feeling is there if you look for it.

They dug a hole for scraps and washed up, using water from the billabong and a towel which they hung on the LandCruiser to dry. Another hole, dug further away and with a pile of earth to scatter on top, provided the lavatory. Another handful of water was used to wash hands and faces and for cleaning teeth.

In their tent, Helen and Jack held hands for a little while, until Jack drifted off to sleep. David was snoring loudly within a few minutes. Helen thought about the farewell party and wondered briefly if she had forgotten to thank someone.

She turned over inside her sleeping bag and went to sleep.

Helen woke slowly, more slowly than usual. Usually, she would suddenly be awake and get out of bed almost at once. Today was different; not just because she was sleeping in a tent at the start of a new venture, there was something else. The dream re-formed; a hazy recollection of a conversation – an argument – a feeling of great anger; with a catch of breath Helen saw again her father's face. It was much like her own in colour and shape. She remembered how she had suddenly thought of him when she was looking in the mirror in David's bathroom. That must be why she had dreamed about him. She rarely even thought about him these days; he had been dead since she was twenty. At the time she had needed him most, he had a heart attack and died in his sleep.

It was time to get up.

For two weeks the search went on. They moved camp three times as the search area narrowed. Helen was quite flattered that David seemed fascinated by the way she went about the job, scientifically dividing the land on the road map into squares, measuring the squares against the Landsat image, trying to equate the one with the other.

'It's a bit like trying to find a small black car in a car park as big as Victoria,' she said one day, a bit exasperated.

'A car park full of small black cars,' Jack said. Perhaps he intended to be funny, but his voice was tired.

On the sixteenth day, it was really hot. Over 39 degrees and not yet noon. They arrived back at the camp, after another unsuccessful foray. Helen sighed as she pulled off her hat, and rubbed the back of her neck. She rubbed it carefully, remembering that the sweat and dust could act like fine sandpaper and make her skin tender and sore.

'Are you all right, Jack love?' Helen watched her husband lean on the door of the LandCruiser, tired, with a mess of red dust and sweat in his hair and on his face. In fact, his whole body looked red and sweaty, what she could see of it, barely clothed in red-dusted and sweaty shorts and boots.

Jack smiled and said he was fine, just hot. Helen looked down at herself; Jack wasn't the only one who looked a mess. Only David managed to look reasonably cool after a day in the sun; he was really used to this climate. After all, he lived way up here.

26

She persuaded Jack to take it easy for the rest of the day. His way of resting was to take inventory of the supplies, which were in good shape and lasting well, he reported, just as he had planned.

For a brief time, maybe half an hour, she wondered if the excursion would end in failure. She knew that David was having problems relating the oddly-coloured Landsat images to the country around them. He said he understood that the colours of the map were created by the computer, to make differences apparent, but it confused him. Helen had been hiding her impatience, knowing that Jack sympathised with David; about all Jack could ever see was the difference between agricultural land and the rest. Still, as the days went on, David had become more familiar with the maps and sometimes set off at high speed in pursuit of something, some rock shape, of which he was suddenly reminded. He would end the chase shaking his head and saying that his uncle's uncle would have found what they were seeking on the first day.

Helen shook herself out of anxiety. They knew that if the particular rock formation existed, if the cave existed, it was somewhere hereabouts. It must be here, and they would find it. The trouble was, as Helen said over dinner that night – canned curry from Campbell's factory in Shepparton, specially sent over to Perth at her request – the trouble was that at ground level everything always looks different. She drew a circle on the ground with a stick, and a smaller circle in its centre; alongside it she drew a figure resembling a capital M with very broad serifs. 'Look at these. From up there, the circle could be anything. But if you knew it looked like this – ' She jabbed the capital M. 'From the side – you'd know straight away what it was.'

She threw the stick aside. Jack and David went on looking at the circle and the letter M.

'Well, I don't know.' Jack looked at David, who shook his head.

'Oh, for goodness sake, it's a hat, isn't it.' Helen picked up her straw hat, which had been at the side of her chair since the sun went down, and dropped it between the two men. 'See?'

'I was thinking you meant something much bigger,' Jack said. 'You know, more like a mountain or a lake.'

'A place to keep cattle in,' David said, but without much enthusiasm.

'A hat. Just a hat.' Helen stood up; stretched her arms above her head and yawned. 'I'm for bed.'

She watched as Jack and David checked that the fire was completely dead and they cleaned up the few dishes that had been used.

She was inside the tent when she heard David speak.

'You know what, Jack, I've really been looking for something big. Do you think I've been missing something?'

'I doubt it. I mean, a cave isn't all that small, is it?'

Something in David's voice, a quiet excitement, an agitation, had caught Helen's attention and she listened as the two men moved closer together, talking quickly and quietly, no doubt not wanting to disturb Helen.

'I don't know. Maybe I wasn't watching carefully enough. How big is a cave? How high are the rocks that hide it? I've had an idea of its size; you know – just an idea – but I can't read Helen's maps. Maybe I've been wrong all this time.'

'Let's not get too involved in this.' Jack's voice was anxious now. She could imagine him making that familiar gesture, patting the air down with his hands, as though it would keep their voices low. 'We'll talk to Helen about it in the morning.'

Thinking she might join in the conversation, Helen opened the flap of the tent.

'There's that low ridge of hills fifty kilometres from here.' David pointed, his arm a black arrow against the rising moon. 'I didn't think they were what we wanted because there wasn't much of them and they aren't very high.'

'Were they on Helen's map? A ridge sounds like a pretty noticeable feature to me.'

'Not really. They're like these over here, not much to them.' He pointed to a low group of hillocks a hundred metres away, little more prominent above the flat sand than the ridges of a crocodile's back above its body. 'From above they probably don't show up at all, and even from the side they aren't very prominent. I just called them a ridge because my uncle's uncle did.'

'Not very noticeable from above or ground level, eh? Not like Helen's hat – noticeable from both?' Jack picked up the hat, turning it slowly in his hands.

'Well, it was to the Arundijilaba. If they called it a ridge, they must have seen it clearly enough.'

'I doubt if it's what we want, David. But we'll tell Helen in the morning, eh?'

Jack patted David on the shoulder. David looked off for a moment in the direction of the 'ridge' and then went into his tent. Jack too stared off into the night, before turning towards the tent.

'Did you hear that?' Helen nodded.

'Could be our search is over, dear,' he said.

'Maybe.'

Jack seemed keen to talk about it, but the possibility of a new phase in their search was, Helen decided, too nebulous. They could talk about it tomorrow.

They didn't leave for the ridge until after breakfast the next morning. But by six o'clock, in the bright light of morning, the two men had set off in the LandCruiser, heading east.

Helen watched them go, with a little regret that she had chosen to wait for them while they explored the ridge. The trouble was, she thought, that where she was right now seemed 'right'. This was the point she had pinpointed, as closely as it was possible to pinpoint the 'black car in the car park the size of Victoria',the place where the black car should be. Right here.

As the dust from the LandCruiser's trail settled and Helen could no longer see it, she went into the tent and studied again the maps. There is no such thing as women's intuition, she thought. Nonsense. So maybe Jack and David would find the cave after all.

She didn't hear the whisper of the willy-willy until it suddenly rose to a screech. The tent was held down by big rocks, so she knew she was safe, but the small tornado seemed to hover around the campsite for minutes, spinning faster and faster, picking up more and more small, sharp rocks which it hurled against the green canvas until Helen was sure that at any second a rip would appear, a rip which would allow the wind to fling the tent, its contents and her along the ground until everything was destroyed.

She held tight to the frame of the tent, its metal flexing and bowing as the whirlwind tightened its grip. Suddenly, as suddenly as it had started, the willy-willy spun away.

Helen opened the flap of the tent, pushing away a drift of sand.

She watched the spiral of wind move rapidly away from her, inside a tube of red earth which twisted as it rose. Willy willies were always disconcerting. They started up as soon as the sun became hot enough and nobody could predict when one would come or how powerful it might be. Most of them were small flurries that did nothing more than coat the surface of a mug of tea with fine red dust, or make your eyes water. This kind of willy-willy was a rarity.

Both the tents were undamaged, although there was nothing to show where the fire had been last night. The ground in the vicinity of the campsite was swept smooth. Thanks to their good housekeeping habits, all the tools and dishes were safely stowed on the LandCruiser, or in the big packing case behind the rock. Helen walked over to check that the case had survived. It should be there still; it was built for this kind of journey and any kind of extreme weather. And indeed the case, although threequarters buried in sand and rocks, seemed to be intact. The men could dig it out when they returned.

In the distance, Helen could see the dust cloud of the retreating willy-willy still making a slight disturbance on the horizon. It could be the LandCruiser; maybe the men were on the way back, but she thought it was the willy-willy.

She turned around to go back to the tent and attempt to clean it up; a lot of dust had blown in during the storm.

She raised her eyes briefly, and saw that the willy-willy had made a change to the nearby low hills. They were only a few metres high, chosen to be the site of the latest camp because they would provide a visible landmark when they were off in the LandCruiser. Now the sand had been blown from the top and what had seemed no more than a pile of loose rocks was changed. A huge slab of rock lay across other, smaller ones. Even as she watched, a rockfall poured small stones down from the top, down the face of the hill she was looking at.

Below the rock slab, among the big rocks, wasn't it possible that she would find the cave? Helen broke into a run, slowed down as she remembered how dangerous it was to hurry through these sharp and unsettled rock fragments, left behind after the passage of the willy-willy. Slowly she drew closer to the hill.

Yes. Yes! Now she could see it. There was a blackness, an absence of light right in the centre, under the great slab of rock. It was not far above ground level. She started to climb, slipped down, started to climb again. After half a dozen scrambling attempts, Helen reached a small ledge from which she could get a foothold and haul herself up to a narrow platform at the entrance to a cave, only a couple of metres above the ground. Just inside the entrance, the floor of the cave dropped; it was a metre and a half lower than the flat shelf at the entrance on which Helen was standing. The air was thick with dust; hot and stale. It was almost dark. Helen stepped gently down to the floor. She regretted that she had not brought a torch with her.

Silly to forget that, she had no right to be here if she forgot the most basic of tools. She ticked herself off for carelessness, mumbling crossly while she felt around the floor of the cave, near the entrance.

The ground was not smooth, of course, there were fragments of rock, some of them possibly having just been split from the body of the cave by the willy-willy's furious beating.

She should go no further. Only a fool would go further alone, and without light. Nobody knew where she was. This wasn't a safe place for a sensible woman to be. Only yesterday she had encountered that snake.

Helen took the high step back to the entrance cautiously. She stood in the entrance to the cave until she saw the dust cloud in the distance. It had to be Jack in the LandCruiser. Willy willies don't come back.

Helen scrambled to the top of the hill and waved. She stripped off her shirt and shorts and waved them until she got a wave in response. Then she pulled her clothes back on and raced across the hot sand to meet them.

'I was right! I was right! It's here!'

'I T WAS THE WILLY-WILLY! Did you see it? It was frightening, really terrifying, but look what it did! I mean, here it is – it opened right in front of me, as though – as though –' Helen was out of breath for a moment as they scrambled over the dangerous scree.

'Like Open Sesame,' Jack said.

'Yes, just like that! Open Sesame, and it did.'

David and Helen, who had gone first, took hold of Jack's arms and hoisted him up to the foothold on the face of the hill, just below the entrance to the cave. He was not as agile as Helen, but Jack did not lack enthusiasm and he used their arms as levers, and more or less jumped the last metre over the lip of the entrance and down into the cave. He landed with a grunt.

'Be careful, love, it's dark and splintery.'

'Is it safe?' Jack sounded excited rather than apprehensive.

'Probably,' said Helen.

They stood, holding on to each other, in silence.

'I can't see, dammit.'

Helen could hear the excitement, and such exasperation, in her voice that it made Jack laugh. She squeezed his arm.

'Maybe one of us should go and get some torches,' she said, not moving.

'I'll go. Don't do anything until I get back.' David scrambled out of the cave.

'Bring something I can push into the ground, David! That stick will do; the measuring stick, you know which I mean? And a trowel!'

They heard David's acknowledgment: 'Will do!' A flake or two of fine rock dust fell on Helen's face; she must remember how fragile this ancient roof was. She shouldn't call out again. They could hear David's boots scrape as he raced across the sand to the tents.

Jack must have felt the fragments of rock moving in the air too. He didn't move. Helen held tightly onto him.

'It isn't safe here, is it?' We should be sensible, Jack. One of us should wait outside.'

'Yes, that's the sensible thing to do.'

'In case – you know – something goes wrong.'

Neither made a move towards the cave entrance.

'Isn't this exciting?' Helen said. She reached across to stroke his face, as though to say 'Here we are together in another adventure.'

Making as much noise as when he left, David returned. He handed each of them a torch. He dropped a spade and a few other tools, including the measuring-stick, just inside the entrance to the cave. David himself carried a lamp, which he flicked on and then held high.

The air was dusty, glittery in the bright light, due no doubt to their scrambling arrival, and it was hot. As the lights moved a small group of bats took wing and left the cave, screeching, skilfully dodging the humans who tried with less skill to avoid contact with them. The bats' agitation caused more rock particles to fall.

There was an earthy smell in the air; dry, almost sweet.

'Smells like a silo, doesn't it?' David said, sniffing hard a couple of times. 'You know, on farms: hay or something. That and the bats. Nice, though.'

A lone bat skittered past them, releasing a few fragments from the roof.

Jack pointed his torch up; they looked at the roof of the cave critically. It looked solid enough.

35

'We shouldn't all be in here together,' Jack said. 'One of us should be outside. In case the roof caves in.'

'You're right,' said Helen.

Nobody volunteered to go.

Most of the flakes she had felt must have been floating around in the air, Helen decided; stirred up by the willy-willy and their arrival in the cave. It was probably safe.

'It's probably safe as long as we don't shout,' she said.

David held the lamp a little lower now, so that most of the cave was bathed in its light. It wasn't very large. It was like being in an upturned bowl. The roof was almost within reach of a stretched arm. In the harsh brilliance, the shadows seemed darker. They seemed to move abruptly as David took a step forward.

'No! Wait!'

David stopped.

Helen's torch lit up the ground in front of them. The bright light seemed to fragment, skid about on the sand. Rock splinters lay on the same red earth as outside the cave, but only for a very short distance. Helen breathed in sharply as she saw how the earth blackened within an apparent curved line. Not gradually fading to black, but abruptly, as though the curve marked the line of a shore, the edge of a deep hole. From this line the blackness went right up to the far wall of the cave. It was as if they were standing at the edge of a pool of black water.

'There are rocks and stuff on it,' David said. 'It can't be wet.'

'That's right. Jack, give me that stick.'

Brushing David aside with a mutter about weighing less than him, Helen first tried to push the heavy, metre-long stick into the blackness. She tried again. She knelt down and tried to penetrate it in several places, as far out from the edge as she could reach. David was right about the smell; it was like fresh grass, new-mown hay, there are some native flowers that smelled like this.

Helen went on poking gently into the blackness.

'It's like trying to find land mines,' Jack said. 'Mind one doesn't go off.'

Jack was whispering. Helen stood up.

'I'm going to stand on it. If I'm right and those stones are as heavy as they look, it will bear my weight.'

She stepped carefully forward, and tamped the black soil delicately with the toe of her boot. When nothing gave way, she moved her foot forward boldly, and then her other foot. After a moment, she tested the ground by stamping on it, pressing firmly, trying to gauge its resilience.

'Well,' she said, 'I don't know what it is, but it looks like peat.'

'Peat!' David was so surprised he swung around, and the lamp made Helen's shadow dance crazily along the walls.

'I can't smell anything but those bats, can you?' said Jack. 'Wouldn't peat have a smell of some kind?'

'There is a kind of smell here, I think – a sweetish smell. David's right about that. Clover, maybe. A fresh sort of smell. Of course, it's hard to discern it under the bat – guano, is it? David, there's vegetation around here, isn't there?'

Helen was crouching again, rubbing her fingers over the ground.

'Well, yes,' David said. 'But not that sort. Doesn't peat depend on lots of water? It can't be peat. There's none here. Not within living memory. Dead memory, come to that; my uncle's uncle knew all the stories from his uncle and they don't mention anything like that around here. They had water once, but way back in the Dreamtime.'

'Water?' Helen looked up at David. 'There are stories about water?'

'Yes of course. All aboriginal stories are about water. Well, a lot of them. Especially up in these parts.'

Jack had found a place to sit down on the lip of the cave entry. He shone his torch in Helen's direction, to help her. 'If there was water around, doesn't that automatically mean there'd be something growing?' Jack smiled apologetically. 'Not that I know much about these things, of course.'

'Yes it does, dear. Water means vegetation, even if only a little and rarely. The stuff out there – ' Helen waved an arm vaguely towards the land outside the cave, 'there's not much of it and it gets precious little help from the climate, but a little water goes a long way with some of these desert plants.'

She scraped her fingernails on the surface of the blackness, and rubbed what she had picked up in her fingers. 'Something grew in here for many years, something with a high acid content. As it died, it compacted into the water, under the water, and carbonised, turned to peat. I'm sure of it.'

'If there was that much water here, I still don't see how nobody knew.' David put the lamp down and passed Helen the trowel for which she was snapping her fingers and pointing.

'Well, people don't know everything, do they.'

Helen dug a small sample of the black soil from the edge and walked carefully off the dark area. 'Let's have a quick look at this. Then I can get down to some real work.'

In the sunlight, outside the cave, Helen was delighted to be able to show the others the densely packed vegetable fibres in the specimen. There was no doubt – it was peat.

She led the way back to the camp.

While Helen worked on her sample, looking at its structure under the small but high-powered microscope she had brought with her, Jack and David made lunch. Jack was a dab hand at making damper and the smell of the hot bread soon brought the scientific work to a temporary halt.

Jack passed round the cheese and the pickles. Helen sat on the ground with the others, eating as quickly as she could, anxious to get back to work. She finished long before the men.

'It's not *proper* moss. Sphagnum moss; that's what makes peat where peat belongs. It's funny here; Australia I mean. We've got thousands of plants that don't appear anywhere else and quite a few of them seem to imitate plants found elsewhere. This is more than probably something very like sphagnum moss. Extinct centuries ago, I shouldn't wonder.'

As she spoke, Helen gently teased apart strands of moss and put samples of it into plastic bags, which she labelled and sealed.

'Does this finish it, then?' David stood up and looked around at the neat and tidy tents, the swept area in front of them. 'You've proved your point, right? So what happens now?'

'We all go home, I suppose.' Jack's regret was audible in the quiet voice.

'Not quite yet.' Helen put away the last of the plastic bags, now arranged in upright rows in a tin box which had held teabags.

'I have to take samples in an orderly fashion; you know that, Jack. Check out the cave floor; see what else I can find, if anything.'

'Are you going back in now? This afternoon?' Jack looked tired, Helen thought. Maybe he needed a good rest after all the excitement. It was already nearly three o'clock; she could wait.

She could spend the time thinking. Planning; how to go about things. Writing up what had happened so far.

'Actually I could do with a rest,' she said. 'Tomorrow morning, shall we make it? Get another early start?'

'Why not?'

While they were preparing dinner that night, David was persuaded to tell some of the legends he had learned as a child about this area of the desert. The stories seemed to be simple and yet there was a whole way of life wrapped up in the simple homilies and memories.

Helen was curious to follow up his earlier mention that water figured largely in local stories. She knew, of course, that water was of such importance to Australian outback life, and always had been, that it was bound to have a significant place in local history, traditions or stories.

After the meal, she asked him about the Arundijilaba, and their history. They relaxed over a glass of port – a celebratory bottle of very good port – and David visibly struggled to find a starting place. His problem, he said, was that he rarely thought of his family, especially his uncle's uncle, except with respect and a somewhat remote affection.

David had been given a Western education and his early holidays walking in the bush with his uncle's uncle – Charlie – had soon given place to playing football with the other kids, and study.

'My uncle's uncle had to teach me the Arundijilaba ways – that's the way it was done; we weren't taught by our fathers – so I learned it all from him. Uncle Charlie was great. There were so many legends, so many stories.' David took a sip of port, silent for a moment, looking into the fire.

'There was one story Uncle Charlie made me learn word for word. I can't remember it in his, nor even in the stumbling translation my Dad made for me into English. Not entirely; but it started – I think it started: "There is a Great Lizard who lives alone in the sacred place. We speak of him in whispers. We must obey him as he is the Great Lizard who speaks to us all. The Great Lizard gives us good hunting. The Great Lizard is careful of us and takes no revenge. Because we are the Great Lizard's people we are not revengeful with others. The Great Lizard keeps us from all harm if we listen to the Great Lizard's words." '

He spoke quietly, his eyes half-closed, correcting himself as he hesitated here and there.

Helen thought it sounded like poetry, as there was a cadence in David's voice, a lilting, that seemed rhythmic.

David knew no more about the Great Lizard, except that membership of the Great Lizard's family had brought great distinction on David's ancestors. Or so they believed.

'And yet you say they died out, more or less?' Jack poked the fire, which was dying too.

'We all lose our beliefs, don't we, if we don't work at keeping them going?'

'Too deep for me, David. I'm off to bed,' Helen said. She wanted a chance to think alone, and quietly, about the implications of the discovery.

As she undressed, she rehearsed in her mind the notes she had written during the afternoon, and how they would shape up into the scientific paper she would write when they got back home and the excitement was over.

As she lay in bed, the plans shifted, moved to the back of her mind.

Helen smiled into the darkness: 'Proud of me now, Father?'

She saw herself again, a small child nervously pleating the sash of her pink silk frock as she tried to repeat unfalteringly the poem her father wished her to learn. Every Sunday she spent an hour with her father in his study, and every Sunday she recited to him. Almost every Sunday, she failed to please him.

Jack and David stayed up a while longer.

Too excited to sleep, Helen listened to the men as they discussed the nature of 'faith', which neither of them laid claim to having.

Eventually their voices faltered and they went off to bed.

Helen was up first and made breakfast. She put together in a backpack the tools she would need for a thorough look at the bog. To the backpack she strapped a grid made from aluminium, which folded out to provide a large square divided into smaller, ten-centimetre squares, and the metre-long stick, which was graduated in centimetres. She packed graph paper and heavy black crayons, two cameras and lighting for them, and extra batteries. And the Polaroid camera, for quick results. She put bottles of water in the Esky, and plastic mugs.

The others awoke, and they ate quickly, hardly talking. As the moment to start out on the expedition to the cave arrived, Helen was delighted to see that David was as excited as she was, and Jack too was humming as he gathered the tools together.

'It really is exciting, isn't it?' She picked up her share of the equipment and led the way back to the cave.

They placed the lamps so as to provide as much shadow-free light as they could.

The peat was contained in an area almost 10 metres across and a little less than eight metres to the back wall of the cave.

Helen and Jack placed the grid carefully across the central front section. They tapped it firmly into place with U-shaped pitons, and Helen took several photographs. She rearranged the lighting between each series of shots, so that shadows would be created and provide some depth to the photographs. On a rough plan of the area she drew squares to match the grid. She numbered the squares, and then scratched the outline of the squares onto the peat.

Now they could start.

Using a trowel, Helen made the first cut. The trowel was straight-sided and cut a deep and clean incision into the black soil. Another cut at right-angles, and a third, and the fourth cut allowed Helen to remove an amount of peat ten centimetres deep. She measured the depth, corrected it by digging a very little deeper. Now she had the means to measure what she did with accuracy.

By lunchtime, they had cleared the top ten centimetres of the peat from within the one-metre square, and from another metre alongside the first. There was little to show for the hard work; a few animal bones near the top, a few stones further down.

There was no change in the colour or composition of the peat, as far as Helen could determine with the naked eye.

They started again after lunch. This time Helen planned to tackle the next ten centimetres down.

Jack dug gently into the second square while Helen watched him, resting her aching shoulders – digging through peat is a strenuous task. David had brought an apple with him and sat in the entrance to the cave, eating it while he was trying to remember more of the legends his uncle's uncle had told him. Every so often, he would tell them a fragment of a story.

'That's funny.' Jack lifted the trowel nearer to a lamp. 'What do you make of that, Helen?'

Whatever it was, it wasn't just a rock. Helen picked up the small piece of something different, and held it close to the lamp.

'I'd better take it outside. Don't dig any more for a minute.'

Just as she had to get used to seeing in the dark, Helen had grown accustomed to waiting a minute or so before her eyes ceased to squint in the bright light of the desert afternoon. She sat next to David, who finished his apple and threw the core as far as he could throw it.

Helen opened her hand, and looked at the small object Jack had found. She gently brushed away the fine shreds of black fibre that partially obscured its shape. Without any doubt, it was a finger.

It was black, perfectly formed; a spatulate, graceful finger with a visible pattern of whorls and loops on the fleshy side and a trimmed fingernail. It was thin, but entire.

'Good grief!' Helen held out the finger for David to see. He reached out to take it; saw what it was, and obviously changed his mind.

'Jack! Jack! Quick, come here!' As she called, Helen wiped her free hand as though she might soil the finger if she touched it.

'You found a body!' David was excited. 'Part of one, anyway! There must have been someone through here, some poor bastard drunk who fell in the bog and died there. How long ago would it have been, Helen?'

'I don't know. I can make a guess, but I don't know.' Helen looked blankly at David. 'We have to find out if there's more of the body there, Jack. Maybe it's the only bit left; maybe – '

'I felt the trowel go through it. It resisted more than the peat. I think I cut it off – somebody.' Jack sat down abruptly.

For the next three hours, until long after the sun had gone behind the purple hills, they struggled to find the outline of the 'poor bastard drunk'. The rest of the right hand was soon seen, beautiful in its blackness, like liquid tar shaped into a tenderly curved sculpture. The naked arm, its muscles shrunken but still clearly defined, led to the area where the head must lie, but Helen wanted them to take the work of clearing much more slowly. The body lay on its side, one leg bent up and across the other, as though the man had died comfortably. For over an hour, they worked slowly, uncovering the lower part of the dead man, leaving the head until last.

'What do you reckon, Helen? Fifty years?' As he helped smooth away the peat with a dampened brush, David started to speculate. 'What sort of bloke would he be, wandering around here? A tribal man? Do you reckon he just vanished and his family gave up looking for him? Nobody from a town would just disappear. I wonder if there's a police record of him going missing?'

Helen paused and looked with alarm at David. 'The police! Oh, I really don't think we want them involved, do we?'

'Look, Helen.' Jack had been brushing the area of the man's neck with a soft, dry brush. A few strands of dry, matted hair appeared. Then the outline of a face. Helen took over from Jack and soon, with delicate, sensitive strokes of the brush, the man's face was cleared of peat.

His eyes were closed and he seemed to sleep. Although the peat had crushed his face, distorted it under the pressure of time, and it was difficult to see exactly what he had looked like in life, the man seemed at peace. His eyelids were softly wrinkled, the eyebrows curved gently above a finely-shaped nose.

When they had cleared him completely, they looked at the dead man in silence. This peaceful body had once been alive, had laughed and wept, had known love and sorrow. Jack traced with his finger the eyebrows, the closed lids, the nose, the full-lipped, gentle mouth. The dead man lay there, black as the peat around him, at one with it. Part of it.

'What do we do now?'

'I don't know, David. What do you think, Helen?'

'We get some expert advice. And quickly. I have a feeling this is something more important than we can imagine.'

The disquiet Helen felt did not surprise her. She knew that they should have left the body untouched from the moment the finger was identified. Other specialist scientists would have made more knowledgeable exploration than she had. They could perhaps have identified the man, and maybe she had, in her eagerness, destroyed some important evidence. And yet she had taken photographs, and her measuring technique was not unlike that used by archaeologists.

'Should we cover him up again, Helen? I mean, won't he spoil if he's out in the open like this?' Jack's practical commonsense shook Helen out of her contemplation.

'Spoil? Oh, I don't think so. The peat's quite dry, so the body must be too.'

David was looking at the man as though he might be able to recognise him despite the damaged features. This disconcerted Helen; the body was just that – a body.

'What about falling stones; stuff blown into the cave?' David said.

'Oh God, I don't know.'

Jack looked up at her. Helen felt his surprise; she was very rarely at a loss.

'We must protect him, Helen. Either cover him up or take him somewhere safe.' Jack spoke firmly. David nodded equally firmly.

'You're quite right, of course.' She started to chew her lower lip while she thought about the dilemma. She was aware that Jack, although he probably had a few ideas about what to do, kept silent. She remembered that this was how she first grew aware of Jack, when they met all those years ago. She remembered him quietly waiting for her to give an opinion, not impatient with her as her father was, not even merely courteous about it but waiting as if he knew her opinion would be valuable. She had become secure through Jack's understanding and respect over the years. She smiled at him, and he nodded back.

'You're right, of course, David,' she said. 'We must protect it. I think the damage has been done now – '

'You mean the finger? Oh dear, is that going to be a terrible thing to have done?' Jack was rubbing his face, clearly nervous.

'No, I don't mean that; you couldn't help that. No, I mean perhaps we shouldn't have uncovered it. I got carried away – not like me at all, is it, Jack? Still, if it is a problem, it's done now. We had better get it out, I think. We should take as much peat out with it, underneath, as we can so that it is minimally disturbed.'

'Right, do you want to mark out where we should dig?' David was visibly keen to get on with the job. He started to scratch an outline around the body with the measuring rod. 'Is this about right?'

'Look, let's stop for a minute.' She didn't shout, not in a cave whose rocks were apt to split. Helen wanted a chance to think the problem through. 'Let's get a drink.'

She scrambled out of the cave and fetched three cups and a bottle of water from the Esky which she had left at the foot of the hill, keeping cool under a space blanket. Jack followed her out, and David too, more slowly.

'Here; drink this.'

'Drink me,' said Jack.

'What?'

'Drink me – you know, Alice in Wonderland. The bottle that had a label on it: Drink me. This is all very Alice in Wonderlandish, isn't it?' He sipped the cool water appreciatively.

'He doesn't look like an Arundijilaba, like an aborigine,' David said.

'We can't know who or what it was until it's been looked at by someone who knows about these things,' said Helen, firmly.

'Like who? Another scientist?' There was an edge to David's voice. He wiped a drop of water from his mouth. 'I mean, this was a man, right? Not just some scientific thing; not a rock, or a bit of dead plant life, or something. A man.'

'We must treat him with respect; you're quite right, David.' Jack leant across and patted David's knee. 'I'm glad you reminded us; sometimes we all forget these things, don't we, Helen?'

His placatory tone irritated Helen. This discovery wasn't a person, it was a body, long dead; long gone. When it fell into the bog, how it got there and how it came to be preserved were far more interesting questions than its identity. Some itinerant aborigine, sheltering from the heat, no doubt. Nothing more. It was a scientific puzzle now, nothing to get all namby-pamby about.

'I need better equipment. I have to find out how old that peat is and just how long that body has been in it. I could take samples back to Perth, of course, but I don't want to leave the body exposed for longer than necessary. I can do the job *in situ*, given a bit of help.'

'We'll do all we can, Helen.' Jack's offer was prompt.

'No, no. Not that kind of help. I'll need to contact – someone – an archaeologist, I suppose. Maybe someone with experience of ancient soils. There's someone in the back of my mind – who the dickens is it? He gave a paper at the Soils Conference a couple of years ago. He'd spent a sabbatical working with this kind of thing in Europe. Interesting stuff. Walters? Walker? I'm pretty sure he's in Adelaide.'

David gathered up the plastic cups and took them back to the Esky. He stood looking back up at the cave, his face thoughtful, withdrawn. Helen watched him as David crouched down and picked up a handful of soil, letting it trickle slowly through his hand. For a brief moment, Helen had an image of a man she had seen on television, letting sand drift through his fingers by a pond outside a Nazi concentration camp, where his family had died in the Holocaust.

'Jack, I have to get to a telephone. Quickly.'

Helen scrambled down away from the cave, leaving the body where it lay. She thought about covering it, but could think of nothing she could do to protect the body. Nor could she think just what protection it needed. It was out of the bog now, but still in the same temperature as it had lain in for years – centuries, perhaps, if her guess was right.

'We should have brought a radio. Or one of those telephone things you can take around with you. I never thought of it.' Jack sounded disturbed; perhaps he felt that his planning expertise had failed him. She reassured him hurriedly.

'They don't work up here, dear. And never mind what we could have done; what can we do now is the issue. Whatever it is, we must get on with it, and quickly.'

Helen fastened the Esky, gathered together the tools lying around.

'Need we mark this place, David? Shall we find it again easily?'

The land around the outcrop did seem singularly lacking in features. There were similar outcrops every hundred or two metres, with similar shapes around them. The sand was grainy, strewn with stone fragments, undisturbed by animal or human tracks passing over them, and all of it unremarkable.

'No problem.' David grinned. Helen realised that he thought it a simple matter to remember this location; he saw clues and pointers in the surroundings which she couldn't see. Not all his Uncle Charlie's teaching had been forgotten.

'A phone.' Helen looked at David. This was his territory. OK, he knew how to find his way back to the cave, now could he find a phone? Quickly?

'I'll go. It'll take a while, but I reckon if I go straight in that direction I'll get to the weather station by tomorrow morning. There's nobody there, but the phone should be working.' David faced into the north-east, tapping a foot on the ground. 'I'll need to take some water and a bit to eat. I won't stop tonight; just keep going, right? Who do you want me to ring?'

It had not occurred to Helen that she wouldn't be making the initial contact herself. It was clearly best if David made the long, rough drive to a phone, but how could she expect him to talk to the man in Adelaide, a scientist she had never met and who would not find it easy to believe the message she would send?

'No, I'll come with you. Jack, you stay here and make sure –' She shrugged; nothing could happen to the body unless another willy-willy came through as bad as the one that uncovered the cave. Not very likely. 'You stay here so that we can find our way back, all right? And rest.'

Jack nodded; he understood her need to go.

'I'll ring the lab in Perth. Talk to Teresa Vandenburg. No, I'll ring her at home. She'll be there until half past eight in the morning. I won't want to say too much – the words are important.'

'What will you tell her?' Jack looked anxious, which made Helen feel a little irritated. She could manage this side of things very well.

'I'll just say I've found what I was looking for.' Jack was looking sceptical. 'And found more than I was looking for. Right?' Jack nodded. 'I'll tell her it's important she doesn't tell anyone. She's to track down the man at Adelaide Uni who knows all about bodies in bogs and get him over here. Walters or Walker, something like that. Or another expert. Quickly. Very quickly.'

Helen could imagine Teresa's shriek when she heard the phrase 'bodies in bogs' and the wild questions she would throw down the phone line. She hoped she could cope with it.

'Don't tell her anything else, Helen. The fewer people who know about this the better.'

'Of course I won't. She's to tell nobody at the lab, nobody at all. Only the man in Adelaide; she'll persuade him to come, I know. She can persuade people like nobody I know. Better she talks to him than me.'

'She persuaded me to buy that awful safari suit last year,' Jack said. He shook his head with disbelief. 'I never wore the damn thing.'

'Do you need anything? Is there anything she should send?' David was getting some food and water together, putting them in an Esky. He stood up and moved his shoulders around as though to loosen them up, readying himself for the long and difficult drive across the desert.

'I don't know. I can't think.' Helen got up and paced around. 'No, I can't do anything until that man from Adelaide makes contact. Oh, I'll have to ring her back – when, David? – to find out if the man's coming and then we can make arrangements to meet him in Perth.'

'We'd better stay there, at the weather station. We can stay a day or two, no hassle. I've got plenty of food and water. Enough diesel. Take our sleeping bags. You can sleep in the LandCruiser.'

It was clear that David had already thought of the need to stay there until Teresa called back. Helen felt relieved; she wasn't the only one thinking ahead.

'What's-His-Name – the man in Adelaide – he may want to talk to me. How long should we wait around for his call, David? If he rings, I'll give him some details but in absolute confidence, of course. No hint of this must get out. We don't want other people barging in on us.'

This is my discovery, she thought. Mine. Nobody else must get in on it.

'Can't wait too long. If your friend is as good as you say, he may settle for her invitation anyway.'

'I hope so. And if he needs anything special, he'll have to bring it with him,' Helen said.

'Let's be off then.' Without fuss, David swept the dust imported by the ride through the hundred metres where the willy-willy had been blowing, out of the front seat of the LandCruiser. He crunched into gear and they left. Jack and Helen waved. She knew Jack would stand there, worrying about her, watching the dust trail until it faded into the eastern horizon, a smudge against the indigo sky of late evening. Jack was probably hoping that she would be able to stand back and let other people handle all the problems. She knew that he also appreciated that she would do no such thing.

'Good to get a bloke who knows what he's doing involved, eh, Helen?'

Helen didn't take offence. She knew what David meant and it was a relief. 'It's going to help for sure. If we can get him to come over, it means that other hands are going to get dirty too.'

They stopped briefly to eat; a scratch meal, tinned corned beef and beans, tinned peaches, bread. They cleaned up what little mess they had made and sat together for twenty minutes, on a couple of canvas chairs, watching the stars become visible and the moon grow into an almost impossibly huge size as it hung over the land.

'It's funny to be sitting here, quietly, doing nothing, when back there is the most important thing I have ever done.'

'It's good to have a break, though. You're not – '

'- as young as I was, yes David, I know that. I shan't do too much. I know my limitations.'

'I didn't mean – '

'Don't worry about me.'

'It's Jack, really,' David said, sounding reluctant as if he were telling tales out of school. 'He worries about you.'

'Well, if he doesn't, nobody will. Let's face it, it takes it out of you, this desert. Struggling around, getting into caves; the dust and the hard work.'

David shifted slightly. 'Well, if you're both all right then.'

When they set off again, he concentrated on the driving, steering a bouncing way through and between the scrubby trees and anthills. His headlights were on high beam, picking up the occasional night hunting bird, a dozing kangaroo or emu startled upright into immobility by the light.

'I do wonder sometimes if it's become a bit much for Jack.' Helen looked at David's profile. He seemed not to be listening. 'But I suppose we're both all right. Excited, that's all. Concerned for each other, of course. He mustn't take on too much, right?'

Even as she spoke, Helen's thoughts had moved on. She had read, years ago, a book about bodies found in bogs. Somewhere in Scandinavia; Denmark, perhaps. She remembered with a degree of clarity which surprised her the photographs of one such body; a middle-aged man – maybe her age – who had been strangled to death. The rope was still around his neck. The book suggested it might have been some sort of ritual death, or a punishment. He had a leather hood over his head, and his face – she remembered the face – was as contented as though he fell asleep at the end of a pleasant day among friends.

Maybe the body she had found had ended his life peacefully. Maybe he had been murdered for some occult reason. Did the local aborigines do that kind of thing? She must ask David – but not now when he was concentrating on the road. Maybe the man had been sick, or lost, alone in the searing hot desert. He certainly looked at peace, she thought.

She could see herself quietly acknowledging letters from other scientists, letters sent to congratulate her on the discovery of the ancient waterhole, the remnant of a watercourse as yet unidentified. Others would follow her lead now and trace those ancient lines.

Her scientific paper would start – it would start – she would write a first-class abstract in plain and simple language and put something simple at the beginning, quietly stating the facts and judiciously calming down the enormous surprise and significance of the discovery. 'An unknown ancient bog was discovered – found – in a remote part of the Western Australian desert during a search to verify findings made in the laboratory.'

She nodded to herself a couple of times and, as David raced ahead in silence, Helen had only herself to share the excitement.

CHAPTER 3

THE WEATHER STATION WAS WELL PROTECTED. It looked incongruous; a single metal building little bigger than a suburban garage surrounded by ten-foot high cyclone fencing with a razor wire top. The constant wind had caused red sand to pile up in drifts around the base of the building, as snow would have drifted in another world.

The gate, made of closely-meshed, centimetre-thick stainless steel wire, and bolted fast with a huge padlock in place, looked impenetrable.

'I can't climb over that,' said Helen.

'No need.' David opened the tool compartment of the LandCruiser and hauled out a huge pair of wirecutters. 'These'll do the trick.'

And indeed they did. Within a few seconds he had unfastened the gate, opened the door to the weather station with a snip through the large brass padlock holding the door shut, and stood back to allow Helen to enter first.

'I'll put the kettle on, eh?' he said, and went back to the LandCruiser.

Helen looked with interest and pleasure at the stacked weather-sensing equipment. Almost all of it was enclosed in glass containers to keep out dust and insects. She wondered with some embarrassment if her presence there would upset some of the delicate sensing mechanisms. They were both hot: the temperature in the station must have been affected by their arrival, not to mention the movement of air around the instruments.

There was a metal folding bed in a corner with a plastic bag on it containing pillows and grey blankets.

'More comfortable for you than the LandCruiser, Helen,' David said, testing the thin mattress with his hand.

'Yes, I'll be fine.'

Another bag on the bed held what looked like towels and soap and a couple of toilet rolls. A box marked with a large red cross stood on one end of the bench. There was an office chair, a lamp much like the ones Helen used back at the camp, boxes of stationery. Little else. No computer. Just a telephone.

Helen found the number in her address book and pressed the buttons. The phone rang for a couple of minutes before it was answered.

'Ian?'

'Teresa?'

'Is that you, Ian?'

'No, I'm not Ian. It's me, Helen Lytton. Can you hear me?'

'Helen? I was dreaming – I thought it was Ian – what's wrong?'

'Nothing's wrong. I need your help, Teresa.'

'My help?'

There was a rattling sound on the phone. Then silence. Then a very loud swear word that made Helen smile.

'Hold on, will you?' There were fumbling, groping noises. A cough; another cough. Helen could imagine Teresa struggling to wake up.

'Christ almighty, it's only four in the morning! More fumbling noises. 'Shit, I caught my foot in the duvet. Hang in there while I get a cigarette, will you? Right, what do you want?'

'I'm ringing from a weather station in the Nor'west. Can you hear me all right?'

'It's a lousy line; can you do something about it?'

'No chance. It's a satellite phone and I'm hooked into it through a line from the weather station. Best I can do is this.'

'OK. Start at the beginning, hey?'

'Better sit down, then. It's a bit complicated.'

'Right. Go ahead.'

'I'm ringing you – '

'I gathered that; go on.'

'Because I found what I was looking for and more besides.'

'That's great! Even at four am. Gee, that's – '

'There's more, Teresa. It's important you don't tell anyone about this; anyone at all. Except one person. I want you to ring a man at Adelaide Uni – I can't remember his name but I think it might be Walker – '

'Oh, that's helpful. Go on.'

'Yes. And it might not be Adelaide Uni, but I am sure it's one of the South Australian ones.'

'Cuppa?' David came in with two steaming mugs of tea.

'Who's there with you? Is it Jack?'

'No, it's David. He's helping us with the project.'

'I thought you were Ian when the phone rang. What project?'

Teresa's lack of focus was exasperating.

'I know you thought I was Ian. You said "Is that Ian". Look, Teresa. This is important. I want you to ring that man in Adelaide and get him over here, as quick as possible.'

'Where?'

'I'm at the Bandergoorup Weather Station.' Helen glanced at David as she said the name: he nodded.

'Look Helen, I'm pretty resourceful but are you serious? I'm to call a man whose name I don't know – and you don't know – at a very large university – and it may be the wrong one

– and ask him to rush across the country to some place I've never heard of?'

'The man in Adelaide is an expert on bodies in bogs. That should help, eh?'

'An expert on – ? Oh my God! Have you found one? Was there someone – oh my God! Why the guy from Adelaide, though? Why the secrecy?'

'I found one all right. A man. An aboriginal; probably from David's own tribe. We found him yesterday. Will you do as I ask now?'

'David's an aboriginal? Is he a scientist?'

'No, he's a primary school teacher. Teresa, please – '

'A teacher? Really? I'm sorry, that sounds so – damn patronising. Forgive me, I'm half asleep and stunned with it.'

'That's OK.'

'Yes, I'll find him. How does he get there? To – where was it?'

'How does he get here, David?' Helen offered the phone to David who took it from her and gestured to Helen to sit down on the camp bed. As she did so, he passed her a mug of tea. She started to sip it as she listened to David giving instructions to Teresa.

He suggested the man from Adelaide could rent a four-wheel drive vehicle at the airport in Perth. He spelled the name and location of the weather station carefully, making Teresa repeat it twice.

'If you get him to ring me, we'll wait here at the weather station and find out how he'll be travelling. It's not all that easy but I reckon we'll find each other.'

'I hope so.'

'She says she hopes so.' This for Helen's benefit.

Helen caught his eye and added another thought to the conversation.

'Oh, Helen says if he's not there to get another one.'

'Another one?'

'Another expert.'

This time, David grinned and made a 'thumbs up' sign to Helen. 'She says she'll get him, Helen.'

'Tell her I'm counting on her to do so.'

'Helen said she's counting on you. I'll give you the number here.'

She had to repeat that twice, too. Then he hung up.

They were both tired. After she had drunk the tea, David took the mugs to rinse out from the kettle still plugged into the cigarette lighter in the LandCruiser. When he came back into the station, Helen was almost asleep.

'I'm just going – ' He nodded in the direction of the chemical toilet, outside the back door. When he came back, he nodded again.

'Good night,' Helen said.

She heard the LandCruiser door slam. Then she heard nothing more until morning.

They woke at almost the same time; Helen heard David come quietly into the station. They exchanged 'Good mornings' as Helen went out to the toilet. On her way back she stopped to watch the morning sky turn from deep indigo through every shade of violet and red into the bright gold of the moment just before the sun rose. It never ceased to enchant her. Dawn, dusk – they happened so quickly in Australia.

There was more tea waiting when she finished washing her face and hands from the container of water in the LandCruiser. Tea and a sandwich.

'Feel all right?' David said.

'Great, thanks.'

'I was just thinking that your friend will have had to wait a while before ringing the uni. Not likely they'd have someone on the switchboard at four in the morning, eh?'

'Oh God, I hadn't thought of that.'

'Still, she'll be right now. Only half an hour difference between Perth and Adelaide. Bound to be someone there now. Who's Ian?'

Helen looked at David, her mug of tea warming her hands.

'Oh, Ian. He's Teresa's boyfriend. Funny chap, really. He's gone fishing for a few weeks.'

'I fish. Nothing funny about that.'

'No, he's gone fishing in Nepal. He's like that. Very rich, mind you, so he can afford to be eccentric.'

'Maybe he'll climb Everest while he's there, eh?'

'I doubt it. He's done that once.'

'So is she eccentric, too? Your friend?'

'Teresa? Well, maybe a little. Ian's good for her; she's good for him, too, I think. Makes him laugh, you know? And he taught her to drive fast cars and fly.'

Helen was aware suddenly that she was gossiping about her friend. Not a thing she did usually. Time to change the subject.

They chatted about science and teaching for a couple of hours then lapsed into comfortable silence. Helen rather wished there was a radio, or a magazine, at the station but in their absence she fell to thinking about the discovery again.

She was jarred awake by the phone ringing. David was outside but came hurrying back as she picked up the receiver.

'Hi, Helen! Look, I'm sorry it took so long to get back to you. Adelaide Uni didn't answer the phone until nine o'clock.

Well, it did but it was only the night security guy and he wouldn't fetch anyone to help me.'

'Never mind that. Did you find our man?'

'I had this brilliant idea – I mean, you said not to tell anyone about it, didn't you?'

'Yes, Teresa. Did you get him?'

'I'm telling you, aren't I? I had this brilliant idea – '

Helen took in a deep breath but said nothing. This was Teresa's moment.

'By that time I had a plan, right? I said to the switch girl "Hello? My name is Teresa Vandenburg and I'm writing a book about a murder and I believe there's someone there who knows all about – " Anyway, after a while I said I wanted to talk to the man who knows about old soil and that. You know, bogs, I said. And bodies in them. And she told me who I wanted. Wasn't that brilliant?'

'Brilliant. And – ?'

'Well, within a few slow-moving minutes, this man came on. He was a bit cautious at first.'

'What is his name?'

'Walker, like you thought. So I told him the true story, after I made him promise to keep it all a close secret. I could tell he was indulging me, that he thought I was just a screwed-up American woman getting fancy ideas about science. Nevertheless, he was interested and, as I went on, his interest became stronger and even urgent. He wasn't about to rush headlong into any woman's fantasy, though. Very sensibly, I thought, he asked me to give him half an hour to check out a few things. Fifteen minutes later, he called back. He said "Yes of course I'll come. If there's half a chance she's right, this is something I must see." He said he could leave more or less straight away, he had a couple of people to tell – he'd say he had urgent personal business. Then he asked how to get to you.'

Now they were getting to the point.

'This was a problem to which I had given a lot of thought during the last couple of hours, Helen. Your instructions had been minimal, you were going to discuss the logistics of actually getting Antony Walker to Bandergoorup with him, right? And I had a better idea.'

'Please, Teresa, cut to the quick, will you?' Helen had waited patiently but it had been a long time.

'I'm meeting him at Perth Airport. The Qantas flight at lunchtime. And we'll be with you by late this afternoon!'

'Impossible, Teresa. He can't get here that quickly.'

'Oh yes he can. I'm taking Ian's plane – I'm flying him up!'

It was all organised. The small airfield where Ian housed his plane was putting together a flight plan, organising fuel, and everything else she would need. She had rung the Perth Laboratories and pleaded 'urgent personal business' to attend to.

'Hats off to Dr Walker, for that one. So I'm packed and ready to go. All I need is to know where to land near you up there.'

Helen handed the phone with a quick explanation to David. He gave Teresa directions. There was a landing strip a couple of hundred kilometres from the weather station at Bandergoorup, built to serve a rarely-used meatworks. The man who owned the meatworks lived on the edge of the landing strip; David would contact him and make sure the strip was clear for her to land. And that was all. Couldn't be simpler.

David locked up the weather station as well as he could after ringing the Meteorology people in Perth to explain the 'dire emergency' that had caused him to break in. They weren't pleased, as he remarked to Helen. Not even the promise of a generous cheque from her calmed the senior officer down but as one of his people was due to visit the station within the next few weeks, and this was the first break-in in the seventeen years since the weather station was erected, he conceded that the chain and padlock could be replaced quickly – and at Helen's cost.

'Thank you, Mr Clark,' Helen said. 'Thank you for your understanding.'

'That's all right, Dr Lytton,' he said, sounding as though it were anything but all right. 'It's a bugger being caught short up there, I know.'

When she hung up, David was grinning.

'Not the best excuse, Helen. Not the best.'

'Well, it's a kind of emergency, isn't it?' Helen smiled too.

They got into the LandCruiser and set off for the meatworks to arrange for the plane to land safely alongside it.

As it turned out, there was only one hitch. Not exactly a hitch, but the small four-seater plane was fuller than Helen had expected. When the plane landed, she saw that Dr Walker had brought someone else with him.

'Who's that?' Helen's voice was shrill; an extra person was not part of her plan at all. She hurried across the red, recently scraped and graded ground to meet her visitors, leaving David and the owner of the meatworks to wait.

The younger man to alight from the plane held out a hand as Helen drew near. 'I'm sure you won't mind, Dr Lytton. This is my father, Peter Walker. He's retired now, but his background could be useful. I haven't briefed him at all, as promised.'

In the background, Teresa shrugged. Helen gathered that Teresa too had protested about the additional visitor.

They all shook hands, and Helen noticed that Teresa seemed to have warmed to Antony Walker. As they started to unload the plane, Teresa muttered into Helen's ear that the man had the darkest eyes she had ever seen. 'Almost black,' she said. 'Deep and mysterious like unplumbed pools. Sheer Mills and Boon. How could I send his father packing?'

Teresa moved away from Helen to help Antony Walker lift out a heavy case. She grinned at him and he smiled back, a little disconcerted, Helen thought.

The Walkers looked very much like each other, except that the father was taller, more spare and bony inside a loose cotton shirt and jeans. Antony wore shorts with his cotton shirt. They were wearing boots. Both had grey hair and their eyes had those smile lines at the corners.

Their smile was the same smile; wide and trusting. Helen decided she liked both of them.

'Hey, Helen. I had to leave a case behind to make room for Peter. It was the beer and wine, which seems a great shame, but I can pick it up when I fly back for more supplies.'

'More supplies?' Helen said, profoundly hoping that trip wouldn't be necessary.

'She made us both hold a six-pack of beer, and a bottle of white wine on our laps,' Antony said. 'She left the rest in the boot of her Volkswagen.'

'Teresa refused our offer to help load the plane, Dr Lytton. My son brought quite a bit of stuff – camping gear and a few instruments. They're packed in pretty solid cases. Teresa must be a strong young woman.'

The plane was just about empty by now. They picked up what they could carry, the two men still nursing the wine and beer under one arm.

The older man loped alongside Helen comfortably, seemingly not at all curious about the nature of the instruments his son had brought with them.

'We didn't bring much in the way of personal things. I think Teresa was quite relieved about that. Her plane isn't a jumbo, of course, is it. Noisy, too. I'm afraid I slept most of the way here.'

Antony Walker had heard his father's comment and sidestepped neatly from Teresa's side to join Helen.

'I tried to pump Teresa about your work up here, but she was very cagey about it.'

'I asked her to be,' said Helen.

'Yes, she said so.'

Helen could feel his glance and showed nothing but polite determination to keep moving away from the plane. She could see David and the other man, a much older and overweight man dressed in tight football shorts and a black singlet, waiting in the shadow of the meatworks building. The owner of the meatworks had a hand up to shade his eyes as he watched them approach. Another person in on the discovery. Too many; too many.

The case Helen was carrying was heavy. She stopped to rest for a moment and the small group stopped with her, putting down their loads. She saw David start across the strip towards them.

'I took the precaution of looking up your background in the university library before I agreed to come,' Antony Walker said. 'I hope you understand that?'

Helen nodded. 'Yes, quite right.'

'I was reassured about your credentials, although they are not in my field, of course. I must say that I am very curious to know how you came to be looking for a body in such an unlikely place.'

'It was the last thing in my mind when we set out on the expedition.'

'You're at the CSIRO in Fremantle, too, I think you said?' Antony had ignored her comment. He sounded casual, almost offhand as he asked. Helen hadn't mentioned her affiliation with CSIRO, but maybe Teresa had.

'Yes. I've just retired.'

'Ah.'

Helen looked at him, seeking an interpretation of the 'ah'. She saw only courteous interest.

'And Teresa?' he said. He glanced at Teresa, who was taking animatedly to Peter.

'Yes, she works there. She's not a scientist, though.' Just in case it mattered. 'She works in the Computing Section.'

'Support work; you know,' Teresa said. She had heard the last exchange and joined them, slipping an arm through Antony's. His elbow immediately bent, making a right-angle in his arm, a formal and rather clumsy support.

Helen looked at Antony; he nodded. He would know about support work. Scientists usually relied on other people for expert help with their computing needs.

David joined them and picked up two of the cases, leading them off to where the other man waited.

When they reached him David introduced himself and Barry O'Donnell. He told the newcomers by way of introduction that Barry owned the Lakeview Meatworks and lived there permanently even though the work was only seasonal.

'Bloody lonely this time of year,' Barry said. 'Nice to have a bit of company. Was the strip OK?'

Helen wondered what he meant, but Teresa answered. 'Yeah, great. Thanks.'

'You can park your plane in that shed, if you like.' Barry pointed it out; a large, corrugated-iron shed glittering in the sunlight.

'We can do it, Teresa,' said David. 'Barry knows how, I reckon.'

'Too right,' Barry said with a grin and the men set off back to the plane. Barry was chatting affably as they moved away. He didn't seem curious, Helen was relieved to notice; just sociable and friendly.

'The Walkers seem nice,' said Helen as she and Teresa watched from the side of the runway.

'Yes. He is nice. Both of them. Mind you it wasn't easy talking on the way here. You know, noise.' Teresa waved an arm around.

'You managed to get to know each other, I think.'

'Well, a little.' Teresa's voice was unpersuasively meek.

'A little?'

'Well, we chatted about Antony's work and mine. Somehow the fact that the plane belongs to my boyfriend came up, as did the fact that Ian and I have no wish to marry. Antony told me he was divorced and has no children. That's all, really.'

'All! It sounds to me as if you were interviewing each other,' Helen said.

'Well, I'll be – ! So it does!' Teresa sounded amused.

The men rolled the plane into the shed which was big enough, and empty enough, to be a hangar. From the distance, Helen watched Barry put chocks under its wheels. It wasn't the first time a plane had been kept there, obviously. It would

68

certainly be safe. David and Antony stacked the spare fuel in a corner, in an area where other fuel was stored.

When the plane was empty, and its cargo safely disposed of, the LandCruiser and its passengers came back to join the women. David opened his door to let some fresh air in as Barry got out to talk to the women. The Walkers got out slowly, stretching and seeming happy to be able to relax.

'I was just telling them about me,' said Barry. 'Occurred to me you might like a drink before you set off back to wherever. A shower, too, if you're feeling the heat.'

It sounded like a good idea but they were all eager to get to the campsite.

'Another time, perhaps,' said Helen, shaking Barry's hand.

'Thanks, Barry, for the use of the strip. And the garage.' Teresa smiled. David closed his door. The Walkers got back in. Teresa accepted a hand from Antony as she climbed into the back of the LandCruiser, followed by Helen.

'A tight squeeze, but we'll manage,' said Teresa. She seemed to Helen not entirely sure that they would manage. It was a very tight squeeze. Teresa had to sit very close indeed to Antony.

Barry seemed reluctant to see them leave. He kept a hand on the open frame of the window as he spoke. 'Visiting scientists, eh? CSIRO people, I expect. Seen them up here before.' He was only a little curious. A lonely man, Helen thought.

'Scientists, yeah. Who else would visit these godforsaken parts, hey?' Teresa grinned and Barry laughed at her cheek.

The Walkers and Teresa waved. Barry nodded in their direction. As the passengers settled into the LandCruiser in their cramped conditions, Helen watched the elderly man, surely carrying too much weight for this merciless part of the world, walk slowly back to the verandah of the large and isolated house built next to the meatworks. He sat down in a rocking chair. He waved as the LandCruiser bounced away. The passengers waved back.

'Jack will be surprised to see all of you.'

Helen was aware that David was apprehensive. Jack had not expected two men; even Teresa would be a surprise to Jack. No doubt David wasn't sure if they had done the right thing, agreeing to Teresa's plan to fly the Adelaide scientist up.

'Hey, everything's going to be fine!' As if she understood David's thoughts, Teresa patted his arm and settled her slim bottom more firmly on the hard cushion as they bounced along. She was obviously looking forward to the adventure. Helen watched her friend with pleasure and wished she felt as relaxed.

It was almost dark when they got back to the camp.

The LandCruiser stopped in a skid on the loose scree. Antony Walker, who had been asleep for the past couple of hours, woke suddenly and jumped down from the vehicle. Rather than get involved with Jack's possible anger, or so Helen thought, David went around to the back of the LandCruiser and started to unpack the luggage and equipment.

Teresa ran across the few metres separating them and took Jack in her arms for a squeeze, as Helen walked towards him smiling hugely, reassuringly. It's all right, Jack; she tried to send a wave of comfort to him. Peter Walker got out more slowly, stretching his legs and arms as he walked with his son towards Jack.

'Oh don't look like that, Jack! I had to come – it's too exciting for me not to come! And I got Dr Walker up here a

70

whole lot quicker than if he'd had to drive up, now didn't I? So stop looking cross.'

'But how did you do it?'

'Simple; we flew.'

Helen shook her head slightly; Teresa was being a bit too casual.

'I mean, how could you organise it so quickly?' Jack sounded almost jealous, Helen thought. As if he should have been the one to arrange for the journey.

Civilities were exchanged cautiously. Now that they were at the headquarters of their expedition, a phrase Jack used with something of a flourish, Helen thanked Antony Walker for coming on so sketchy a briefing. He thanked Helen for thinking of him when the need arose.

Jack soon walked away to the edge of the camp, looking up into the star-struck sky.

'He'll be thinking that everything's got completely out of hand, Teresa,' Helen said quietly. 'Look at him. Just standing there, happy to see three of us coming back. Three, but not five.'

There weren't enough chairs but a blanket on the ground was quite acceptable to the Walkers, whose bodies had been vibrating in the plane for rather too long, Peter said.

Jack opened a couple of bottles of wine, and handed plastic glasses of it around. 'It's not the wine you brought with you,' he said. 'I've put that in the fridge.'

Everyone accepted a 'glass'.

'I'll put some more food on.' Jack went off and busied himself opening tins. All that was needed, according to Teresa, who offered her suggestion while extracting a large box from the top of a stack of boxes near her, was a few vegetables as she had found time to buy a couple of quiches en route to the airport.

'Quiche? In the desert?' Peter Walker's wry amusement made everyone smile, a little. Suddenly, the white wine started to work and the group relaxed.

'This is your line of country, isn't it, Dr Walker? It was you who worked on the bog bodies in Europe?'

'If I call you Helen, will you call me Antony? My father's "Dr Walker".' Antony smiled at Helen, who thought what a pleasant man he was. 'Yes, I spent some months in Britain. They turn up there from time to time.'

'I remembered your paper. At the Alice Springs conference?'

Antony nodded. 'When can I see what you've found?'

For a moment, Helen sat swirling her wine in the plastic tumbler. The secret was lost now; soon other eyes would see what she and Jack and David had seen. Antony Walker's eyes would understand more than she did. The body would no longer be her exclusive scientific trophy.

'I'll take you up in the morning; first light.'

'Up?' Antony looked around. The landscape was very flat. Helen could see him wondering about her choice of words.

'It's in a cave,' she said. 'A cave I was looking for; a cave where I was sure I would find traces of water; ancient water.'

'Around here? It seems unlikely.'

'It is unlikely. But it's there. And there's some sort of spring keeping it damp.'

'What led you to even look for it? I mean there's no indication of anything like water here; not from the air. No indication at all.'

Before Helen could start to explain, Peter Walker joined them. He pulled a box with him to use as a seat. 'I thought I'd never want to sit down again, Dr Lytton.'

'Helen.'

'It's a long drive from the meatworks.'

'Meatworks; weather stations,' said Jack. 'How did these places get into the picture? It seemed relatively simple when we set off.'

Peter explained how Teresa had organised their arrival. Jack knew most of it but he clearly enjoyed hearing how the details slotted together. Teresa hovered within earshot and came across now, visibly hoping that all was forgiven: both the extra guest and her own presence.

'Enjoy the quiche, hey?'

Helen laughed. Teresa was not very good at seeking approval subtly.

'The quiche was marvellous. Thank you.'

Teresa sat down on the ground, relieved.

With a sudden thought, Helen said, 'I must give you the money for them. Oh dear, and the petrol or whatever that thing uses. The aeroplane. Is it Ian's?'

'Not to worry. Ian said I could use it and he's rich.'

'Rich?' Antony asked her with a serious expression.

'Yeah, he's rich all right.' Teresa was clearly amused by Antony's concern.

'How does he make his money?' Well, Antony was direct enough. Teresa would like that, Helen knew.

'Nothing very exciting; he saves exciting things for his hobbies. He's some sort of an accountant for big business. That sort of thing.' Teresa waved a hand about vaguely, indicating her lack of interest in Ian's other life.

'So you're one of his "exciting things"?' Antony seemed to realise that he was quite possibly flirting – Teresa didn't seem to be sure either – and he abruptly turned away, not hearing Teresa's guarded reply. Helen enjoyed the exchange and happily neither of them seemed to be aware of her.

Antony abruptly asked Helen if she were enjoying her retirement and as she replied that she was, yes, very much, she could see that Antony felt rather foolish.

'More wine?' Jack and David came over. They had finished their chores; now the group was complete, some on deck chairs, some on boxes, Teresa sitting on the ground.

Helen tried to catch David's eye; she wanted to reassure him that the plans had worked out very satisfactorily; that he had done well to go along with Teresa's scheme.

'Perhaps someone will tell me what all this is about now.' Peter didn't seem to be in any hurry to be informed, Helen thought. He must have been taken on trips before where he was given little information until it was necessary. Maybe he did some sort of 'need to know' work; maybe he was something to do with the government, or the army. Helen took another sip of wine.

Well, he needed to know. They could hardly keep him isolated now from what they were doing.

Peter didn't interrupt as she explained why they were there. The others listened, their faces reflecting the flickering light of the camp fire. Only Teresa seemed to want to interrupt but her frequent exclamations of 'Wow!' were patted into silence by Jack's hand on her arm. Antony watched Teresa, intrigued by her, or so Helen decided.

Helen told the newcomers how Jack had made the discovery, omitting to mention that he had severed a finger from the body. It was important that they all keep the secret because it was of considerable scientific importance. With that aspect emphasised, Helen fell silent, watching Peter's face in the light of the lamp which David had fetched, quietly, while she talked.

'You said your father would be useful, Antony. How come?' Teresa's bluntness made Jack squirm, and he made a small, muttered protest. Helen said nothing; she looked again at Peter, waiting.

'I'm retired now, of course. I'm a pathologist.'

Helen spoke into the silence. 'You can tell us what he died of.' She sipped her wine.

'Yes, probably. I've done some forensic work in my time.'

'The law?'

'I can advise you.'

In the pause that followed Peter's quiet and firm comment, Teresa started to tell the group about the trip; how she had organised it, how helpful everyone had been. Helen saw that David was amused by Teresa's enthusiasm for outback flying and what she saw as its laid-back accessibility. He told a couple of stories, slightly exaggerated, about people being arrested for being drunk in charge of aircraft after a night out on the town.

Jack went with Antony to set up the tent the Walkers had brought, and which they would share, and to move David's few possessions out of the tent he was vacating for Teresa. David had said he was happy to sleep in the open air, alongside the LandCruiser, or in it if the night became cool. Helen and Peter Walker said nothing to each other for a while.

She shifted uncomfortably in her chair. 'I suppose we must report the find.'

'You should.'

'Even if it's old; very old?'

'Even so.'

'It's important to science, Peter. I want to keep it for science.'

'It was a man.'

She shifted uncomfortably in her chair. 'Is that your advice? That after making the discovery of my lifetime I have to tell the police and let them walk in here, take the body away, have an inquest, a funeral, get the newspapers in on it? Be on the ABC news? Is that your advice?'

Peter paused for a long moment, his eyes disengaged from the immediate surroundings.

'If this body is what you believe it to be, Helen, then as far as I can see at the moment, until I've had a chance to examine him, there is no rush. If he has been in your cave for a long time, then a little time more won't hurt, will it?'

'How long?'

'We'll talk about that when I've had a look at him. My son's a scientist, Helen. I understand your position and his. I am truly here to help, not hinder.'

'And you're retired. You don't have any obligation to the law.'

'I can't agree with that, but let's say my obligation runs a little slower, like I do now.'

They smiled, tentatively. Tomorrow would make decisions for them, Helen knew.

CHAPTER 4

A S SOON AS IT WAS LIGHT ENOUGH, the party had a quick breakfast and set off for the cave.

As they walked across the ground around the camp, which was still somewhat smooth since the passage of the willy-willy, Helen explained how her few moments of fright had led to the discovery of the cave. She told them that if the willy-willy had not blown away so much of the accumulated rubble, she might never have seen the entrance.

David said he was sure they would have found it, but it had been taking a long time.

Peter seemed to want to offer Helen his arm but she made it abundantly clear that she had no need of support, and walked vigorously ahead; unlike Teresa who clearly found her sandals singularly inadequate, as Helen had expected when she saw them, to the task of carrying her through the sharp splinters and gritty sand. Without Antony's hand on her elbow, Helen thought, Teresa might well have fallen several times. What a performance!

There was room in the cave for all of them, just. With David's help, while the others kept out of the way at the entrance to the cave, the Walkers set up and adjusted the compact system of battery-operated lights they had brought with them, creating the best possible conditions to look at the body.

'Helen? Would you spread this over the bog, please?'

Helen did as she was asked, shaking open the large, white, plastic sheet across the flat surface alongside the excavation, at the other side of the body. Antony told her to weight the corners with rocks, so that the sheet would be as flat and smooth as possible.

As the preparations drew to a conclusion, David stepped back to the entrance to the cave, seeming to Helen as is if he were torn between wanting to watch and being uncomfortable with what was about to happen.

The Walkers pulled on surgical gloves and turned their attention to the body. It was lying on the flat surface alongside the depression where it had been until discovery.

Helen stood for a moment, looking again at the body she had discovered so unexpectedly. Although emaciated, its skin so shrunken that she could see the location and shape of its bones, the body was perfect. For now.

'We shouldn't all be in here,' Helen said. 'We'll affect the temperature – and the humidity; there's moisture in our breath.'

'Just one quick peek,' Teresa said in a whisper. She moved past Helen and leant carefully over the body. 'Oh my God, how beautiful!'

For a long moment she looked at the sleeping figure of the man, gently shaking her head in wonder. Nobody tried to urge her away. They too looked for a long time at the body.

Antony stirred, took a deep breath. 'We'll make more space for you,' Jack said to him, although his eyes were looking elsewhere. Teresa helped Jack to gather up the empty containers for the lights and they carried them outside the cave.

David gave Teresa a hand as she scrambled down the scree, and turned back to assist Jack. They had left the cave quietly, but the doctor and the scientists were already so engrossed in Antony's work that none of them noticed, except

Helen whose attention was only momentarily diverted by Jack's stumbling descent.

With his father's help, Antony moved the lights around so that he could take photographs from several angles at every stage of his examination of the body and the peat where it had lain. Between making exposures, they switched the lighting system off because of the heat it generated, relying on the cooler, gentler radiance of the gas-powered lamps.

Antony's equipment for taking core samples of the peat was simple to use; Helen was familiar with the technique. Soon there would be an accurate measurement of the age of the deposit and of the length of time the man had lain in it. All Antony had to do was sink the hollow instrument into the peat alongside the body and mark the level at which the body had lain.

He slid the extruded core samples into plastic bags and labelled them sequentially. Dating would come later, back at the laboratory.

He took several samples at different locations, and at different depths. He checked the sketches Helen had made, and added his own annotations to them, then photographed them. Finally, he took samples of the surface of the peat, and small samples of the vegetation still clinging to the body. These too were labelled and put into a box with the core samples.

At last Antony's attention turned to the body itself. He moved a lamp closer and looked for a long time at the damaged face. As he moved the lamp around, it cast shadows over the face, seeming to animate it, Helen thought, as though the dead man stirred slightly in his sleep, as though he moved his damaged mouth, almost blinked, turned his head a fraction.

The man's head was at a slight angle, exposing one ear, surrounded by a mass of hair that seemed long and curly. Although it was dry now, it seemed to Helen that the hair had been wet and tangled when the man died. His ear was perfectly preserved; it had a small lobe, and the curve of the outer ear was almost delicately shaped, like a sea shell.

'Teresa's right,' Antony said. 'It's beautiful. You often see that kind of calmness on these people's faces. Sudden death or not, there's some kind of common acceptance. Silly, I suppose, to think that. Still, it always strikes me that way.'

'It's relaxation of muscles, Antony. Common enough when people die.' Peter's voice was matter-of-fact, but Helen heard the slight catch in his voice. This was an emotional moment for all of them, she thought.

'Here we go.' As he spoke Antony used his tweezers to take tiny specimens of matter other than peat from the body. He identified shreds of cloth, fragments of leather, a splinter of wood. As he called out the details, Helen wrote them down on labels. All the specimens were dropped carefully and separately into small plastic bags, which she immediately sealed. She peeled a label from its plastic backing for each bag and placed it carefully, pressing it down without crushing the contents.

'Look at this, Helen. Did you see it? What did you make of it?'

His voice suddenly urgent, Antony lifted the edge of a length of fabric which lay under the body, pleated and folded as though it had been put there yesterday, and still pliable. The fabric was black, as black as the body itself. It looked to Helen as though it had been placed where it was to cushion the body in rest, like a blanket.

Helen shook her head. 'I hadn't seen that. Clothing? Surely not.'

'See this, Dad? If we get it out carefully – I reckon it's a cloak or something; still intact, I think. He must have been lying on it when he died.'

'Why didn't it disintegrate, I wonder?' Helen watched the small, careful movements Antony was making as he gently lifted the body clear of the fabric and with great precision, and Helen's help, edged the fabric out from beneath the body. His father stood back, waiting for his turn.

'It's the chemicals in the water. Preserves the bodies and sometimes all sorts of artefacts too.' Antony lifted the folded fabric, which Helen had thought no more than a shape in the bog, an impression created by the weight of the body, when she first saw it. It hung, not entirely stiff, not entirely soft, over his arms.

'Helen, get a sheet down, will you?'

She got another plastic sheet from the box in the corner of the cave and spread it flat on the cave floor. Helen took the length of fabric from him and, following Antony's instructions, laid it down gently. With cautious concern and trying to work out the shape as it unfolded, she was able to spread the black fabric out almost to its full size.

'I wouldn't have thought the local people would use clothes – if it is clothing – this elaborate, this big. I wouldn't have thought they would use any at all. And where would they get the fabric? It's been woven.' Helen could see the pattern of the weave, a herringbone pattern, quite clearly.

Antony stood up, stretching his back. He looked thoughtfully at the bog and the depression the body had made. 'It's not all that old, you know.'

'But it must be! There's no visible trace of water anywhere else around here!'

'Oh, the bog itself is pretty ancient, no doubt about that, Helen. But your body – well, I don't know. He's not so old.'

'How old, Antony?'

'At a guess – oh I don't know – '

'At a guess?' Helen was anxious to know.

'Three – four hundred years; not more. Not much more.'

'Or less?'

'I doubt it. This sort of stuff is reasonably predictable.'

'It's not sphagnum moss, though.'

He was rather surprised by Helen's comment, she could tell. But then he was a soil scientist and probably had assumed that she had little experience of the vegetative components of soils. And indeed it was a special area of knowledge and Helen had very little of it. Just enough to know she was right.

'It works the same way as the European bog material. My guess would be about four hundred years. Not ancient.'

'And not an aboriginal, I think.' Peter Walker had been quietly examining the head of the body. He stood up, his eyes still on the body. 'We must get him to some place where I can have a better look. I can tell you quite a lot without being too invasive at this stage, Helen.'

'Not an aboriginal? But that's not possible! His colour – and this place – there were no white people here then! Not four hundred years ago!" Helen was almost shouting. What was going on? Her bog man, her discovery, was being turned into something else.

She hurried out of the cave, angry and confused.

'They're wrong! It can't be right!' She shouted her protest as she scrambled down the scree. Jack and Teresa were chatting at the foot of the outcrop. Teresa had a plate in her hands, heaped with sandwiches, ready for a working lunch when the scientists stopped for a break. When they heard Helen's cry, and saw the anger and bewilderment she knew must show in her face, they came over to her, clearly concerned. David stood a little way off, smoking, watching. Helen regretted her outburst but it really was becoming too much to bear.

'What's wrong, dear? What's upset you?' Jack put an arm around Helen's shoulders.

'They say he's four hundred years old!'

'Wow!' Teresa said. 'And that's a problem?'

'Oh Teresa, that's not all. They say he's not an aboriginal.'

David threw away the cigarette first and stamped on it to kill any possible sparks. 'Of course he's an aboriginal,' he said. 'He's a black man. He's like me.'

'I know, that's what I said. I mean, I know there's stuff – tannin – in the bog and it acts as a dye – I mean, I know that – but of course he's an aboriginal.'

'What are they doing with him?' Helen was surprised by the intensity in David's voice. He sounded as though there was an accusation in his question

'They're talking of getting him out, putting him some-where safe, where they can work more on him.'

'No. They can't do that.'

David brushed Teresa aside, almost dislodging the plate of sandwiches, and strode to the foot of the outcrop. He started to climb up to the cave. Helen hurried across to him.

'What's the matter, David? They know what they're doing; I was just disconcerted, agitated. Don't take any notice of me, please, I'm all right.'

David stopped when Helen caught his arm. He looked up at the cave entrance, barely visible behind the piled scree. Jack came over to them, harried from behind by a worried Teresa. Helen looked to them both for support.

'Is there a problem?' Jack said.

'It isn't right. I can't let them do it.'

'Do what, David? What's worrying you?'

'Those people.' David jerked a thumb in the direction of the cave. 'This is a man they are dealing with. A man. An Arundijilaba; one of my own people. I can't let them move him.'

'But David, they're scientists; they know what they're doing.' Helen was puzzled again; what was wrong with everybody?

'We don't allow our dead to be moved. They stay where they are put. Where they are buried.' David's voice was flat; uncompromising.

There was a surprised silence. Helen struggled to gather her wits.

Jack recovered first. 'You don't believe that, David. What sort of superstitious nonsense are you talking? You aren't an Arundijilaba, you're an educated man!'

Whatever David thought of Jack's remark, he showed no sign of changing his decision to go into the cave. Gently, but firmly, he removed Helen's restraining hand.

'Hey look, David,' Teresa said. 'Let's talk about this. You know the Australian government – both Federal and State ones – are real sensitive to aboriginal beliefs about their people. Hell, I was reading about it in the *Bulletin* last week – all the museums are giving relics back; there's no way anything can be done legally that would offend the aborigines.' Teresa talked calmly, and at last David turned his eyes away from the cave and looked at her.

'I can't explain it properly,' he said. 'I want what my grandfather wanted. He spoke for all of the people hereabouts and he told me a dead man shouldn't be touched. Unless he can come alive again, a dead man has to be left in his grave.'

'Well, there aren't many who can come alive again, are there?' Jack smiled faintly.

Helen watched as the attempt to lighten the atmosphere seemed to work.

'He said it could happen.' David suddenly squatted down, one knee bent and the other leg stretched out. He looked tired, Helen thought. Tired and worried. 'My grandfather was very particular about that. And when the old man spoke he was always right. Always. Even when he said something stupid, he was always right.'

'He couldn't have been, though, could he?' Jack continued his distracting chat. Teresa climbed up to the cave to tell the Walkers that lunch was ready. They followed her out, slid and scrambled down the scree, and went to the tents. Helen went with them, and as they scrubbed their hands, she explained how disconcerted she had been by their pronouncements. She was embarrassed; her display of petulance was hardly that of a scientist.

Peter reassured her that everyone understood; they were all under stress. He patted Helen's shoulder and rather than feeling patronised, she felt grateful. Antony hung up the towel they had used and led them back to the others, grabbing a sandwich from Teresa's plate as he joined her.

While they were eating, Jack again said that David's grandfather couldn't have been right always, could he? Helen knew this tactic of Jack's; start a discussion, be a bit provocative, distract the person who's upset. It always worked with her when she was talking about her father.

David took up the point, not looking at the Walkers. 'The old man was never wrong. Like his father, and his grandfather. All the way back. We had to believe that, too. His word was the law.'

'Well, things have changed, haven't they?'

David said nothing more. Jack fetched a box and sat down with him, being there if needed. Another tactic familiar to Helen. Food and water were consumed in silence. Antony was visibly tired after the concentration of the last few hours.

Helen hoped the silence was a friendly one. It seemed unlikely that everything was back under control – some sort of control. When they had finished eating, she made a muttered excuse and went off to her tent, followed by Teresa. Helen sat down on a camp bed and put her face in her hands.

'I don't know what to do, Teresa. I don't know how to handle things any more.'

She heard the crunch of footsteps coming towards the tent, and looked up before the footsteps stopped.

'We have a problem, Helen.'

When she heard Antony call out to her, she gave a despairing look at Teresa, who shrugged her shoulders as though to say: 'There's nothing we can do now, events have moved on too quickly.' Helen stood up and pushed the tails of her shirt firmly into the waistband of her shorts. She took a deep breath, and looked with a rueful grimace at Teresa.

'What is it, Antony?'

Antony pushed aside the tent flap and stood in the entrance. He started to explain the predicament.

The problem which he and his father had perceived was that the body had to be moved to a place where it could be kept at a temperature of about four degrees Celsius. It was impossible to conduct any kind of examination in a tent; the heat would cause the body to start deteriorating immediately.

Antony and his father wanted the body taken to Perth. They could arrange with one of the major hospitals there for the provision of a storage place for the body – 'there'll be room in the hospital morgue' – and for help with the examination.

Their idea was that Teresa should fly the body back right away. If they cut a large enough amount of peat to hold the body, and put a layer of it on top, it would not be damaged during the flight.

The body and its container of peat would weigh a tonne or more; the logistics of getting it out of the cave were urgent matters for consideration. Antony looked around expectantly.

'Can we get moving, then? Any ideas about getting everything out safely?'

'I can sort that out.' Jack had followed Antony to the doorway of the tent. He had already taken a notepad and pen from his pockets. 'I'm an engineer by trade.' He walked away from the tent. Through the open flap Helen saw him start making a rough drawing and some calculations, looking up at the entrance to the cave, where Peter Walker was standing, waiting.

There was a sudden eruption.

'You don't get it, do you?' David was furious. 'You just can't walk in and steal a body like that; I won't let you! He's one of my people, right? Leave him alone. He has to stay where he was buried.'

'He wasn't buried there,' Helen said, quietly, reasonably. 'He fell into the bog, and died there, David. There was no funeral, no ceremony.'

'Most aboriginal people went without ceremonies those days. Leave him alone.'

David took up a position at the foot of the outcrop, where there were already the scars and scrapes of people's boots going up and down into the cave. The signs of so many intrusions, Helen thought.

'Let me at least prove to you that this man isn't an aboriginal, David.' Peter Walker stretched his long legs from crevice to crevice as he descended the rock face. 'Let me spend a couple of hours with him, in a properly protected environment and then, if I am wrong – if he is an aboriginal – I will guarantee that he will be returned here and reburied.'

Helen wasn't so sure about that, but what mattered now was to calm David down.

For the moment, he seemed satisfied, or so she hoped.

The problem was very far from solved. As Teresa pointed out, once she had a dead body aboard she would have to make some kind of explanation to the airport officials. Out here, she said, they couldn't construct a coffin and even if they could, a box of that size and shape would arouse suspicion, even among the informal and friendly airport staff. They were not unaccustomed, Teresa reminded them, to keeping an eye out for drug runners who brought their merchandise into Australia via south east Asia, and the small airports were sometimes seen as easy targets. Which they were not.

No, a coffin-shaped box would have to be opened, and promptly.

Then it would be stored in a hangar until officials came to look at it. And someone would surely ring the newspapers and the television stations.

For an hour they tossed the questions back and forth. Whom should they call in Perth to arrange reception of the body, and how many – how few – people needed to be told? At what point, if any, must the police be brought in? Could Peter's offer of a private return of the body to the cave, should it be an aboriginal, be feasible if they couldn't keep the whole adventure a secret?

It was David, somewhat to Helen's surprise, who came up with the solution.

'Look, I've got an idea. But I want to know that you all agree. First up, if this man is an aboriginal, we put him back and leave him where he belongs. Right? No more science. No cops. He's left alone, reburied. What do you say?'

Helen thought she was the only one who had a problem with David's proposal, but she knew that it would be proof enough to send photographs with her article to a publisher. There would be enough data to validate her claim; that was all she needed.

Satisfied by the silence, David nodded.

'Barry O'Donnell. The Lakeview Meatworks. It's got refrigeration; you can do your – postmortem – your examination – there.'

Within five minutes, David was on the way to the meatworks with Antony Walker alongside him. As he was climbing into the passenger seat, Antony asked Helen to go back into the cave again and spread some loosened peat over the body.

'I'll see if the meatworks bloke has some sacks we can use; much better covering than peat now, I think. Anyway, I'll ask him.'

Helen went to the cave as soon as the LandCruiser pulled away.

She hadn't noticed before that sometimes it was cooler in the cave than outside. The rock protected it from the sun and the spring moving slowly deep below it did not get warmed as it pushed through the earth.

The scientists had checked the temperature at the level where the body had lain; there it was cold, so cold that Helen was reminded of the chill desert air at night in winter. Now the body was out of its chilly, almost damp grave and these few people who knew about it had an obligation to take great care of it. Of him.

Antony and his father had carefully replaced the almost weightless, distorted body in the hollow grave. Helen reached out a finger, not quite touching the black face, and marvelled again at its serenity.

Could Peter be right? Surely this was a black man; how could a white man have got here long before any white men were supposed to have reached the continent?

The peat, like soft black straw, settled easily back onto the body. For just a moment, Helen almost wished it was still undisturbed.

She stood for a few minutes in the mouth of the cave, her eyes looking off into the distance, unfocussed. Peter Walker came over and held out his hands to help her descent. He said nothing. She was sure that he understood how difficult it was for her to relinquish this extraordinary event, and to let others take over.

She smiled; a faint smile, but the best she could manage. Peter nodded, reassuringly.

'He isn't black?' she said.

The pathologist wasn't entirely sure, but almost so. He had made measurements of the dead man's head and found, he admitted somewhat to his surprise, that the proportions were Caucasian rather than aboriginal. Of course, as he explained, if the aboriginal were not a fullblood, then the standard formulae would not be valid; the man's head could have inherited the dimensions of his non-aboriginal parent. But four hundred years ago?

'It's not likely there'd be much opportunity for him to have a white parent, is there.'

Helen sat back, puzzling over the mystery.

There were other differences, too. It was not just a matter of taking measurements. The nasal cavities seemed wrong; and the jaw was not in the least prognathous, unlike the jaws of aboriginal people.

The man looked fairly young, Peter said; maybe forty or so. Of course he was just guessing from a very sketchy examination, but the man's face certainly looked young. Even through the distortions caused by the centuries of pressure by the peat, he didn't seem very old.

Peter Walker and Helen chatted about age, about getting old, and soon Helen felt better. Nothing seemed as urgent and terrible now.

The hours passed. There was nothing to do but wait. The decision had been made and all Helen could do now was go along with whatever seemed the best thing to do. She hoped they were making the right moves.

Going in and out of Helen's tent, gathering tins and containers, Teresa was organising a meal, with Jack's help. Idly watching them, with her mind on other things, Helen knew that, in truth, Jack wished Teresa weren't there. She was very efficient, but in a way quite different from Jack's tried and true formulae for success. He, for instance, opened cans in the order of need. She opened them quite randomly. She had already opened the tinned rice pudding and decided that tinned tomatoes would go very nicely in the corned beef stew. Three tins? Maybe four? She had opened four without discussing with Jack how many were needed.

Helen could hear Jack arguing very politely with Teresa about this unseemly haste. Jack said, half humorously but Helen recognised the irritation in his voice, that he thought Teresa was behaving with typical American disregard for economy, for thrift. Helen suspected that her husband rather hoped that there would be a lot of food left over, so that he could very pointedly not say 'I told you so.'

After a while, the preparations for the meal quietened down and Helen joined Jack outside their tent. She asked him why he was pacing about, looking irritated. She tried to hide her amusement. She had seen Jack and Teresa get on each other's nerves before, and it always ended with Jack in a tizz and Teresa trying her best to apologise for some, to Teresa, quite incomprehensible offence. As seemed to be the case now.

He started to explain and Helen, hoping to soothe him quickly, firmly tugged at his sleeve, drawing him into the tent.

Within moments, Teresa came bustling into the tent after them, with a briskly-yelled 'Knock knock!' and asked Jack to come at once and cook the tomatoes properly. Then she saw his face and knew she had done it again.

By the time all this had been sorted out, and good cheer had taken over, and Peter Walker had been brought in by Helen on the act of reconciliation, the meal was ready.

They set aside a more than appropriate quantity (as Jack put it) for the two men away at the meatworks and enjoyed a companionable dinner.

'Will you be able to find out much?' As Teresa gathered up the plates, and went off with Jack to 'tidy up', Helen turned to Peter, who had been quietly thinking, visibly thinking, for the last half hour. Helen guessed he was thinking about the job that was ahead of him. His answer confirmed her guess.

'About his death? Enough, I think. I can look for physical damage to the body. The internal organs will probably have gone – bacteria, Antony says. The bodies in Scandinavia – the ones which you remember – '

'The sacrifices to the gods, yes.'

'Well, they were either hanged or garrotted. Antony says the ropes were still in place around their necks. Some were beheaded. I can look for that; foul play. Blunt instruments. Trauma.'

'He didn't look frightened.'

'Or as if he'd suffered; no.'

'Do you have enough equipment – instruments?'

'Yes, I can manage. Antony told me nothing about your discovery but he did suggest I bring my "little black bag" with me.'

'Your "little black bag"?'

Peter took out a pipe and with a small 'Do you mind?' to which Helen shook her head permissively, he lit it with a few puttputting sounds as he drew the flame from his lighter into the bowl.

Abruptly, Helen was with her father, sitting on the sofa opposite his armchair in the living room. Her mother stood behind him, signalling the right responses while he asked Helen about her day at school. As she answered, falteringly, hesitantly, he pulled some shreds of tobacco from an old rubber pouch, and tamped the tobacco down into his pipe with a forefinger. He made puttputting noises as he held a lighted match to the tobacco, clutching the worn yellow bowl of the meerschaum pipe in fingers that curved like talons as he sucked the fire down.

'Odd how smells take you back,' she said, wondering if her brief experience had been visible on her face.

'The tobacco? Yes, I believe it's the sense most linked to memory.'

'I was with my father.'

'Has he been gone long, Helen?'

'Not long enough. Forty years. More.'

She could feel Peter's interest but by not acknowledging it, she gave him no encouragement. He puffed on the pipe again.

'Well, you were asking about the "little black bag"?'

'Yes. Yes, I was.'

'Do you know, I think the phrase came from England. They had a few famous people doing my job back in the twenties, thirties. When they gave evidence at a murder trial, the jury usually went along with whatever the pathologist told them.'

'Were they always right?'

'They certainly thought so. Usually, perhaps. Maybe. There's some doubt. One or two of them were dodgy characters.'

'And they invented the "little black bag"?'

'Well, maybe the media did. But certainly in every photograph of these famous men setting off to view another grisly murder, there would be a caption: "Sir Bernard Spilsbury, the Home Office Pathologist, arrives at the scene with his Little Black Bag." That kind of thing.'

'It sends a shiver up the spine.'

'Well, yes, I dare say the media played that up. Certainly the bag is useful. Spilsbury would be carrying a few instruments; obviously, he would need to have them. You have to do as much as you can *in situ*. The evidence might be there; important information almost certainly will be.'

'And you brought yours.'

'Yes, without thinking about why Antony suggested it. Yes. Odd, really. Habit.'

'How will you start?' Helen wasn't sure she really wanted to know but the image of her father lurked still behind the sweet, blue smoke.

'Oh a few measurements, of course. Settle his race, anyway. Then a snip here, a snippet there.' He glanced at Helen, and she sensed his reluctance to say more. Peter was not going to indulge her question. It seemed as though he knew she was asking only because she was in need of distraction.

There was an irruption of loud, assertive music. Teresa came out of her tent, holding up a radio from which the racket of pop music blasted. Peter and Helen waved her away as she came laughing over to them, turning the noise level up.

Jack came up behind her, reached around the radio, and firmly switched it off. He glared at Teresa who grinned at him, happy to have provoked him again.

As he opened his mouth to say something impolite, or so Helen assumed in slight alarm, they heard the LandCruiser's engine.

David was back, and Antony was smiling very happily.

'Everything's set, Dad. The bloke at the Meatworks – ' He snapped his fingers to remember the name.

'Barry O'Donnell.' David was already loading two plates with the evening stew.

'Yes, O'Donnell. Well, he's fine about it. He's putting the cooler on now and by the time we get the body there – ' Antony glanced sharply at David, who nodded. 'Well, everything will be ready.'

'He's got a cooler? For the bad guys?' Teresa handed the two latecomers bread, and forks.

'A cool room. When he's processed the kangaroos, he has to keep them – the carcases – chilled until the refrigerator trucks arrive and load them up.'

'Kangaroos? That is one nasty thought.' Teresa went off in the direction of the bottles of water.

'The restaurants in Melbourne and Sydney seem to like it!' David called after her.

'Probably all those American tourists,' Jack suggested, just loud enough.

'Naughty, naughty.' Teresa nudged Jack with a sharp elbow as she gave a bottle of water to each of the returned travellers. She sat down.

'What did you tell him?' Helen's nervousness could be heard in her voice. She tried to calm it down. 'You know, does he understand that this is a scientific affair, and must be kept absolutely secret?'

'Yes.'

Antony ate in silence, while the others waited, until every last scrap was gone. David ate little, but Antony asked for, and received, another plateful. Teresa emptied the cooking pot onto his plate, shooting a triumphant glare at Jack whose proof of her extravagance was fast disappearing down Antony's throat.

When he had finished eating, Antony took a last swig of water, rubbed his hand over his mouth and stood up.

'O'Donnell gave us some sacks, too. And some bits of fencing. So we're all set. Let's get on with it, then.'

'What, now?' Jack looked surprised.

'Better now while it's still light enough to see what we're doing. Then we can be off right away. Better to go at night; the temperature's lower, eh?'

David held up a hand, stopping the others before they really got going. He cleaned the last trace of stew from his plate with a hunk of damper, and drank a healthy draught of water. Helen wondered what was coming now.

'I want you to tell me what exactly you plan to do with the man,' he said, looking at Peter.

'We need to take him to a place where he can be kept at the same temperature as he has been lying in since he died.'

'I understand that. What then?'

'Then, I hope, I can tell you how he died.'

'Whether he died naturally or not?' Helen asked, in a quiet voice, almost as though she did not want to know the answer.

'Yes. I might be able to tell you that.'

Helen took the empty plates over to the cooking stove. She could feel the focus of attention switch to her. There was a large boulder sheltering the stove from errant wind; she leant against it and continued the discussion.

'Does it make a difference?'

'Heck, Helen, it would have made a hell of a difference to the guy!' Teresa reached over and took another piece of damper from the basket on the ground between her and David.

'Peter knows what I mean.'

'It might. It may be necessary to contact the authorities.'

Antony stirred uncomfortably. Helen glanced at him, his impatience was visible; he wanted to get on with the job.

David exploded. 'Shit! I can't go along with all this; all this talking back and forward about him! Leave him alone. Let him rest. He's a man, a dead man. You said you would bring him back here and forget about him.' He jumped up, started pacing about, agitated.

'We're talking about a number of possibilities, David.' Peter took out his pipe, changed his mind and replaced it in his pocket. 'If the man is an aboriginal – and remember that I think he is not – then if the rest of the party agrees – ?'

Helen saw how sharply David watched for the firm nods she and Teresa gave at this invitation.

'Then we shall bring him back and replace him in the place where he was found. That is my promise.'

'What about the project, though? Will it be a secret: it should be kept a secret.' David's voice was angry, not reassured.

Peter turned to Helen. She had hoped he would field all the questions; she wanted more time to think.

'We can certainly keep the cave's whereabouts a secret.' For a moment, she chewed her bottom lip, thinking.

'Not really, you know.' Teresa pointed to the scars on the face of the outcrop.

'I can make those invisible.' David's assurance was final, certain.

For a moment, Helen wished all the problems were invisible, too. That she could have the time to bring them into focus one at a time, slowly, sorting out the details, the whys and why nots, one by one. That was the way her father used his mind; he would concentrate on each single issue with a ferocity that had scared everyone in the family.

Antony moved forward again. Helen made a slight gesture which stopped him.

'I want to write a paper about it,' she said.

'Go public, you mean? No! No, you can't! This man is not your property!' David leaned over Helen, shouting in her face.

'Nor is he yours, young man.' There was such authority in Peter's voice that David backed away, silently. He took a deep breath, and shrugged his shoulders apologetically.

'I'm sorry, Helen, I didn't mean to – but look, he *is* mine. He truly is. Nobody else but the Arundijilaba were here before the white man came; nobody. There was only the Arundijilaba – and the Great Lizard.'

'The Great Lizard? Hey, what was that?'

David looked at Teresa, with the expression almost of contempt which Helen was growing used to seeing.

'He was – he is – oh I'll tell you later. I have to take responsibility for that dead man, surely you can see that? I am Arundijilaba; I am the grandson of the son of my great-grandfather; I have a family responsibility here. He must be returned to the earth within three days.'

'Three days?'

'Oh Helen, help me. So much is coming back – I'm remembering all sorts – It's as though my grandfather is standing right here, telling me what to do but I can't hear him properly. Three days, yes, three days and I don't know why.' David sat down abruptly.

Helen, despite David's appeal, could think of nothing to say. Teresa looked concerned. She went over to the stove and came back with a cup of tea, which David took from her and started to sip gratefully.

Antony looked at his father, who offered him no solution, Helen could see.

The sky was beginning to redden as the sun settled lower. Soon the blue sky would glow and everything around them would seem to be rinsed in golden light. It was a magical time of day. Helen shivered.

'Is it getting cold?'

Nobody answered her. They were waiting, she knew, for her to say something to reassure David. But what could she say?

This was the most important event in her life. It would be the crowning achievement in a life which had been uneventful, a life without highs or lows. Since getting her PhD there had been no outstanding successes; reasonably competent research, a dozen publications, a couple of papers at conferences. Enough to satisfy a grudging father, perhaps, had he lived, but not much.

Not much at all.

Helen knew that publication of the discovery of the body would immeasurably enhance a paper on the discovery of an ancient water source, and a bog. She would be able to publish her paper anywhere, in the most prestigious scientific journals. *Nature* would be happy to have her paper; there would be seminars, conferences, demands for reprints from all over the world. She could write a book!

'All I can say, David, is that we understand your point of view. Be patient with us. Let us find out a little about the body and then we can talk again.'

David had to be satisfied with that. She watched him tighten his mouth, cutting off a response he must have thought impolitic. He would wait – but that decision would have to be made soon.

'Can we get on, then?' Helen could hear the impatience in Antony's voice. For him, the most important problem was about to be resolved.

Helen looked at David. He nodded.

CHAPTER 5

ANTONY AND PETER WENT BACK INTO THE CAVE, turned the lamps on and got to work. Helen followed them up the scree and watched from the entrance to the cave. The men covered the body more thoroughly with the straw-like peat Helen had spread gently over it, packing it in firmly where they could. Gradually the body started to look like an Egyptian mummy, still bandaged and mysterious. The form of the man was there – head, torso, limbs – but in this case, unlike the mummy's, the shape was twisted as the man himself had lain in his moment of death.

'It looks solid enough, what do you think Helen?' Antony stood back, allowing Helen a better view.

'Yes, I would think so.'

Now that they seemed satisfied with the top and sides of their packing, the Walkers started to remove peat from underneath the body. They worked very carefully, digging and scraping away at the peat to make a tunnel under the body until they had the same depth of peat under it as was lying on top; some fifteen centimetres. The base was solid. It was still connected to the bog at the head and feet.

'Do you think we should sprinkle some water on the block, Antony? Keep it damp?'

'I don't think it's necessary, Dad. It's not going a great distance.'

Peter went down to the camp and Helen watched as he and David struggled back up to the cave, carrying the sacks and a bundle of fence palings. David left his burden reluctantly but went back down the scree after a long look around at the well-lit scene of the excavation.

With the help of his father, Antony laid several sacks brought back by David over the mound, and strengthened the construction with a row of fence palings over the sacks. Under the body they made the tunnel broader until it became a deep slot.

The block of peat containing the body was like a bridge now. Antony threaded ropes under the block and placed another row of palings on top of the ropes. A layer of sacks went on top of the palings. The ropes were brought over the top of the block and tied. As they pulled the ropes tight enough, the palings were held in place.

Once the ropes felt secure, with a glance at Helen, who nodded, Antony sliced through the peat at each end of the block.

Antony waved Helen over with a quick gesture, while he kept his attention on the block.

'The fabric, Helen. Can you take it?'

Helen carefully covered the length of fabric within the plastic sheet it was lying on. She folded it loosely, and only a couple of times, in case the fabric proved to be fragile.

As they finished their work, Jack arrived at the cave entrance. Helen was so engrossed in what she was doing that she was startled to hear his voice, and the note of triumph in it.

Jack had worked out a way to get the one-tonne load out of the cave. It wouldn't be easy, he said, but if they worked together, it should succeed.

'It's like building the pyramids in reverse.' His voice was deeper than usual, with excitement. 'All we need is to make a sort of ramp. See how I've done it here?' The drawing was neat and businesslike. 'The ramp will slope gently down from the cave mouth. We lift the body over the lip of the cave and slide it down. Couldn't be simpler, really.'

He waited for the praise which didn't come. Helen felt sorry for him but she could see how impractical his idea was. 'Need another few minutes to think about it, dear.'

Jack looked at her, surprised.

'It weighs a tonne, Jack, easy. Too heavy for us to haul about like that.' Antony led the way down from the cave, followed by his father and Helen. Jack looked around the cave at the solitary light left on before he followed them.

'Well, if you don't think it would work – . I wonder if we could – ' Jack wandered off to the tent, chewing the pencil and studying his plan.

'Don't worry about it.' David was laughing at the worried expressions around him. Helen felt a spurt of irritation with him – one minute he was anxious to stop the work in its stride, now he was solving all its problems.

Antony muttered something to the same effect, which wiped the smile off David's face in an instant. 'Now I trust you,' he said. 'I didn't then.'

For a second, the two men looked with considerable aggression at each other. Antony must have seen something he respected because Helen was relieved to see him relax, nod, and back off.

'OK, let's get on with it, then,' Antony said, calm now. 'What's your solution, David?'

'Look, I thought about all this stuff,' David waved his arms to include the problem of shifting the load down from the cave, 'while Antony was checking out the cool store. So I asked Barry to bring his ute. He's got a ruddy great tackle on it for hefting big reds in and out. If he can shift some of those bucks he can shift this. He said he'd follow us once he'd got the cooler going. Any minute now, I reckon.'

'That's great, David. Well done.' Peter grinned with pleasure, and looked at Antony, encouraging him to do the same.

'Will he find us?' Helen wasn't sure she wanted the meatworks man closely involved but it did seem like a good idea.

'Oh yes. We've made a pretty clear track for him.'

'What we really need is a block and tackle.' Jack came back to the group, briskly efficient again. 'It occurred to me – '

'The meatworks?' Antony asked him. Jack, surprised, nodded.

'On his way, mate.' David laughed. 'Good idea, eh?'

Helen hoped Jack was pleased. He seemed gratified that his idea was the one likely to work.

The Walkers went off to clean up after their work, and Helen took the opportunity to let Jack explain how his ideas would have worked just as well. And so they would, she thought. He's good at that sort of planning.

The ute wasn't very big, but it was as strong as a ute could be.

Knowing that a heavy weight was involved, and part way up a hill at that, Barry explained that he had brought with him a section of a metal chute used for hauling dead kangaroos aboard. He looked without curiosity at the coffin-shaped block of peat, merely asking what it weighed: did they have an idea? The answer didn't worry him, he laid the chute as a ramp against the inside wall of the cave, leaning against the exit. The chute had rollers fitted into it and with a few strenuous heaves, the men were able to get the block of peat onto it. Once they had struggled successfully to get the excavated section of peat close to the lip of the cave, Barry was able to swing the block and tackle around far enough to get a good grip on the chains he slung around the block. Antony guided him slowly as the machinery took the weight and even more slowly as the great block slid very slowly over the edge.

Everyone held their breath, except Barry who repeated that he had shifted bigger things than this in his time. With what he seemed to think was far too much fuss on the part of his spectators, the block was nudged into the tray of the ute. The chains were removed, and ropes fastened securely across the block to hold it in place.

'Are you ready to leave?' he asked, looking around at the strained faces.

'Leave?' Helen was unsure of his meaning.

'Well, you're not going to stay here, are you?' You can all bunk down at my place until you've sorted this out.' He jerked a stained thumb in the direction of the block of peat. 'Tons of room.'

'We'll follow you, then.' Antony was keen to get going, Helen saw.

'Hang on; we've got to pack up yet!' Teresa looked around, clearly in a panic about getting everything stowed away.

Jack took charge. Within twenty minutes, the LandCruiser and the trailer were loaded, and there was no sign of their camp. Only the scrapes on the hill below the cave showed where they had been.

Helen looked back at the scene of her extraordinary success and wondered how it would stay in her memory. At the moment it looked just like any other expedition's end. Except for the looming, black block of peat on the back of the ute.

'Can you find your way back here?' Jack asked David.

There was no answer. Helen was amused to see David merely look at Jack, as though the question had been something of an accidental insult.

They piled into the two vehicles and went away.

When they reached the Lakeview Meatworks, Jack pointed out to Helen the safety fence all around the buildings. 'Could be useful, you know.'

Helen had sudden images of marauding television crews, officials, other scientists. 'Yes, it'll keep them all out,' she said.

Jack peered at her, apparently surprised by the intensity in her voice.

They drove through the gates, which had been left open, and parked the vehicles outside one of the sheds across the yard from where Ian's plane was stored. They had pulled up under a long metal awning, alongside an unloading bay. Barry hurried into the shed to open the big access doors and switch on the security lights, which flooded the yard, and the lights on the unloading dock.

The meatworks proper consisted of a transportable office and three large sheds, two of which comprised two rows of self-sufficient cool stores, the sort of huge refrigerators like small rooms which Helen had seen in butchers' shops. Each cool store could be refrigerated independently of the others, reducing the power needed when little meat was in store.

The third shed was the largest. It was equipped for handling carcasses and preparing them for the restaurant trade. One end was fitted with a travelling conveyor system, with huge hooks to carry the animals from the loading bay to the skinning table.

Several long steel tables were arranged in the central area, with large bins alongside. At the end furthest from the skinning table, trolleys were stacked together, next to a row of sinks and disposal chutes.

'God, isn't it revolting. Makes me wish I was a vegetarian.' Teresa shivered. The room was very cold.

'You don't have to eat kangaroo. It's a choice,' said Jack.

The expression on his face made it quite clear that his choice was firmly against eating it.

'Don't you have to kill animals out of the sight of each other?'

Helen wished she hadn't asked, but it was an interesting, purpose-built place, not unlike a laboratory with all this stainless steel.

'It's not a slaughterhouse. They're dead when they get here.'

Barry was a little short with her; she could imagine that he was not too pleased by the negative reactions of his guests.

'Oh God, yes. Shooters. Men with spotlights.' Teresa shivered again.

'Mostly farmers. If they didn't shoot the pests, they'd lose their crops. We get plagues of the bastards up here. Doing them a good turn, having the meatworks.'

'Apart from which, kangaroo meat is very good indeed,' Peter said. 'It's a low-fat, low-cholesterol meat. Very good for you; in fact, it's better for you than most of the other red meats.' He looked around, approvingly. 'This is a splendid place for us to bring our work, Barry. It's obviously spotlessly clean and hygienic. We should probably scrub one of those tables down before we bring him in; is that all right with you?'

Helen fetched the folded fabric, still wrapped in the plastic sheet. On Antony's instructions, she laid it on a table, opening the folds so that the relic was merely covered, not completely enclosed. She took a handful of tissues, a small bundle of them, from her backpack and placed them by the plastic.

The women left the men to get on with the job, and sat on a couple of plastic chairs, chatting about animal welfare and the boredom of eating vegetarian food. At least, Teresa was chatting.

Visibly placated by Peter's praise, Barry hastened to gather detergents, disinfectants, brushes, cloths and a couple of buckets of hot water. Although everyone was feeling the chill in the air from the huge air-conditioning plant above them, they set to and scrubbed the table clean. Jack wheeled a trolley over and that was scrubbed, too.

'It's going to be cold work, Antony.' Peter said he was warm because of the scrubbing, but he pointed out that he could see his breath.

'Not to worry, mate.' Barry led the way out of the shed. Helen and Teresa followed. They had not been asked to help with the scrubbing, rather to Teresa's surprise.

'I thought for sure we'd be expected to do the domestic chores,' she said.

'This is laboratory cleaning,' Helen said, smiling.

'It's still bloody cleaning, though, right? Women's work.'

A row of metal lockers was ranged at one end of the loading dock. Barry took a pile of folded sweaters from one of them. From another he brought out several sets of thick, quilted overalls.

'Hats in the end locker: choose your own colour. Gloves if you need them.'

While the women chose a sweater each and gratefully pulled them on, Antony and Peter tugged protective overalls over the sweaters they selected.

'We'll never get our lab coats over these,' Antony said.

'Can fix you up there, too. Regulations. White coats, aprons, the lot. They're inside, in plastic bags. Hygienic, like you said.'

'Then we're all fixed up.'

'Yes, Dad, and ready to go.'

They turned to the load on the ute. Another critical time. Antony cleared his throat nervously. Helen watched, her hand to her mouth.

Barry started up the motor and the conveyor system came alive with a cough and a clank. It was operated by a portable device which hung from the ceiling of the loading dock. The row of hooks moved off, swinging with the momentum. When a hook came round to the edge of the loading dock, Barry stopped the machine briefly. While David stood in the ute to guide him, he made a couple of quick starts and stops to get the hook exactly in position.

'Excellent!' Jack was very impressed.

He's enjoying this, Helen thought. She hoped his confidence would be justified.

The hook was lowered until it was almost lying on top of the block of peat in the back of the ute. Barry jumped aboard and pushed the hook under the chains which lay diagonally across the block. He stepped back onto the loading dock and, with a deft manipulation of the control device, he raised the block clear of the ute.

'All clear!' Jack said, although Barry seemed to know that.

David used his weight to limit any tendency for the block to sway. In a few moments, the block was on the loading dock, swinging gently at head height.

Antony fetched a trolley and with the same care, the block was lowered on to it.

Barry looked amused by the applause, which Jack led, but for the people watching it had been a splendid performance, Helen thought, and it was a great relief to see the block still safe and secure.

Within a short time, the body in its protective casing, was safely held in a temperature of four degrees Celsius. The temperature gauge over the door was large and easily read. Helen felt the first sag of relaxation for hours.

Barry pointed out the cupboard containing butcher's implements but Peter said he could manage very nicely with own instruments. However, he said he was pleased to see that a sterilising machine was alongside the cupboard.

The lighting in the shed was cool, as it had to be, very bright and efficient.

'Tomorrow is going to be a good day, I can feel it.' Antony smiled.

The men took off the protective clothing, and put their selections into an empty locker so that they would be readily available next day. While they changed, Peter told David and the women that the facilities here were much better than they had dared to hope.

Everyone was relieved now that the major task was over.

'God, I'm so hungry I could eat – '

'A kangaroo?' Jack couldn't resist teasing Teresa, Helen thought. What was it about those two that set each other off?

They walked over towards the house, Barry falling behind a little as he locked up the shed – Antony and Helen watched him without comment to make quite sure that it was secure. He replaced the padlock on the big metal gates, giving it a tug to reassure the others.

The house was separated from the meatworks by a small row of stumpy eucalypts. Each had an old tyre around its base and showed the signs of regular watering by hand: a deep trough in the soil inside the tyre.

Barry told Helen and Antony that Lakeview House had been built forty years ago, when the meatworks had been somewhat bigger and in use more of the year. In those days the kangaroo meat had gone to factories to be processed into canned food for dogs and cats. A little had found its way into the illegal trade, padding out beef intended for human consumption, but it was much more strictly controlled now. Barry made a living from the few months the meatworks operated. Not a fortune, as he explained cheerfully, as they walked across the yard, but enough.

They caught up with the others near the front door.

'You don't seem particularly excited by our discovery,' Peter said to Barry. Helen noticed the 'our', but decided on reflection that Peter had every right to claim some part of it.

'Nah, well, we get a few bodies around here. Not often, mind. People go off the track, you know? No water, no sense. Picked up a couple in the last six or seven years.'

They crossed the open verandah to the front door. Barry led them along the wide corridor inside the house. It was painted a faded pink and was lined with reproductions of bush scenes, two them the same ones as were in David's house, although these were bigger versions. Helen wondered if either of them were the size of the original.

Most of Barry's house consisted of a living room, at one end of which was the kitchen. There were many windows, some fitted with glass louvres, designed to catch every breeze. Several small, compact bedrooms lined another, shorter corridor, at the far end of which was the bathroom. Barry explained with considerable pride that everything operated from solar power; the house was heated, cooled and lit by

111

stored, solar-generated electricity and the cooking stove was similarly supplied. Barry had long given up the use of bottled gas. 'Couldn't rely on the supplies,' he said when Teresa asked about it.

There was a fan hanging from the ceiling in Jack and Helen's bedroom, switched on already to cool and circulate the air a little. A large air-conditioning unit hung on the wall in the living room, humming quietly. Helen liked fans, and wished they had installed them in their house in Perth instead of the air-conditioning which she found too drying. Jack liked to be really cool though. Something to do with his metabolism, he told her. And fans don't make you really cool.

While he was fixing a late-night drink for his guests, and some cheese and bread for Teresa, Barry told them a story or two about the dead bodies he had found: one had been an old grandmother, left to sit in the shade while her son-in-law and daughter walked fifty kilometres from their wrecked car, in searing heat, to find shelter. When Barry answered their cries for help, they were on the ground outside his house, pretty near exhausted. The old woman was dead when they got to her; still sitting under the thorny bush where she had been left.

Teresa went outside to have a smoke. It seemed to Helen that Teresa didn't hear Barry say she could smoke right where she was; he was a smoker himself. Antony got up after a moment and followed her to the verandah. The sound of their voices, talking, laughing, drifted in through the open louvres.

'This one's a bit different, though. This body. Did David and Antony tell you?' Peter lit his pipe. As the sweet, blue cloud of smoke reached her, Helen closed her eyes and banished a memory.

'Said something about it being pretty old.'

Helen leant forward. 'It's four hundred years old. How about that, then?'

Barry whistled. 'Jesus, Mary and Joseph, that's a pretty long time to be dead.'

'That's why it's terribly important that we don't let anyone know we have found it, Mr – Barry. You do see that?'

In a hushed and confidential way, which he seemed to think would be reassuring to Helen, Barry said that he did indeed see that telling people could have awkward consequences. He didn't much care for officials, he said, not since the meat-substitution trouble a couple of years ago. He minded his business and expected others to do the same. Anyway, he was too old for a lot of fuss.

He promised – 'on my solemn oath, on my mother's grave' – not to say a word to anyone about it. Helen, embarrassed by Barry's confidences and dramatic gestures, was anyway grateful for the undertaking.

After wonderfully refreshing, hot showers, Helen and Jack slept in a bed made – so Barry told them with great pride – by Barry's father as a wedding present for his son. The rich red of the jarrah bed and the floorboards contrasted with a snowy white counterpane, and a collection of old and beautiful rugs. Sleep came easily, helped by the gentle clicking and murmuring of the fan.

'Tomorrow's problems will take care of themselves, Jack. Goodnight.' But he was already asleep.

When morning came, Helen was astonished to be shown a huge quantity of frozen provisions in a cool store not much smaller than one of those in the meatworks. Barry was right when he told her that having extra guests was no problem at all.

Breakfast was a large and friendly meal, with plenty of good coffee, whitened with 'long life' milk.

Barry's toaster made eight slices at a time, to Teresa's evident delight, and the strawberry jam and marmalade were delicious.

Very soon, the time came for the work to start. Peter picked up his 'little black bag', and Antony his camera.

Teresa offered to help 'in any way she could' and was clearly disappointed to be asked to stay in the kitchen and clean up.

'I knew it,' she said loudly to Helen. 'Sooner or later, it gets back to domestic chores.'

'You can help me organise lunch,' said Jack. 'I'll leave you others to get on with the scientific stuff.'

Teresa looked at the ceiling, pantomiming a lament for her assigned role of working again for Jack. Helen laughed at the performance.

'Go on, you'll enjoy yourself,' she said.

As Jack started clearing the table, with Teresa's resistant help, the Walkers and Helen left, with David and Barry following on.

Inside the coolroom, the Walkers 'suited up', and with the help of David and Barry they removed the packing, the sacks and fence palings, from around the block of peat. David and Antony pushed the trolley alongside the scrubbed, stainless-steel cutting table, and lifted the surface peat away, putting it into a big plastic waste-bin.

At last, with infinite care, and with Helen resisting the urge to offer advice or help, Antony and Peter removed the body of the man from the peat. Moving him onto the cutting table was a simple matter, the man himself weighed very little.

Barry was impressed but not overawed by what he saw. 'Skinny little bugger, isn't he?' he said.

'Notice that smell, Dad?'

'Sweet – can't identify it – not the peat – odd smell. Recognise it, Helen?' At Peter's invitation, Helen moved closer and sniffed.

'No – maybe some sort of spice? It's pleasant enough.' She moved back a little, out of the way.

'Reminds me a bit of your tobacco,' Antony said, his hands busily moving shreds of peat away from the body.

'No.' Helen spoke too sharply and the men looked at her. 'I mean it doesn't smell in the least like tobacco to me.'

After a moment, Antony turned back to his work. Helen felt the flush fade from her cheek.

When Peter Walker opened his 'little black bag' and Barry saw the glint of surgical instruments, he decided to leave them to it, carefully closing the heavy door behind him. David stayed where he was, inside, leaning against the steel wall, watching. Helen, hugging her arms deep inside the borrowed sweater, kept her distance, too. But she watched carefully.

There were no garments; the large piece of fabric was the only one to have survived. The skin, or rather the dermis beneath the skin, looked exactly like leather. They could see the pores, the marks of accidental cuts and minor damage incurred during life, on the legs. There were hairs still attached to the body, although the face seemed to be clean-shaven. The hair on the man's head was shoulder length, and had a strong natural curl. Peter shook some liquid from a bottle onto a piece of gauze and stroked a section of the hair; it was fair, with a reddish cast, but fair.

As this became apparent, the two men working on the body paused, and looked at David. He nodded, but indicated that they should continue.

Helen held her breath.

'There's a finger missing.'

Peter said it quietly, but David heard. 'That's how he was found. It got cut off.'

Peter looked at Helen for a moment, then turned back to his work.

There was more flexibility in the body than they had anticipated and Peter was able to make accurate measurements of the cranium, using the callipers he carried with him.

'I didn't really need confirmation; this is a white man. From what I can tell about the fusion of his cranial plates, the man was about the age I had thought; around forty.'

'You're sure he's white?' David sounded relieved but Helen was puzzled.

'Yes, quite sure.' Peter continued his work, delicately, sorting through the remains of the white man.

'The internal organs are gone but the bones are fairly intact.'

After a short time, Helen drew nearer to the table, as Peter stood up and arched his back.

'Well, the cause of the man's death is clear. He'd fallen and broken the femur of his left leg; the break is as easy to read as if it happened yesterday. No attempt had been made to treat it. Shock; exposure; extreme heat. Being alone and unable to move would bring unconsciousness and death quickly in this climate.'

'Poor man,' Helen said. Peter glanced at her, seemingly surprised.

'Yes. Yes, it was a painful end,' he said.

They worked for a couple of hours more. David watched, no longer looking agitated about the possibility of the man being an Arundijilaba, but as fascinated as Helen was by the skill of Peter Walker and the sensitive handling of the dead man.

At last the work was done. Peter sighed, stood up and looked with a sudden and visible access of sympathy at the body. He gently moved a strand of the blackened, damp hair back from the man's forehead and lifted it clear of his neck. Antony pushed his father's fingers away abruptly.

'What's that?'

Helen and David moved towards them, but were waved away by Peter, concerned to keep the space and atmosphere free of contamination.

Antony and Peter bent over the head of the dead man.

'There's something round his neck,' Antony said. 'Look, almost at the back of it.'

Antony gently lifted the dead man's hair out of the way and slid his fingers around the object he had found. He lifted it up and moved it around the neck so that it was lying in his hand. Helen could see, although she was not close, that the thing was made from wood, and there was a hint of metal – probably that had caught Antony's eye when his father first moved the hair.

While Antony held the object clear, Peter carefully explored its dimensions.

'It's fastened on to something. I think it's a piece of leather – would you say leather, Antony?'

Antony looked carefully and nodded.

'Like a necklace or a pendant would be?' Helen's voice sounded to her as if it came from a long way away.

'Yes,' Antony said – and his voice sounded the same.

117

They took photographs, then Peter gingerly cut through the leather thong, a few centimetres from the knot.

With great care, Peter slid the artefact across the body, pulling gently to free the leather thong. It lay in his hand, black, fragile, but unmistakable.

It was a crucifix.

For a long moment nobody spoke.

'Helen?' Antony said.

She could only shake her head.

They covered the body with sacks, not speaking to each other or to David who looked puzzled by their sudden taciturnity. He had seen that something had been found, but Helen realised that he had not seen what it was. It seemed inopportune to tell him at that moment.

The Walkers washed their hands carefully, scrubbing their fingernails. Neither spoke. Helen and David waited by the door.

The pathologist and the soil scientist, each clearly lost in his own thoughts, walked quickly across to the house. Peter carried the crucifix in both hands, carefully cupped. Helen walked behind them, looking towards the house for Jack. She looked back to see David securing the door behind them, then he hurried to catch up.

Teresa and Jack were sitting on the verandah at the far side of the house, sipping cold tea from tall glasses. Barry was looking at the struggling patch of a herb garden outside the back door, and seemed rather relieved when he saw the Walkers approaching.

'Know anything about this sort of thing, Helen?' he called as they drew near.

'No. It's parsley, I think.'

Distracted and clearly not willing to stop, Helen and the others walked past Barry onto the verandah.

'We have to talk, Helen. Can we go inside?' Helen knew that Antony meant: Can we talk in private? She walked towards the door, pulling off the sweater.

'Yes, of course.' She asked no questions: Antony's face was set and Peter looked worried.

David came up behind them as they turned towards the door. 'They found something,' he said. 'I don't know what, but they found something all right.'

His excitement caught Teresa's attention.

'What is it, Antony?'

'Can we all come and hear about it?' Jack asked, already on his way through the door.

Antony looked at Helen but she could give him no clue as to how secretive they should be. She shrugged slightly – there were already so many revealed secrets about this venture that another one couldn't do any harm.

Antony sighed, and nodded.

Barry came up on to the verandah and said he would put the urn on for coffee, so please hang on a tick until he got there.

Helen went to the bathroom. As she left, David went in and Antony was waiting in the hall. None of them spoke.

In the living room, they waited for Barry, who was bustling about at the other end of the room. Antony was silent. He smiled reassuringly at Helen, who was not at all reassured. Peter was holding the artefact in his hands, as though it were alive and very precious. He's holding it like a young animal, Helen thought.

Teresa gave a grunt of impatience and went to help Barry. She put a collection of mugs on a tray, added a bowl of sugar, a carton of milk, and a packet of biscuits. Three teaspoons and a handful of paper napkins. She spooned Nescafé into the mugs. Barry filled the cups from the urn and carried the tray over to the coffee table around which the group was sitting.

'The discovery first,' Helen said, holding her hand up to stop Teresa who was about to distribute the mugs.

Every face turned towards Peter's hands. Slowly, he unfolded them and displayed the blackened object.

The silence absorbed them. Teresa put her hands to her face, and Helen thought she had never seen her friend so moved. For herself, Helen was thinking about her paper: 'And we found two artefacts; a length of woven fabric and a cross. A Christian cross.'

'He must have been a Christian, then,' she said.

'Unless he stole it.' David was trying to sound unimpressed, Helen decided.

'Was it wrapped in that material?'

'No, Jack. It was around his neck. Look, there's the cord it was on – a piece of leather.'

The crucifix was not the sort of small symbol Helen was accustomed to seeing as an item of jewellery. With eyes used to measurement, Helen estimated that the cross was at least twenty centimetres from top to bottom and about fourteen wide. The wood was remarkably well preserved with only a few deepened grooves to show that it had been immersed in peat for four hundred years. The pieces of wood were almost two centimetres thick and square in section.

The worn leather thong ran through a metal ring that had been inserted into a hole in the top of the cross.

'What a marvel!' Teresa held out a finger as though to touch the form of the man on the crucifix. Antony as gently stopped her.

'We shouldn't touch. We don't know how solid it is.'

The Christ figure was about sixteen centimetres high. It was exquisitely modelled, with a face of such agony, such beauty that it made Helen bite her lip as tears came to her eyes. The arms and legs were elongated and twisted, the muscles standing out as though the torture of suspension were still distorting the man. The thorned crown, black now from the peat, was complete with minute thorns which pricked Peter's gloved fingers as he moved them across the surface of the crucifix.

He jumped slightly.

'How could anyone wear it? It's sharp, isn't it?' David said.

'It may not have been so sharp when it was worn, David. The metal may have – eroded, or something. I don't know. It's not my field. Antony?' Peter turned the crucifix in his hands, slightly rotating it.

'I only know what bits I picked up in Britain. It's uncorroded, though. Hell, you can see every detail. No, there might have been a bit broken off. Let's have a look.'

Antony took the crucifix from his father, holding it in his own gloved hands, and lifted it close to his eyes. 'Yes, I think I can see it, just a tiny break in one of those twigs.'

'Thorns, Antony.' Helen corrected him.

'Well, yes, thorns. I suppose so.'

'Why didn't we see it before? I mean, when we were looking at him – it's big enough. How did we not see it?' Helen said.

Peter explained that the crucifix had been almost around the back of the man's neck, tucked away at the side, concealed by his hair.

'What exactly does this mean, Antony? What does it tell us about the man?' Jack wanted to get things settled, organised, straightened out and catalogued. Helen felt a stir of anger; why couldn't he just relish this wonderful moment? Why ask questions?

She spoke up, diverting her irritation by answering. 'It's obvious the man was a Christian. Is he white, Peter? Did you settle that?'

'Oh yes, his hair was blond, with a touch of red to it. Celtic, maybe.'

Helen glanced at David, relieved that there would be no more difficulties with him.

'So, our man in our bog is a four-hundred-year-old white man, a Christian,' Helen said.

'OK, Helen, but how on earth did he get here? Aren't we talking about the sixteenth century, for Heaven's sake? Isn't that quite a bit before Captain Cook?' Teresa sounded frightened.

'Two hundred years before him.' Antony looked up at Helen. He looked as though the responsibility for this new revelation was not easy to bear.

Jack passed around the coffee, putting a mug on the coffee table in front of each person, but nobody added milk or sugar, or even picked up the mugs. 'It's a very large piece of jewellery for someone to wear,' he said. 'I mean, they wouldn't be moving around in those Elizabethan costumes, would they? Doublets and hose and stuff? Not here?'

He was right, Helen thought. Jack was quite right: who would wear a piece of jewellery as big as that – here in the Outback?

She suddenly had a picture of Sister Gabrielle, the nun who had visited Marlbeck Primary School to give confirmation classes to the Catholic children in Helen's class.

'Nuns wear them. Or they did before they started wearing ordinary clothes. I remember nuns wearing them.'

'Not just nuns, surely.' Teresa sounded excited. 'I mean all sorts of religious people. Weren't the Mormons busy in Australia at some time? Maybe it belonged to one of them and it was lost or something.' Teresa's voice faded away as the illogicalities of her suggestion seemed to occur to her.

'Here, let's have a look.' Barry leaned over, taking a good look at the crucifix. 'That's not a Mormon thing, whatever they are. It's Catholic; don't you know that? Non-Catholics have empty crosses. This is a Catholic cross. That's Jesus,' he said, unnecessarily, 'and that makes it a Catholic cross.'

'Was he murdered? Was it some sort of persecution thing?' Antony glanced at Teresa, half-amused by her question but too preoccupied, Helen saw, to smile.

'He broke his leg somehow. I assume he tried to shelter in the cave and he died there. It can happen.' Peter was matter-of-fact.

Helen sighed. 'It seems it did happen. It's easy enough to fall on those rocks.' She was thinking hard but getting nowhere.

'Poor bastard.' Barry picked up his coffee, added milk and a large amount of sugar. 'Lonely way to go, eh?'

Teresa pointed to the crucifix. 'But how in hell did it get here?' She looked at Helen for an answer.

Helen thought she knew the answer. 'Where's the fabric – is it still where I put it? You didn't move it?'

As Peter shook his head, Helen stood up and set off at a brisk walk out of the room and across the verandah.

'Come on, somebody – whoever's got the key! I want to see that fabric.'

David hurried after her, and got ahead quickly enough to open the door to the cooling shed before Helen reached it. The others followed. Helen walked over to the plastic-covered shape. She turned to see if Antony was following, and was relieved to see him coming across through the trees.

'Can I open it, spread it out?' she said.

'I don't think we can damage it.'

Peter was still holding the crucifix so Antony used his gloved hands to open the fabric wide. Now Helen saw what had been invisible to her before.

It had sleeves, which had been folded inside.

'He must have folded it up when he dragged himself into the cave. He must have folded it up to lie on. It must have been hot and he didn't realise how cold it would become when the sun went down.' Helen spoke as if she could see the man, struggling with a broken leg into the safety and shelter of the cave.

'Those rocks are dangerous,' she said. 'I've nearly fallen many times. He fell and broke his leg and was alone.'

'Does this tell us anything about the man, though, Helen? I don't see what you're getting at. Why are the sleeves so significant?' Peter was clearly puzzled.

'It's not just the sleeves; it's the thing itself. It's not simply a length of fabric, a blanket or a cloak, Peter. It's a soutane,' Helen said. 'You know, a soutane. A priest's garment. It fastens up the front and it has sleeves and they wear a crucifix over it. It's a soutane, Peter. The man's a priest. A Catholic priest.'

124

CHAPTER 6

'WELL, THAT'S ALL RIGHT. There were priests all over the place then.' Jack sounded as if he were trying to reassure himself, Helen thought, and not making too good a fist of it.

'Do you think so?' Helen needed reassurance too.

'Boats; they got around to all sorts of places.' Jack waved an arm around the Pacific Rim.

Peter Walker was gently turning the crucifix over, looking at it from all sides. 'Up here? I don't think that's likely. Not that long ago.'

'Is it safe?' For a moment everyone except Peter, who was completely preoccupied, looked at Helen, puzzled. She felt herself blush; imprecision was not her usual style. 'I mean, is it safe to have the thing in our hands? Might it fall apart, crumble or something?'

Peter looked with alarm at Antony, who shook his head. 'It's OK to take it out of here. Look, the wood's fragile, probably, but the metal is perfectly solid. Silver-gilt, I would think. Or pure silver. If we handle it carefully, we should be all right.'

Teresa had been over to the sinks and came back with a small but sturdy cardboard box which had held a couple of dozen bars of soap. It was a little wider but about the same length as a shoe box and had CARBOLIC SOAP. ABSOLUTELY PURE printed on the lid.

She packed a few centimetres of the loose peat from the bin into the box.

'Is this a good idea?' she asked Antony.

'Brilliant,' he said. He was not smiling. Helen wondered what he was thinking.

Peter gently laid the crucifix on top of the peat, and Teresa picked up another handful of peat from the bin. She tucked it around the artefact, and patted it down. Peter put the lid on and only then did he seem to focus again on the people around him.

He slowly pulled off the gloves which had protected him, and the crucifix.

'What now, Antony?' he said.

This was no longer a simple matter of finding a dead man, Helen realised. Simple! Well, it had seemed so compared with this conundrum. For some reason, whatever reason, the fact of the man being a priest had both puzzled and alarmed them all.

'You're sure his death was accidental?' Antony asked, as though ticking Item One off a list.

'Yes.'

'You're positive he's a white man?' Item Two.

'Positive.'

'And you're certain, Helen, that this – ' he waved at the soutane, 'is a priest's thing – a garment worn only by priests, even then?' Item Three.

'I think so, but I may be wrong. I can only relate it to paintings I've seen: I think so.' Helen nodded.

Item Four was hers to ask. 'And you, Antony, you're certain about the four hundred years? Give or take a few?'

'Yes; quite positive.'

For a moment Helen had the full attention of the others. She pushed her bottom lip out and pursed her mouth, thinking.

'We must try to find out who he was. Is.' Helen took the cardboard box from Peter and left the cooling shed almost as quickly as she had entered it.

The others followed her back, more slowly, to the house.

Lunch was tuna sandwiches, made by Barry and Teresa, although none of them probably could have said what was in them at the time they were eaten. The discussion went back and forth for hours.

It seemed to Antony and Helen, at first, that the appropriate thing to do was to get in touch with the University, any university almost, but Antony was keen that Adelaide University should be the contact point. He believed that the protection of a University's interest in identifying the man would help in any dealings with the police, or the church, or the politicians.

'Politicians?' Teresa was aghast at the thought that 'their' body could be a matter for political interest.

'I can imagine all sorts of reasons why they might want to take it over. Local prestige, for one.' Jack sounded uncomfortable with the idea. 'And it will arouse a lot of interest, you know. Any politician who gets his name connected with it will be able to bask in glory anywhere in Australia.'

'If it gets out, it will go further than that.' Helen was pouring coffee for the group, as they sat around in the living room at Lakeview House. Barry, who seemed not particularly interested in the discussion, had gone into the kitchen where he was putting away the bread and the butter. He came back after a while, carrying a plate of cheese, pickles, dried fruit and crackers.

'Honestly,' Helen said. 'This is something much more than just a local nine days wonder.' She handed a mug of coffee to David.

'Well, it's a scientific thing, of course.' David sounded as though only scientists would find the body interesting.

'No, it isn't, David. Surely you can see that? Just because it isn't an aboriginal man doesn't mean that he's any less likely to stir up controversy and huge interest. More, maybe.'

Antony was stirring his coffee, only part of his mind on what he was saying.

'More, eh?' David stood up and paced around the room for a few moments. Everyone watched him, Helen feeling a little edgy.

'So a white man is more interesting than a black man, isn't that what you said?' By now, Helen could see that David was really angry.

'It isn't at all what Antony was saying, and you damn well know that, David. Sit down and shut up.' Helen was surprised at how strong she felt. All her vacillations and uncertainties seemed to have dissipated. Hooray for the subconscious mind, she thought. Well done! Her left – or was it right – hemisphere seemed to be back on call.

David did as he was told, abruptly. After a few sips of coffee, he took a slab of cheese from Barry's proffered plate and subsided into affected disinterest in the proceedings.

'Look, let's be pragmatical about this.' Helen looked around at the people in the group. 'Let's just work out what we know, what we need to know, and where we can turn next.'

'While still keeping it a secret?' Peter shook his head. 'I don't think we can count on that, Helen. At best we have only a few days to make discreet enquiries, and then someone is going to get hold of the story and blow it wide open.'

'We know,' said Antony firmly, trying to override his father's pessimistic comment. 'We know that our body is white, fortyish, and appears to be that of a priest. All right, is a priest.'

From the corner of his eye he must have seen Helen lift her head sharply at his diffidence about the identification. She accepted his correction with a sharp nod.

'Barry assures us, and he has to be right, that the crucifix is a Catholic one.'

Barry mumbled: 'Right on!' through a mouth very full of cheese and pickled onion.

'And he had with him a soutane,' added Helen.

'A cassock,' Barry said, nodding.

'A what?' Helen was surprised. 'Is that the same thing, Barry? I remember knowing they wore soutanes – is it the same thing?'

Barry nodded. 'Black thing, long, buttons up the front. Cassock.'

'So where do we go from here?' Antony raised his shoulders, then dropped them, in a gesture of uncertainty.

Helen had an idea. 'Are there any stories, David, any legends, anything your grandfather taught you that suggests that a priest somehow found his way here?'

'A priest? No, no priests. Most of his stories were about the Great Lizard and he was more sort of spiritual than physical, you know? And there were stories about my grandfather's grandfather and his grandfather and so on way back to the beginning. They made the law. What they said, we did. No priests. Not that I can remember.'

'All those men. Were women never recognised as anything?' Teresa snapped another cracker in half and nibbled on it.

'There were some women who were important. I can't remember much. There was one story. If I can get it right. Probably can't.' David was struggling with a memory long lost.

Helen switched off; she was thinking about the likely course of events if they were to seek the support of a University.

'Can't remember her name,' David said. 'She lived with the Great Lizard, I think. She was chosen for being a good woman, you know? Her children were special, too. One of them anyway. The story was something to the effect that she was on our side, the Arundijilaba's side, and would talk to the Great Lizard about us and get help if there was a drought or something. Can't remember her name. She was some woman, though; very powerful.'

'Sounds a bit like Our Lady.' Barry gathered up the plates and piled them on the kitchen counter.

Peter snapped out of his reverie. 'You know what occurs to me?' He stood up. 'Isn't there some sort of establishment – a priory, abbey, something of the sort, halfway between here and civilisation?'

'New Norcia, you mean?' Jack said. 'Remember it, Helen? We passed it on the way up from Perth. Funny place, really; there were some boys there playing with a pet kangaroo when we went by. A big place, I mean a real church and a school and a hotel – and other big buildings in the middle of absolute nowhere.' Jack remembered it not too well, but had clearly been impressed.

'I've been there!' Teresa said, keen as mustard. 'You know what migrants are like; went there the first year I was in Australia. It's an abbey, I think. Benedictine monks run it.'

Helen struggled to remember something the CSIRO librarian had told her about New Norcia: what was it?

'There's a Library there! Sheila Stanley told me about it; apparently it's all catalogued in Latin.' She jumped up.

Antony joined her; he held out his hands and grasped Helen's in them. 'You're right, Helen. That's the next move!'

They danced around a couple of times, excited. Helen hadn't felt so exhilarated for ages; well, not since she discovered the cave.

She caught Jack's puzzled stare and stopped, feeling herself blush again. She let go of Antony's hands and pushed her own hands deep into her pockets.

'Antony's right,' she said. 'The Library at New Norcia must have some sort of records about the early days here, surely. I mean Western Australia didn't have much else happening before Captain Cook.'

David glared at her.

'I'm talking about recorded history, David. Of course your people have been here since forever but I'm talking about recorded history. Written-down stuff.'

'Who's going, then? And how?' Jack, as always, brought Helen to an awareness of the need to plan carefully.

'I can fly there. There has to be a landing strip even if it's just part of the main road up from Perth.' Teresa was pulling her sandals back on, after sitting barefoot during the morning.

'I wouldn't know what to look for,' said Jack. 'Not really.'

'None of us does, Jack.' Peter shook his head a little. 'I think I know less than most people, though.'

'Antony?' Helen looked at the scientist.

'Yeah, you come with me, Antony.' Teresa sounded enthused by the idea. Antony looked at her quickly, hesitated too long.

'No, Helen, I think it should be you. You're a scholar, you can talk in a scholarly way with whoever runs the Library. I could do it no better than you, and it's your project.'

Helen felt a surge of pleasure at being handed back her discovery, and so graciously. 'OK. When? Need we let them know we're coming?'

Barry offered to ring New Norcia and alert them to the imminent arrival of an aircraft, a female scientist and an American female pilot. All of which he did, to the amusement of the rest of the group, who were listening in and enjoying the way Barry dropped each scrap of information, hoping to cause a stir amongst the Benedictines. It caused nothing of the sort; his disappointment was short-lived, though, as he told the women they would be well-received and welcomed at the Guesthouse. They could stay as long as they wished, for a small charge.

It was agreed that, during their absence overnight, nothing would be done with the body. They would take with them Polaroid photographs of the priest's garment. Antony suggested that he could safely ring a conservator he knew at the Museum in Sydney and get expert advice on taking appropriate care of the soutane – the cassock.

There was no need to say exactly what they had found, or where, or that it had been found in the company of a dead body.

Helen and Teresa hurried away to pack overnight bags. Helen decided she should take a camera, and a photograph of the crucifix too. Antony went into the cool store to take a photograph of the soutane, and when he came back into the house, he took a couple of photographs of the crucifix, carefully placing it against one of Barry's rather lurid blue cushions so that the shape and pattern would stand out more clearly.

Helen put the photographs and the camera in her handbag and slung it over her shoulder. As she left her room, Teresa caught up with her. She, too, was packed and ready to leave.

Peter was standing by the aircraft, waiting. He said that he had spoken to Antony about it and had decided that his work was finished, at least until there was a need for more investigation.

He proposed to accompany the women to New Norcia, find a way to get to Perth from there, and fly back to Adelaide.

'I shall be ready to come back at the drop of a hint,' he assured Helen. She felt somewhat uncomfortable about his leaving them. They had been through such an exciting event together and Peter's calm, skilled decisiveness had helped to keep the group functioning together.

She said goodbye with regret and a hug.

Within half an hour of the decision being made to go to New Norcia, the two women and Peter Walker climbed into the plane and took off. They waved to the men left behind, who were already sitting with chilled beer in tall glasses on the verandah, waiting until it was time to barbecue some defrosted steaks for dinner.

The plane touched down on a smooth stretch of land used as an airstrip behind the abbey. Helen was surprised to see so many buildings in front of them. They made their way quickly to the Guesthouse, where they found that they were indeed expected; Barry's phone call had made everything very simple.

They were fortunate in that, despite the school holidays being in full fling, there was a room available for the women to share that night.

'A cancellation,' the welcoming monk said, with a smile. 'You must have a very good reason for being here.'

Teresa said the monk was just being charming, but Helen felt a *frisson* of disquiet, wondering if the Benedictine monks had some kind of instinct about missions like hers. Like hers? Was there ever such a strange and unlikely mission as this?

She wanted to ask the monk if the white garment he was wearing were a soutane, but felt it would be far too personal a question. She would look the words up in a dictionary, once they were safely tucked away in the Library.

While the women were signing in, the monk suggested that Peter might find a room at the hotel; he would be more likely to get a lift to Perth in the morning. This Peter was happy to do, and walked across to the hotel, arranging to meet Helen and Teresa again in a few minutes.

Teresa picked up a leaflet about New Norcia. 'Established in 1846 to save the local aboriginal population,' she read. She frowned. 'Save? Should be serve. A bit of political correctness wouldn't go amiss.' Were they Arundijilaba, Helen wondered, but remembered that David said that his tribe was linked only with the small area around Barwick.

Dom Joseph, who described himself as the business manager, took them across the courtyard to their rooms. There were fifteen rooms for visitors, he told them, and they were well-used.

'People seem to relish the opportunity to get away from the city. We have a lot of people here for retreats, seminars, that kind of thing.'

Helen saw how fascinated Teresa was; she had smiled with approbation at the monk's title – obviously a sign of worldly efficiency – and she was watching Dom Joseph with great delight on her face.

'So you don't do the old things,' Teresa said. 'Praying and being silent – the Thomas Merton things?' Well, she had at least read a book or two about monks, she wanted him to know. Helen studiously looked away from the monk.

'We do a lot of praying, Mrs Vandenburg; oh yes, a great deal. We live the monastic life totally; our world is not determined by what's going on outside this place but we recognise its value to us.'

'Money, you mean. Funding.' Teresa nodded wisely, as Helen winced.

'Yes, we need to make money. But more importantly you need us.'

Dom Joseph stopped; they had reached their room. He looked at Helen with a look of incurious certainty which made her feel she was blushing.

'Should you have any more requirements, the Guestmaster will be on duty in the morning.' He told them where they would find a meal, that dinner was already arranged for them. He walked quickly away, his arms folded beneath the length of fabric which fell from his shoulders and covered the front of his robe.

'The Guestmaster!' It seemed that Teresa like this title, too.

Once they were indoors again, Helen said, 'What did he mean – "you need us"? Teresa, does he know?'

'Of course not, silly. They all talk that way: Chip says the Vatican is stacked with priests telling non-Catholics how important the Church is to them. Some of them don't like it one little bit.'

'I hope you're right.' Helen, a long-time member of the Australian Skeptics, disliked this sudden rush of superstition, and unpacked quickly. Teresa, who finished first, chatted on about her brother and his experience in Rome. Chip worked in the American Embassy.

As Helen washed her face and hands in the small bathroom, she wondered how to approach Dom Joseph about the man they had found. She could hardly say: 'Excuse me, but we have found a dead priest – are you missing one?'

'One thing we can do, Teresa, is check if they're missing one here.'

'What?'

'You know, why did they come here? Was one of their people over here long before 18-whatever and is that why the others came?'

Helen ran her fingers through her dampened hair, a practical alternative to brushing it.

Teresa picked up the leaflets and turned back to the first page.

'No, they were sent out from Spain to do that one job. In 18-whatever. No mention of earlier visits.'

'We must ask.'

A few minutes later, they walked with Peter through the olive trees in the courtyard to a garden bench where they sat and talked about their problems until the smell of fresh-baked bread drew them to the dining room.

They ate alone, though not in silence, and decided it was too late to seek out Dom Joseph and start asking questions. A stroll around the monastery seemed in order.

The church was elaborately Spanish in design, reflecting the nationality of New Norcia's founder, Dom Rosendo Salvado.

Buildings ranged on both sides of the road through the settlement. Imposing structures in red and white, with towers, colonnades, arches. Statues of saints decorated every niche, and there were many niches.

In the distance, they saw an old monk walking slowly, alone with his thoughts. He was the only person they saw although Helen remarked that she could hear children's voices coming from somewhere.

They slept easily, despite the heat of the night. Teresa was quite sure there was a bowl of pot pourri somewhere in the room, or a sachet hidden away. Helen reminded her that they were sleeping with an open window; perhaps there was a herb garden outside. The scent was delicate, fragrant, sleep-inducing. Although it was quite different, it reminded Helen of the faint scent she had noticed when they were looking at the dead priest.

Early in the morning, Peter knocked on their door. While he waited for them, he was greeted by the Guestmaster, Dom Francis, who introduced himself and hoped that Peter had enjoyed a good night. Helen and Teresa overheard the conversation and came out to join the men in the courtyard. After more introductions, they strolled towards the dining room together.

The Guestmaster made no enquiries about their visit; tourists were frequent and always welcome visitors, providing they did not interrupt the monastic life going on around them. He made this point gently, and with humour.

However, this did seem the opportune moment for Helen to give some idea of the reason for their visit.

'I want to do a little research on the early days of the Church in Western Australia,' she said. 'Fossick, if I may, in your Library. When can I meet the Librarian?'

The rebuff, when it came, was no less devastating for being politely expressed.

'I'm sorry, Dr Lytton, but I'm afraid the Library is out of bounds. You are welcome, of course, to visit the Museum but the Library is not available to you. Perhaps Dr Walker can take on that aspect of your work?'

Teresa got her breath back first. 'Do you mean – ' she paused, knotting down her incredulity, 'that Helen can't use your Library because – she's a woman?'

With no change in his calm and pleasant demeanour, the monk nodded.

'But that's archaic!' Teresa couldn't hold back, despite Helen's vigorous wave.

'It's an old Church, Mrs Vandenburg. We have a number of old traditions. Females may not enter the Refectory, where we monks eat, nor the Cloisters, nor the Library.'

'Nor become priests,' Teresa snapped. 'It's outrageous.'

'You're not a Catholic, Mrs Vandenburg?'

Teresa shook her head. 'No, thank goodness.'

'It's hard for some Catholic women to accept these rules too. But our Rule here is very old. We have to accept many restrictions. We do so gladly.'

'You've changed the subject,' Teresa said.

'Yes.' Dom Francis smiled happily and Teresa had to smile, back, just.

Peter explained that he was a medical man, not a scientist and he would be no use at all in the Library. There was no way that Dom Francis could change the rules; Helen could not go into the Library. Was there any other way that Dom Francis could help, he asked. Could the Librarian himself assist her?

Helen said she would have to think about the situation and the three downhearted visitors went into the dining room for breakfast. Dom Francis went off, still smiling.

'I'll bet he has a slap-up breakfast,' Teresa said in an aggrieved whisper.

'If he did, it would be a few hours ago.'

Breakfast was another pleasant meal. They were not the only guests of the Benedictines, as they knew, and this morning they encountered the others. A small group of senior children from a Catholic School in Fremantle was at the end of a three-day retreat in the company of a teacher. The teacher breathed sighs of relief as he waited for his toast to cook and told the women about the strain of keeping an eye on so many children for so long.

A middle-aged couple, the woman dressed in shorts, a halter-necked top and too much jewellery, seemed to be annoyed by the noise the children made. They finished their breakfast quickly and left the room, apparently in a huff.

At the table beyond them, a man in his sixties sat alone, reading while he ate his cereals. When the scrambled eggs arrived, he picked up another book, leaving the first one open but face down next to him. Fresh coffee was brought out, the man made room for it, and a third book took its place.

Teresa nudged Helen. 'See that? Either he's a very picky reader or some crazy scholar.'

While her toast browned, Teresa did some more thinking. Helen saw the pursed lips, the puzzled frown.

'You know what?'

Helen waited.

'Spending the next couple of days here just sitting around reading like that man over there while you do whatever you are going to be allowed to do, could be a bit mind-blowing. It seems to me a great idea to take Peter down to Perth. I can fill up the plane with extra fuel, pick up some grog and stuff, then tomorrow I can fly back to New Norcia. What do you think?'

'Good idea,' said Peter, sipping his second cup of coffee.

'When will you get back?' It sounded like a good idea to Helen, too.

'Late in the afternoon, it'll be,' Teresa said, with an implication that her program was very tight.

Helen smiled; she knew that Teresa planned to stretch her trip as long as possible so that she wouldn't have to spend hours sitting about waiting.

It was agreed and, after breakfast, Teresa set off with Peter.

Helen washed, brushed her hair into a neat shape, checked that she looked 'respectable' and went in pursuit of the only Benedictine who seemed likely to be able to help her.

The Librarian was, as librarians always are, courteous and unobtrusive in his questions as Helen explained that she was a scientist, with an interest in ancient water courses.

'I am also interested', she said, 'in the early days of the Church around here.'

It sounded so weak, so insincere, so unlikely. But the Librarian had probably heard stranger reasons for delving into his recondite collection and simply offered to bring out to her the books which contained the kind of information she needed.

'Do you read Spanish?' he said. 'Latin?'

Helen felt a mite embarrassed to say that she read only English.

The monk was not disconcerted. 'We have many books in English', he said.

He showed Helen around the Museum; perhaps, she thought, as some kind of apology for not taking her into the Library, whose open door was so tantalising. As they walked around, Helen's eye was caught by a display case. It held a few open books, some church plate, and several relics of the days of the founder of New Norcia.

There were paintings of Dom Rosendo Salvado and Dom Joseph Serra, Spanish monks with hungry faces and Old

Testament beards. They wore their robes – their soutanes, Helen thought – with a large crucifix strung on a cord around their necks and then stuck through the belt.

'Their crucifixes are much bigger than yours!' The Librarian nodded. 'Yes, it was the fashion then.'

'Was it an old fashion?' Goodness, how weak her question sounded, how contrived.

'Oh yes, I think so. Look at some of the paintings here – it goes back a very long way.' The Librarian was right; such paintings as there were of monks showed many holding or wearing crucifixes as big as the one Helen had found, and some of the paintings were very old or showed events which happened centuries ago.

Many of the men in the paintings were monks and many were priests. The black soutane was a garment common to many of the paintings.

'Back four hundred years – even then?' It was no good, she couldn't think of any other way to ask than directly.

'The sixteenth century? Oh yes, certainly. No doubt at all.'

'And they would stick the crucifix into the belt of the soutane?'

'Well, it would keep it out of the way, I think, don't you?'

'Soutane? Is that the right word?'

'We usually call it a robe. A soutane is the long black coat priests wear, rather than monkish robes. A soutane or cassock; either word.'

'Thank you.' Helen sighed quietly. Now that one was settled.

She caught the expression of amused curiosity on the Librarian's face; a glance which was immediately replaced by polite patience.

He seemed not in the least disconcerted. Probably, Helen thought, schoolchildren asked him questions as odd as that all the time.

He seemed to be waiting, very politely, but she sensed a little impatience. Doubtless he had work to do elsewhere. What a place to be doing it: miles from anywhere, nothing else to distract them. Still, maybe that was the idea. She thought of the haunted look of the man in the first picture: the Founder, who travelled an incredibly difficult journey to this appalling desert of a place.

Chastened to think of that lonely man setting up in business – God's business – so far from everything else, Helen told the Librarian that she was interested in knowing just when the very first priests arrived in Australia, in Western Australia in particular.

'Did any die here? I mean, have you records of them all, the early ones. Are any of them missing?'

This time the Librarian did display some small misgiving. He blinked.

'Those who died in the Order are all buried here and accounted for, Dr Lytton. I can't promise you to find records of the – disposition of the others.'

With a humorous twitch of his mouth, the Librarian went to fetch her an appropriate source of the information. Back in the now empty dining room, Helen sat down at the table where they had eaten breakfast. She put her briefcase on the table, and drew out her notebook, a pen, and the small camera which was reliable for taking photographs indoors.

'May I suggest that you get permission before taking photographs?'

Startled, Helen turned to see the man who had been at breakfast, the man with all the books. He was looking at her camera with some severity.

'Yes, of course. I appreciate that necessity.' Helen was pleased to hear an asperity in her own voice.

'Good.' The tone of voice was pleasant enough, but the brevity of his answer stung. The man took off his jacket, and sat down at a table a little distant from Helen's lodging.

Helen watched him sort out his books, which he took from a large plastic bag. With an abrupt movement, made as he tried to save a book from falling to the floor, he knocked another of the books off the table. It fell with a clatter. Helen immediately gave the man the look of intense irritation people give each other in libraries when noises interrupt their concentration.

'Serves him right,' she thought, and opened her notebook.

'I'm sorry I disturbed your work.' The man was at her elbow again, looking quite pointedly at the notebook's blank pages.

'I was thinking.' Helen wasn't going to give in.

'Yes, I see that.' The man smiled, surprising Helen with his obvious amusement. He knew he had riled her and was clearly trying to make amends. 'May I introduce myself?' He hesitated, ready to retreat if Helen sent him packing with some offhand comment.

'Please do,' she said, smiling back. 'I'm Helen Lytton, Dr Helen Lytton.' Best to make him aware of her credentials, she thought.

'I'm Robert Valindale; Professor Robert Valindale.' Trumped.

They shook hands, formally.

'May I?' Valindale waited for permission, which Helen gave with a nod, and pulled out a chair opposite her. His long arms folded sharply at the elbows as he leant them on the table and cupped his face in his hands.

'Why aren't you using the Library?' Helen asked, still bridling at being excluded. 'You're a man.'

'Indeed. I am also a smoker. The Rule does not permit smoking.'

'Or women.'

'Quite so.' Valindale brought out a packet of cigarettes, and lit one. He did not seek permission by so much as a glance.

'You're Australian?' he said.

'Yes.'

'Then this isn't your discipline,' he waved his hand around, encircling the monastery and its contents.

'No, I'm with CSIRO. I was, that is. Just retired.' She shouldn't gabble on, Helen thought, as if it mattered that this man got her story straight.

Valindale leant back in his chair. 'Then you must be a good Catholic, learning what you can about the early days. It's a great place to start, you know. Fascinating place, New Norcia. Fascinating.'

She was a bit tired of his assumptions. 'Actually, I am not a Catholic and I am interested in only a very small part of Catholic history.'

'What part is that?' Valindale's voice had sharpened and Helen was suddenly scared. *Hold your tongue!* she snapped at herself, and heard her father's voice sharpen to silence her. That was who this man reminded her of. That was why he had managed to ingratiate himself to the point where she was almost telling him the biggest secret of her life.

'New Norcia. Its history.' Helen told the lie easily. That should put him off.

144

'Excellent! Then I can help, Dr Lytton. I'm writing a book about it.'

Oh shit, Helen thought. How do I get out of this?

The Librarian came in and, without speaking, handed Helen two books. She glanced at the titles. They were basic histories, and very thick books. She thanked the Librarian, who smiled and left.

Helen got up abruptly and stood by the window, looking across to the Museum. She thought about the founder's missal, on display in a large glass case, with his rosary.

'What a beautiful piece of jewellery that man's rosary is,' she said. Valindale was still sitting at her table. 'You know, the Founder's. In the Museum.'

She had hoped that he would follow her to the window, so that she could politely retreat to her table and leave him behind.

'Not what he would have called it, but you're right. It is beautiful.'

'I don't really know much about Catholic ways; rosaries and the like. I think there are – ten, is it?' Valindale nodded. 'Yes, ten beads and a space, and then ten more and so on. For repeating prayers, isn't it? Some sort of mnemonic?'

'Yes, indeed.'

He joined her at the window.

Good, she thought. Now he's moved I can stop him going back.

'There are a lot of rituals in the Catholic Church,' she said. 'I prefer a less structured form of worship myself.'

She smiled a little – she hadn't set foot in a church since Fred's funeral eighteen years ago and she only went then because Fred was her cousin.

'Rituals serve many purposes.' The Professor sounded a little pompous. 'And they can be a great comfort. That rosary was a gift from a very important person, very important.' Helen wondered why he didn't say 'The Pope' if that was the VIP in question.

'Rosaries are often given to religious – to members of religious orders – by others who wish to mark their respect and even affection for the recipients of the gift. It's not easy to think what else to give someone who may have taken vows of poverty.' Valindale spoke musingly. 'A chalice, perhaps? But a priest, for instance, would need only one, I think.'

Helen suddenly realised that the Professor was chatting away about very little but it had important significance for her and her quest.

She remembered the photograph in her handbag. The photograph which Antony had taken yesterday of the crucifix they had found around the neck of the man in the bog.

'Do you know about rosaries, then?' she said. 'And about other things; crucifixes, for instance?'

She tried to keep her voice as vague and conversational as his, but she failed and she knew it. Valindale looked at her quite sharply.

'I'm an art historian, Dr Lytton. There's a significant collection of artworks here about which I am researching for a new book. Yes, I know about religious art. Now you must tell me why you ask.'

He took her elbow in his right hand and led her back to her seat at the small table. She had no option but to go where he directed her. Once she was seated, he sat down again opposite her. This time he did not hold his face in his hands, whimsically. He sat up straight, so straight that he seemed to look at Helen down the length of his rather too long nose.

She knew that if she did not take herself in hand, she might start to stammer. Her father looked at her that way sometimes. Watchful, observant, ready to criticise.

'Please don't glare at me,' she said, quietly.

The Professor collapsed immediately. 'I was unaware that I was doing so, my dear woman,' he said. Helen winced at the 'dear woman'. 'I was simply waiting. You have a deep concern about something and it would seem that I might be able to help.'

Helen looked at him. He smiled and nodded, encouragingly. She made up her mind, picked up her handbag and drew out the envelope in which Antony had put the photograph of the crucifix.

Valindale had the good sense not to hold out his hand for the envelope, but Helen was aware of his concentrated attention on it. She took a deep breath.

'I have a photograph – I came across a rather distinctive crucifix recently,' she said, trying to sound vaguely offhand about it. 'It's pretty old, I gather. Maybe as much as four hundred years old. I thought that I might find some clue to its origins here.'

'You came across it in Australia?'

'Yes.'

'And it's four hundred years old? A migrant brought it here, then, or maybe an early settler? A family heirloom?'

'I don't know.'

'May I see the photograph?'

This time his hand was held out and Helen slowly opened the envelope. She drew out the photograph and with her eyes on Valindale rather than on the image of the crucifix, she placed the photograph in his hand.

He looked down at the photograph; pursed his lips.

For a while, a long while, he said nothing. Once he looked up at Helen, then looked again for a long time at the photograph. Finally, he laid it down on the table. He touched the top corners, tapping them until the photograph aligned exactly with the edges of the table.

'I think I know who made this,' he said at last. 'You're quite right to think it's a bit special – yes, it is a bit special -'

Helen drew in a breath sharply, and noticed that Valindale had not missed it.

'It's special because I think it was made by Di Fiore.' Valindale raised his eyes from the photograph and looked at Helen.

'Who was that?' she said.

The Professor was holding the photograph now so that the light from the window fell full on its surface. 'He was a renaissance goldsmith; a very good one, too. He worked almost exclusively for the Vatican towards the end of his life. This looks remarkably like something he made.'

'For the Pope?' Helen was afraid to go on with the discussion. How could a crucifix belonging to a Pope have got here?

'Yes, but not for his personal use. He would have had it made so that he could give it to someone else.'

Valindale gave Helen a look so sharp that she almost flinched.

'Things like this were given to someone of significance from a foreign country. Or to a member of the aristocracy; maybe to a military person who had provided advice or help for the Vatican; a diplomat.'

'A diplomat,' Helen murmured, hoping to distract the Professor.

'Is that where you photographed it? Does it belong now to the descendant of a diplomat; someone who represented England at the Vatican, maybe?'

'No, no, nothing like that.' What on earth should she say: maybe this man could help her resolve the problem, but at what cost? Where was her secret going to be then?

'Look, thank you very much but I think I've said too much already.' She took the photograph out of Valindale's hands, slid it back into the envelope and into her handbag. 'Thank you, but I really must be getting on with my work now.'

Valindale stood up. He looked at Helen thoughtfully, and then sat down again.

'You must forgive me, Dr Lytton. I can see that you are distressed about this Antonio Di Fiore piece. Truly, I have no interest in it other than idle curiosity. If I can help, allow me to do so.'

He went back to his table, and spread his books around in a different pattern.

There was much to think about. Helen knew that her knowledge about the Church, about crucifixes, was almost zero. This man, an academic like so many she had known and trusted, seemed to have more than a passing knowledge about the very topics she needed to study. Could she trust him? What option did she have? She looked at the history books the Librarian had offered; she knew how unlikely it was that she would find anything in them without access to catalogues, without direct searches in the Library's resources.

'Professor Valindale?'

He turned towards her, pen in hand.

'I need your help. Please.'

Valindale pushed back his chair vigorously and returned to his chair at Helen's table. 'My dear Dr Lytton, I shall be delighted to help in any way I can. The photograph, please.'

He snapped his fingers, to Helen's wry amusement, and she handed the envelope back to him.

Again he studied the photograph, this time more carefully. 'Wherever it was found, it's been immersed in water.' He looked up at Helen, who nodded. 'But it hasn't rotted; I mean the wood looks fairly sound?' Again he looked at Helen.

She nodded, and then taking the plunge, she said: 'It was found in a peat bog. I found it.'

There was a long moment of silence. 'And you want to know where it came from; its provenance. Quite right, my dear.'

'Please don't call me your dear, Professor. I'm a sixty-year-old scientist, not a bimbo.'

'A what? I apologise, Dr Lytton, I forget my manners all too frequently. Now, what can I tell you about this?'

Valindale put his finger on the photograph, slowly tracing its lines as though the actual crucifix were under his hand.

He flicked the crown of thorns gently with his thumbnail, as though they, too, were capable of being touched and felt.

'I've got an idea, my – Dr Lytton. Give me a few minutes with the reference books.' He got up abruptly and went off to the Library, taking the photograph with him.

Resisting the temptation to tidy his pile of books, Helen ran her fingers over the top one. She glanced at the title, opened the book at the title page: Harvard University Press, 1991. By Robert Henry Valindale. On the back of the page was a list of his other books. A long list.

Well, that settled the question. The Professor was who and what he claimed to be. Helen remembered the caution Antony had shown when he was asked to fly over to Western Australia; how he had insisted on first checking that Helen's qualifications were appropriate; that Teresa was not ringing him as part of some sort of hoax. Yet Helen had immediately trusted Professor Valindale; there was something about powerful, older men – she always accepted their right to her respect.

Lunchtime came and went. The students and their teacher enjoyed cold beef salads and ice-cream before hurrying off to the transport home. A carload of adult tourists arrived for lunch and a tour. A young couple drove up in a bright yellow sports car, had a glass of wine and left.

Helen spent over an hour and a half alone, filling up on a salad sandwich and a glass of iced water. She went to the Ladies' Room. Looked without interest in the gift shop, where she bought a magazine. Wandered around outside for a few minutes. Back in the dining room, she glanced in the history books, randomly reading an odd page of pious platitudes. She was right; the library's books held no interest for her.

The magazine held her interest for a few minutes as she read a story about a passionate florist and her lover. Extraordinary stuff.

Professor Valindale at last came back. With neither apology nor explanation, he lit a cigarette and was soon immersed in the pile of books he had brought with him from the Library. He stacked them on his table, and an adjacent one, in no apparent order.

After a while, during which he had not spoken, he asked Helen to procure for him a ham sandwich and a cup of tea, which she did.

After half an hour, during which Helen read another magazine story, this time about passion and betrayal in an outer suburb of Melbourne, Valindale stretched and sat back in his chair. He took off his glasses and lit another cigarette.

'Dr Lytton, this is indeed the work of the man I told you about. I was fairly confident of that anyway. But I am delighted to say there is a small mystery about it.'

'A mystery?' Helen wondered what Valindale would say if he knew just how big the mystery was.

'A small mystery, yes.' Valindale put his forefinger down with an audible whack on a section in one of the open books. 'I can't say for sure without seeing the actual artefact.' He glanced at Helen, who guessed he wondered if she had it with her. She shook her head. 'But it looks identical with this.'

With a triumphant flourish, Professor Valindale spun the book around so that Helen could see a coloured photograph of what seemed to her a crucifix absolutely identical with the one back at Lakeview Meatworks. But this one was perfect, the wood was solid and obviously oak; the coloured photograph showed the skill of the smith. The crucifix had been photographed on a bed of purple velvet, much different from the bed of peat in which her crucifix had lain for all those years.

'It's the same,' she said, awed by the beauty of the object in the photograph. 'Isn't it? I mean, they must all look very much alike, but this really does look like mine!'

'It's the same. I am prepared to swear to that.' Valindale looked very solemn.

'Then why is it in this book? Was it stolen – no, how could that be – it's been buried – ' Helen was lost.

Valindale sat down again, after pacing around while Helen struggled for comprehension.

'It has a history, this crucifix. Di Fiore made only three, at the command of the Pope. It's older than you thought, Dr

Lytton, it's five hundred years old, give or take thirty years. Di Fiore lived to a ripe old age; artists did in those comfortable times.'

'Who did he give them to?' This to Helen was the crucial question.

'You're not a Catholic, of course.' Valindale shook his head slightly, as though it were a pity Helen would not fully appreciate his comments.

'You see, Dr Lytton, the three crucifixes were kept by the Pope until he met men who were personally dedicated to his service.'

'Catholic kings, you mean? Henry the Eighth before he opted out?'

Valindale closed his eyes briefly, wincing at Helen's summing up of the loss of England by the Church.

'No, these were priests. Have you heard of Ignatius Loyola?'

Oh for goodness sake, Helen thought. Yes, indeed she had heard of him. 'Yes, of course. He started the Jesuits.'

The Professor folded his arms, assumed a familiar teaching stance, and gazed across the room above Helen's head.

'When Pope Paul the Third gave permission for the Society of Jesus – the Jesuits – to be established, he gave them a special place in his heart. The Society became responsible directly and only to him.'

'Right.' Helen wished Valindale would get on with it.

'According to this book – and it is a very reliable textbook, Dr Lytton, or I would not be quoting it to you – one of the Di Fiore crucifixes was given to St. Ignatius Loyola by the Pope as a token of esteem.'

'Oh my God – then it must have been stolen or something?' How the hell had it ended up here, around the neck of a priest in Western Australia?

Valindale held up a hand to stop her. 'No, it still exists. It is kept in the Vatican Museum. That is the one in the photograph in this book.' The Professor gently tapped the illustration.

'The other two – what happened to them?' It was like getting blood out of a stone, Helen thought, why doesn't he hurry up?

'The second one was given to another Jesuit, perhaps the most famous after Ignatius himself. Francis Xavier. You have heard of him?'

'Yes.'

'He was a great friend of St. Ignatius Loyola. A close and personal friend. It must have been a great loss when St. Francis was sent to India to perform the work of a missionary. On the eve of his departure, the Pope presented him with the second of the Di Fiore crucifixes.'

'He went to India? ' Helen's thoughts were racing; could the second crucifix have been left in India and found its way to Australia from there?

'Oh yes; India, Japan, south east Asia; he travelled far and wide.'

'But those places are just north of Western Australia. The crucifix could have been lost there and somebody brought it down here! Couldn't that have happened, Dr Valindale?'

'It could; but it didn't.'

'No?'

'I'm afraid not.'

'Do you mean that one, too, is still where it belongs? In some museum?'

'Yes, indeed.'

'The third one, then? Where is it supposed to be and why is it here? It has to be this one, doesn't it?'

'The third one – vanished. The reference book says that nobody knows what happened to it. Maybe the Pope knew, but he was silent about its disappearance. St Ignatius Loyola said nothing about it.'

'Where did it go? Why here?'

'I can't answer that. The Jesuits, you know, were involved from the start in politicking, somewhat unseemly it appears to us, but they were round and about influencing the courts of the world from the start. A lot of covert, secret work was being done. Maybe the crucifix was used in some way during that time. I simply don't know.'

Helen stood up and walked over to the window. There were some children playing football with their father. The family car was parked outside, on the edge of the road. The car was covered in the red dust of this part of Western Australia. It was so far, so very far from Rome.

'I doubt if you will ever know its true provenance, Dr Lytton. People acquire things, carry them around the world, lose them. Take my earnest counselling to heart, if I may offer it, and have a museum look at the piece. Sell it, or give it to the Church, but make sure that that marvel of the smith's work ends up in protective custody.'

Professor Valindale gathered up his books into a single, unsteady pile. Helen watched him, surprised.

'You're giving me advice? Aren't you proposing to do anything about it? Are you leaving it to me to make decisions about it?'

'Yes, I am, Dr Lytton. You're a scientist. You're not a Catholic. I feel sure you will make a rational, scientific decision about the disposition of the Di Fiore. Two exist. I hope the third continues to exist, even if nobody else ever knows about it.'

He opened a notebook, and seemed prepared to start work.

Helen shook his shoulder. 'Look, you can't leave it there. If I were to tell you – ' She hesitated.

The old man held up a hand. 'I am not interested in any adventures, Dr Lytton. I am an art historian and subject to stroke. I do not wish to endanger my health by becoming embroiled in your mystery. I wish you well in its resolution.'

Helen stood back, moved but astonished by the sudden weariness that seemed to have overcome the Professor. 'That's it, then? Thank you, thank you for your help.'

'Yes. I have much work to do. Thank you. And goodbye.' Professor Valindale picked up his pen and began writing. Helen carried the heavy reference book: *Art Treasures in the Vatican Collections* from his table to hers. She gathered up the other books given to her from the Library into a portable heap and picked them up. She returned them all to the Librarian's office.

With his permission, and she was relieved that it was without his supervision, she made a photocopy of the pages about Di Fiore's crucifixes, including the illustration.

She went back into the dining room, and looked at Professor Valindale. He seemed engrossed in his work, but she noticed that he was not writing.

CHAPTER 7

HELEN SPENT THE REST OF THE AFTERNOON in the courtyard, under the olive trees, waiting for Teresa's return. She sipped from a glass of iced Coke bought at the gift shop and studied the pictures of the two crucifixes. A couple of cars pulled up and tourists got out, stretched their legs and arms and looked around at the imposing buildings with curiosity. They took no notice of Helen and she was too preoccupied with her own thoughts to take much notice of them.

At one time, a small child ran over to her and held out a hand as though to draw Helen away with him. She smiled and looked up to see his mother approaching with an apologetic lift of the shoulders. The boy said 'Bye bye' and ran off to join his mother on the way back to their car.

Briefly, very briefly, Helen wondered what it would have been like to have children. Jack would have made a decent enough parent but Helen would not have welcomed the role of mother. Her own mother had found the responsibility too much.

Helen drew the photograph and the photocopy towards her and studied them again.

If Professor Valindale said they were by the same hand, then they must be. She could see for herself how the writhing of the agonised body looked the same, the crown of thorns on both of them was as much a triumphant crown as a twist of thorny twigs, the simple loincloth hung in the same sculptured folds. The measurements of the Vatican crucifix were given in the text alongside the illustration; they matched, too. There was no reason at all to doubt Valindale's judgement.

Where did this take them? Certainly a long way beyond the fact of finding a dead man in an unexpected – by everyone else – bog.

The first surprise had been that he was not an aborigine. Now he was a white man and the possessor, legally or not, of what seemed to be a priceless treasure. Well, maybe not priceless, but certainly valuable.

Helen pondered the implications of Valindale's identification and was no nearer knowing what they should do next when she heard the sound of a small plane approaching.

Teresa landed with the smallest of bumps, slowed the plane to a stop, and jumped out. Helen waved to her. Teresa waved back and walked in something of a hurry across the dusty road to flop down in the chair next to Helen's. Her T shirt and shorts were stained with sweat.

With a polite: 'May I?' she reached over and grabbed Helen's Coke. One large and several smaller swigs later, Teresa put the glass down and sighed.

'Not a long trip, but a hot one. Any luck?'

'Oh yes. Did Peter get off all right?'

'I suppose so. I didn't go over to the main airport with him; I just saw him into a taxi. Nice guy, eh? What do you mean: "Oh yes"?'

'Remember that man with the books last night?'

'The scholar – well, that's what I reckon. Yeah?'

'He is a scholar – and an art history scholar at that.'

'My, my. So?' Teresa took another deep swig of Coke.

'So he identified the crucifix.'

'He did what!'

Helen explained with mounting excitement what Valindale had told her. Finally, she picked up the photocopied illustration from the book and put it on the table alongside the photograph of the crucifix they had found.

'You see? You can see, you don't need a PhD in Art to see it, do you? They match!'

'Wow.' Teresa took a deep breath, picked up the photograph and the photocopy and looked quickly back and forth until she was satisfied. She dropped them on the table and finished Helen's Coke.

'I should get one of these; do you want another?'

Helen shook her head, as she became engrossed again in the crucifixes. Teresa went off to the gift shop. When she came back with a chilled can of Coke, without a glass, the two women sat looking at each other. Helen felt stunned, unable to formulate any ideas at all. She wondered if Teresa's quick wits would handle the situation better.

'Where does this lead us, Helen?' Obviously Teresa was baffled too.

'The Professor wants nothing to do with it. That's one possible source of help gone.'

'Why not?'

'Oh, he's got his own things to do.' Helen waved a hand, dismissing Valindale's rather odd disclaimer of interest.

'So we're on our own – you and Jack, Antony, David, Barry, me. Quite a team but nowhere to go.'

'And Peter, if he's needed.'

'Yeah, Peter.'

A huge articulated truck pulling two trailers the same size went roaring past, a cloud of red dust rising behind it. Fine particles floated through the air, leaving the faintest trace of red on the surface of the table. Teresa covered the can of Coke with her hand until the dust seemed to have settled.

'Not much traffic here. Same up there.' She pointed with her chin at the sky, which was cloudless and almost without colour.

Helen chewed her lip. 'You know, Teresa, the trail has led right up to the blasted Pope. We can't go barging in on him and saying, "Please, your Eminence, what happened to that other crucifix?" Now can we?'

'Guess not. Chip says he's impossible to get to. All sorts of officials in the way and none of them takes kindly to visitors.'

For a moment the women looked off into the distance. Helen felt herself stiffen slowly, slightly. As they turned towards each other, she saw that Teresa had done the same.

'Are you thinking what I'm thinking?' Teresa's voice was sharp, much higher than usual.

'Oh Teresa, do you think he would?'

'Why not? He owes me – and if anyone can get in, he can.'

Without stopping to think the proposition through, Teresa and Helen raced into the monastery office, to a telephone. With permission to make an overseas call, and an offer to pay for it promptly, Teresa looked up the number in her address book.

'Will he be up, Teresa? It isn't the middle of the night again or something?' She remembered too well the delay in contacting Adelaide University, and Antony. It seemed like weeks ago now.

Teresa looked at her watch and made a swift calculation. 'He's seven hours behind us. Ten after five in the afternoon here, so he's at work – it's 10.10 am in Rome. Right. What shall I say? What do we want him to do?'

'Oh lord, let's think. Well, obviously we want him to find out who the third crucifix was given to, where it went. If it's easy to find out, and it may be – that book was pretty old –

160

perhaps he could ring us or fax the information to us here? He may only have to make a phone call.'

'Fax is better – is there a fax machine at the meatworks? Yes, yes there is: I saw it.'

Teresa was pacing up and down the hallway of the monastery. Twice she reached out for the telephone but twice she withdrew her hand. 'No, let's get it straight.'

'We can't not tell him what it's about.'

'No, but you want it kept a secret, don't you?'

'Oh God yes. If we can.'

'Try this on for size: I'll tell Chip we found this thing. If nobody knows anything about it, he's to ring back pronto. Right?'

Helen nodded.

'But if there's more to it than that, he can fax the information. Or – '

'Yes?'

'I don't know.' Teresa looked baffled.

'Give him twenty-four hours. We'll fly back to Lakeview and wait for him to call. We can't anticipate what he'll find out. We might as well be there as here.'

'Right. Hang on while I dial.'

Helen had met Chip – Charles – Vandenburg. As Helen had no siblings herself she had been a little jealous to see how close the brother and sister were. Not close exactly – Charles was six years younger than Teresa; too big a gap for them to have been really close as children, Teresa said, but the affection between them had been constant.

'Hi Chip! How're you doing? You're not busy, then?'

Teresa made a thumbs up sign and held the phone so that Helen could hear her brother's voice.

161

His voice sounded clear and close. 'Matter of fact I'm looking out the window watching the pigeons fly on and off my window sill.'

'Yeah, well. Look, Chip – we've found something. In a cave. A crucifix.'

'You've found a what?'

To Helen's ear, Teresa's description of the crucifix made it sound like any other crucifix but, after snapping her fingers at Helen for the details, she told Chip the name of the book in which he would find the picture, told him the page number, and said he should get a copy of it.

'Yes, got that. It's special, is it?' Helen thought Chip must have heard the urgency in Teresa's voice. He hadn't worked out yet why she was so excited.

'You could say that.'

'You found it in a cave, you said?'

'Yes, in the Nor'west – you know, the Kimberley region.'

'Sure. Pretty hot up there. So?'

'Stress that this is a secret, Teresa,' Helen said.

'Yes, will do.'

'Who was that you were talking to?' Chip said.

'It's Helen. Look, Chip – '

'Say "Hi" from me, will you?'

'What? Oh yes. Chip says "Hi", Helen.'

Helen said 'Hello' quite loudly. She noticed that she was tapping the fingers of one hand against the other. Hurry up, Teresa, she thought; be quick.

'So what do I do when I've found the book?'

'Look, this is important, Chip. Right? You mustn't tell anybody – anybody – got it?'

As Teresa spoke, Helen nodded firmly. She put her ear closer to the phone and listened to Chip's response.

'Right. Tell them what?'

'Chip – '

'OK. It's a secret. Cross my heart and hope to die. What is?'

'I want you to find out about the crucifix. Helen spoke to a Professor Valindale – '

'Valindale?'

'Yes – what was his first name, Helen? – Robert Valindale.' She spelt the name slowly.

'Hang on, I'll write it down.'

'He says he's an art historian,' Teresa said. 'Can you look at the picture in that book and then see if you can find out where the three of them are?'

'Three of them?'

'Yes. The Prof. says there were three crucifixes. One was given to Saint Ignatius Loyola – '

'Hey, that's getting pretty way out.'

'You ain't heard nothing yet. The second went to Saint Francis Xavier.'

'The third went to Santa Claus?'

'I'm not kidding, Chip, shut up. The third – we don't know about the third. That's what you have to find out. Quickly.'

'OK. Doesn't sound impossible. Mission Possible; I like that.'

Helen reached out her hand but Teresa wasn't willing to let the phone go.

'Tell him it's vitally important,' Helen said, firmly.

Teresa nodded.

'Chip? Helen says it's vitally important – get that? – vitally important that you keep this to yourself. You mustn't tell anybody about us finding the crucifix. OK? Get that?'

'Got it – but why?'

'Just accept that we're trying to keep the media and the politicians off our backs here.'

'Hey – is this thing serious?'

'You bet.'

'I think you'd better tell me a bit more about it, Teresa honey. Am I likely to get in trouble over this? Are you in trouble?'

'No, nothing like that, Chip. It's exciting, that's all. And secret. Can you do it?'

'Sure. I'll get onto it right away. Can I call you back?'

'Good on yer, Chip! You're a dinkum bloke!'

'I hope that's a compliment. Teresa? The phone? Are you at home?'

Teresa gave him the phone number at the meatworks; Chip said he would find out the fax number for himself if he needed it.

They exchanged a few brief words of family stuff – 'Mom's fine'. 'Yes, I've written her this month' – and hung up.

Helen paid the bill, not forgetting the cost of the call to Italy, and went to thank the Guestmaster for the monastery's hospitality. She was briefly disconcerted when the Guestmaster said he hoped she had found what she was looking for in the Library – Helen had almost forgotten her cover story. She recovered in time to smile, and say yes she had had an interesting time. Too right! she thought, as she followed Teresa out to the plane.

They flew back to Lakeview House speculating about how Chip would make his search for information.

Dinner at the meatworks was a scratch meal – spaghetti, bottled sauce – as nobody felt like work, except Barry who spent half an hour fixing up a loudspeaker on the verandah so that when Chip called, he could be heard by all of them.

'Had to have this set-up for the kids,' he said. 'Schooling wasn't easy for them being so far away, but at least they could both hear the teacher at the same time.'

It was the first time Barry had mentioned his children. No doubt, Helen thought, they were adults now, living in the city. Maybe Barry saw them often and maybe he didn't. He seemed a solitary kind of man.

Barry decided to do some work on the engine of his ute; he'd done 'enough talking for this year', Helen was amused to hear him tell Jack on his way out.

After a while, David wandered out to help Barry. The ute was drawn up in the centre of the yard, under the powerful lights of the security system which kept the yard brightly illuminated at night, on the rare occasions it was switched on. Barry had told them he only had to worry about security at the height of the season. 'Roo rustlers, you know?' he told them, not that anyone really believed it.

With Barry and David occupied outside, the others sat around discussing Helen's information long into the evening.

At twenty past one in the morning, Teresa was still on the verandah, an open book on her lap. She was half enjoying the cool night air, half dozing. The loudspeaker was on a table further along the verandah; the phone on its long extension cord was on the table at her side. When the phone rang, Teresa jumped and reached out for the handpiece.

'Yes?'

There had been only one ring, but as Chip started to talk, Helen and Jack hurried out, struggling into shorts and tugging T shirts down. They sat around the table, looking at the loudspeaker as though it were a television set and Chip's face were visible on it.

As Chip's voice rang out over the next couple of minutes, Antony and David joined the group on the verandah, both in jeans and sweaters. Barry put in an appearance, briefly, muttered that he would make some coffee and went back indoors.

It wasn't a very good line.

'I called a guy I know who runs an art gallery and he knows your Prof. You could say I have "validated Valindale", right, Teresa?'

'Yuk; go on.' Teresa gave a half-apologetic shrug and smiled at Helen.

'So then I did lunch with a friend of mine who works in the Vatican. He was mighty interested in your find.'

'You didn't tell him?' Helen's voice was too loud, she thought. Too loud and too late to prevent Chip from hearing her. She didn't want to make him disinclined to help.

'Well, I had to say something. Tell Helen I didn't say much and I didn't say you had actually found the crucifix.'

'You didn't?' Helen could see that Teresa was relieved, as she was.

'Well, no, but I think he may have guessed it. He didn't sound too worried though. Not at all, in fact.'

'That's good.' Teresa looked around the group; they all seemed reassured. Helen nodded.

'He rang me later this afternoon and he's set up a meeting with a friend of his who works in the Vatican Library. I'm having a drink with the library guy after work.'

'That's great, Chip! Does this guy know anything, do you think?'

'Well, he's higher up the totem pole than Aldo – '

'Aldo?'

'Yeah, Aldo Imbrogno. He's a bishop. He works in the Vatican offices somewhere. The guy I'm seeing this afternoon's somebody Aldo says is senior enough to help.'

'Hey Chip, that sounds risky. I mean – a bishop! they're real high-ups, aren't they?'

'Nah, dime a dozen in Rome. Well, perhaps not. I mean, Aldo knows about being discreet. He has to be. He's real good at getting around in the dark, if you know what I mean.'

Teresa glanced at the others. 'Yeah, I know. Well, give me a bell when you've seen this other guy, eh?'

'Sure. Talk to you later.'

They hung up.

For a moment nobody spoke. Barry came out with the coffee but nobody was inclined to take any straight away.

'A bishop!' Jack shook his head and looked anxious.

'Sounds very risky to me,' Antony said.

'Oh God. I'm going back to bed.' Helen tugged her T shirt tightly around her, but didn't leave. Jack looked at her for a moment and then he left her to it and headed back to the bedroom.

'We'll just have to wait and see.' Antony patted Teresa's shoulder and left the room to Teresa, Helen and Barry, who asked what had happened. He poured them all a cup of coffee. As Helen filled him in, she had a nasty feeling that the enquiry in Rome had taken off at too great a speed and was already rocketing away from anyone's control.

Then they waited. As they drifted off to their beds, Helen knew that her sleep would be fitful.

Chip's call about his meeting with the bishop's friend was not what Helen had hoped. She took the call, while Teresa was still on the way to the phone.

'He'll help, I think, but he wants to see you. He wouldn't talk to me on my own.'

'Why? Oh God, Charles, why does he want to see me?'

'It's a question of trust, he says. He wants to deal with the parties directly involved. That's a quote, Helen.'

Teresa arrived at Helen's side. Helen quickly told her the latest problem.

'This guy sounds more like the Mafia than Nob Hill. He's another bishop, is he?' Teresa had spoken loudly enough for Chip to hear her.

'I don't know. Maybe. What shall I say?' he said.

'It seems quite unnecessary to me, to us,' Helen said. 'Look, forget it, Charles. I'll write a few letters. I'll get the answers that way.'

'No, listen.' Teresa took the phone from Helen's grasp. Helen relinquished it willingly; she was feeling totally defeated by all this cloak-and-dagger nonsense.

'Chip? It's Teresa. Are you at home? Good, we'll ring back. I have an idea.' She hung up.

'I don't think I can cope with any more ideas,' Helen said. 'I'm going to find Jack and tell him we're going home. I can follow this up from there.'

'Oh no you don't!' Teresa was excited again. 'I said I'd got an idea. Let me just – '

'I can't spend money on a trip to Italy, Teresa. It's ridiculous. It shouldn't be necessary. Dammit, all we want – '

'Is something they're unwilling to give. Information. Right?'

'Yes. Right.'

Teresa pulled the phone towards her. She fished in the pocket of her shorts and drew out a small notebook.

'Got it.' A quick flick through the pages and she pressed the spine of the notebook flat. She dialled a complicated number.

'Who are you ringing?'

'You'll see.'

Teresa waited for several seconds before hanging up. 'Darn it, he's not picking up.'

'Who isn't? What are you doing, Teresa?'

'Doing? I'm going to send a fax. Should have thought of that.' Teresa jumped up, grabbed her notebook and hurried off into the house. Five minutes later she returned to find Helen morosely watching the landscape shimmer in the heat.

'It's OK. It's going to be OK. I know it.'

'What have you been up to? Who did you send a fax?'

'Ian!'

'Who? Ian – your boyfriend? Isn't he in – where is it? – Bhutan?'

'My boyfriend, yes. Look, Helen, he's filthy rich, right? And he is a businessman, right?'

'You haven't told him, have you?'

'No, of course not. I simply asked if he would underwrite a new idea. A bit of venture capital is needed, I said.'

'But there is no new idea, no business venture. What does he have to do with this?'

'I know Ian. He'll be intrigued but he won't ask questions. I asked for five thousand dollars and I know he'll say yes.'

'You did what?'

Helen was furious. She had never met Ian and didn't at all like the implications of what Teresa had done.

'You had absolutely no right to contact him and beg for money! Send another fax at once and apologise.'

'No, hear me out, Helen. Look, we need a trip to Italy, right? To get the information. You can't afford to go, none of us can. Ian can chalk a trip like that off his income tax. Stroke of a pen – seen him do it millions of times.'

It took a long time, and Jack was brought into the argument but in the end Helen agreed that if Ian would provide the money it would be accepted.

It was obvious that Helen was the one who would go to Rome. She was the discoverer, she had spoken with Professor Valindale, she was a credible and established scientist – it was her job to go. Yes, she had her passport with her; a passport was the one item of value that Jack insisted they never left at home. Yes, it would get her into Italy. Yes, she would pack a few things right away. If Ian agreed.

Within an hour the reply came back. Ian had caught very few fish but the one Teresa was offering sounded worth catching. She could collect any cash she needed from his bank, or use her VISA card to a maximum of ten thousand dollars. Any travelling expenses could be charged to his account with his travel agent. He was sending authorisations right away.

'Ten thousand dollars!' Helen was shocked. That amount of money was a ridiculous sum to offer for an unspecified project.

'Well, I thought you might need to go again.'

The glare from Helen made Teresa's enthusiasm falter briefly but within half an hour they were in the air on the way to Perth. A short time later, Helen took a taxi to the main airport and after a couple of hours waiting around, she was *en route* to Rome.

She settled into her seat and opened the book she had bought at the airport bookshop: Tim Winton's latest. It was set in Western Australia and would be a good read. Helen doubted if she would actually read much of it right away as the excitement of the trip was going to keep her alert. In one way, she was wrong; within ten minutes she was asleep and stayed asleep until the break for refuelling at the Singapore airport. On the last seven hours of her journey, she finished the book.

Almost twenty-four hours after she left Perth, the plane rolled to a stop and the passengers gathered their scattered belongings and walked off the plane into Rome airport. Helen's first reaction was a shiver. The clothes she had with her were working clothes for the Nor'west of Western Australia, not for having a meeting with important strangers in Rome. She felt cold – and she was nervous.

Chip spotted her in the Arrivals queue and quickly gathered her and her backpack – she had brought only enough for a maximum of two days. He chattered on about the weather and asked her how her flight had been – all the pleasant felicities greeters offer to arrivers. They got into his small car, a dusty black Fiat, and set off for his flat.

Neither of them noticed an equally insignificant car slide in behind them as they left the airport carpark.

As he competed with aggressive Roman drivers and the congestion of the city roads, Charles told Helen about his recent conversations with people he hoped could help her.

'You know I work in the Commercial Section of the Embassy?'

Helen hadn't known that, but she nodded.

'Well, first up I went across the road to the American Library. I have a lot of dealings with them, of course. Usual things going on: bunch of Americans reading *Time* and *Saturday Evening Post* and the local newspapers to see who's died since they left on holiday.'

He honked at a passing Vespa, whose passenger made an unfriendly gesture back.

'Deirdre – she works for the Library and sometimes I think she has the hots for me – '

Another honk and this time the offending car was a very large Cadillac with Diplomatic plates. The driver ignored Chip.

'The hots for you?'

'Yeah, well, much good it'll do her, eh?'

Chip grinned and Helen smiled back warmly. Teresa had told her that Chip was unavailable to the likes of Deirdre. She thought that Chip had probably been making sure that Helen understood.

'So Deirdre found that book and made a copy for me of the crucifix thing. It's there – on the back seat.'

Helen looked behind her. There was a large brown envelope on the back seat, with 'U.S. EMBASSY' printed on it. 'I got Deirdre to check out your Professor Valindale too. He's legit, like you thought. Professor of Art History, retired but still has connections here and there in the art world. Written some stuff on Spanish religious art; that fits?'

'It does, yes.' Helen looked with astonishment as massive relics of ancient Roman architecture seemed to bestride the road they were travelling on. 'You've done a marvellous job, Chip, tracking down all this.'

'Yeah, well, like I said: I validated Valindale.'

Chip broke off a chuckle as a suicidal pedestrian sauntered across the road in front of him.

'Deirdre couldn't find anything more recent than that book but she checked out the Vatican Art Gallery on her computer and there's nothing listed there.'

'I'm so grateful, Chip. You must be very busy – taking time out to help me must be an imposition.'

'No, as a matter of fact, my boss is at a meeting of the European Economic Community and while he's away I have nothing much to do. I've got a couple of weeks' leave tucked up my sleeve, too, if it's needed.'

He glanced at Helen, questioning her with his eyebrows.

Helen didn't know what might be coming up next in her quest so she could only smile and shake her head.

They waited briefly at a red light. Helen noticed with some alarm that all the cars in the line continued to move forward – very slowly – while they waited for the light to change.

'Anyway, after talking to Deirdre, I rang Roberto Roccazella.'

'Roberto – ?'

'Yes, he runs the Roccazella Gallery; knows everybody and then some. Said he knows Valindale. He's OK, apparently. Then I rang Aldo.'

'Your bishop,' said Helen.

'Aldo Imbrogno, yes. Bishop. Works in the Vatican offices.'

'Was he really able to help?'

'Not really. He was very interested; very curious. Anyways, he suggested we have coffee at this little café under the arch. When I'd been there and done that, he contacted his Friend in Right Places.'

Helen had a moment's recollection of just such a 'café under the arch' where she used to meet her friends out of the sight of teachers and unwanted hangers-on. Odd how little cafés could hide away like that.

'It's real little, this café. Good food, half a kilometre from where I work and the same from where Aldo works. Discreet, too. I biked over yesterday and Aldo walked, I imagine. He usually cuts through a couple of lanes and a park to get there, or so he says. Likes the exercise. And the privacy.'

By now, Helen could sense that Chip was concentrating on the traffic. It was getting denser and slower as they drew into the inner city.

'You know, Helen, to be honest it's all getting a bit much for me. I mean it had seemed comparatively simple to meet Aldo and ask for help. Now we're going to have a drink with someone I don't know. I figure Aldo has been networking, just as I did; so I guess this man from the Vatican Library will be someone equally discreet. But if the crucifix is important, if it's an artwork of some significance, then maybe discretion will fly out the window.'

'I'm sorry, Charles, to have involved you in this.'

'Well, we'll just play it by ear.'

They arrived at the *Corso* Bar a few minutes early but Chip's friend Aldo was already there. He was with two other men. Chip winced. Helen saw the reaction; involving two more men was spreading the intrigue even more widely than Chip had hoped. He told Helen as much and looked with a grimace for her reaction. She tried not to show that she too was disturbed.

Bishop Imbrogno was a small man, with the Roman's love of good food and wine turned to plump comfort. He looked to be about Helen's age but his thick, wavy hair was untouched by grey and his smile was as dazzling as a movie star's. He was dressed in a well-cut black suit. His clerical collar (if he wore one) was hidden under a light scarf.

'That's a lousy disguise, Aldo. They all know there isn't a tie under there.' Chip greeted the bishop with an air kiss, not an unusual greeting in Rome, Helen assumed.

'It serves.' Aldo shrugged. 'They know what they choose to know.'

The short, dumpy man was introduced simply as 'Pietro'; the taller man's name was not mentioned. Helen's hand was shaken and she endured a cold and penetrating inspection by the three men as politely as she could. Both of the strangers wore black suits. Their ties had black and silver stripes, almost identical in design.

Red wine was brought to the table, with extra glasses for Helen and Chip. The waiter poured the wine, replenishing the half-empty glasses of the earlier arrivals. He moved around the table with obsequious deference. They know a bishop when they see one, Helen thought.

'Perhaps we can help with your problem?' The tall man was cadaverous and dignified; although he wore no clerical collar, he looked so much like a prelate of the Church that Chip told Helen later that he was surprised that he was not introduced by his full name and title. He would certainly be familiar in many circles. Chip said there were paintings of popes who looked like him.

Although the man had addressed his remark directly to Helen, Chip answered. 'Not really my problem. My sister lives in Australia and she seems to have found – found a reference to something – ' Chip faltered briefly. 'Aldo offered to help me find out what happened to it.'

'Your sister,' The man glanced briefly, unquestioningly, at Helen, 'is interested in something that is in the Vatican Collection?'

'It's a crucifix,' said Aldo.

Helen caught her breath.

'It's in a book,' Chip said, sounding much too vague to Helen. He was being cautious, of course. 'The book doesn't say so, but it seems there were three of them.'

'The book?'

175

Chip gave him the citation. The cadaverous man did not write it down, just listened passively, his eyes on Chip.

'There were three of these crucifixes, it seems, Aldo.' Chip was warming to the story. 'One for Saint Ignatius Loyola, one for his second-in-command – '

'Saint Francis Xavier,' Aldo said, nodding to urge Chip on.

'And a third one.'

'How do you know this?' The tall man spoke with a hint of asperity in his voice.

My father used exactly that tone of voice when he was impatient, Helen thought. Scared the daylights out of me.

Chip said that 'a certain Professor' had provided the information.

At last the tall man looked at Helen. Carefully, weighing up her age, her probable status.

'Is this true? There is an academic – a Professor interested in this story?'

'Yes,' she said. Keep it simple.

'And I have undertaken,' Chip said, equally simply, 'to find out who the third one belonged to. Then Teresa (my sister) and Helen will know what they need to know.'

'I'm a scientist, Mr – ' The man did not fill in the gap. 'My interest in this is entirely for scientific reasons,' Helen said.

'And you wish to find out the provenance of the third crucifix, if it has ever existed, for what scientific purpose?'

Oh such sarcasm! Helen smiled a little. She was brought up on that kind of acid tongue. She could handle it well enough.

'I want to know if it could have got to Australia. That's all.'

'You have a photograph, I believe.' The tall man held out a ringless hand, curved expectantly. His hand almost reached Helen, his target.

'I haven't got it with me,' Helen said.

Chip had suggested that they should suss out the situation with the 'friend' of Aldo before taking him entirely into their confidence. He had left the photograph in his flat.

'Then we cannot help.' The tall man stood up, looked coldly at Aldo for a moment and left.

'I'm sorry, Charles, Dr Lytton. You must understand that he was doing you a favour by consenting to look at this matter.' Aldo was flushed, annoyed.

Pietro, the other stranger, was a much smaller man with little hair, sharp eyes behind rimless glasses, and neatly manicured hands. So far, he had been silent. He watched Aldo and Charles as they exchanged apologies and explanations. Helen watched him.

'I just don't understand,' Chip said, 'why a simple request for information has to be tied in to a principle. What do you mean: trust him? Why should we trust anyone? I've already said too much; far too much.' Chip sounded angry to Helen. She waited as the men glared at each other.

They subsided into silence.

The bishop wiped his mouth with a red-checked table napkin. He pushed the empty wineglass away from him. He folded the napkin carefully, sat back and looked for a long time at Chip. The silence did not trouble Helen. Many people did their thinking this way.

'Let me help.' Pietro spoke for the first time.

'Can you?' This time it was Helen who spoke.

'I will have to make enquiries about it. I am not involved in the artistic world of the Vatican. My enquiries may need some – discretion, you realise?'

'Yes, but you're used to that, Aldo says,' said Chip. They exchanged a quick and conspiratorial smile. Helen saw the look and concentrated her attention on the bishop, who was still silent, contemplating his empty glass.

'Have dinner with me. Bring the photograph. Aldo will give you the address.' With a minimum of movement, Pietro left.

'Who is he, Aldo? And why the hell did you involve the other guy? Pompous bastard.'

'I had to involve him; he's the one man you need to get into the records. Others have access but he's the one I can approach – confidentially. You know.'

Aldo glanced in Helen's direction. A glance which did not quite reach her.

Chip nodded.

'And Pietro?'

'He is very well connected, Charles. He is a member of the Black aristocracy, yes? You know that these are people ennobled by the Church many years ago?'

'I've heard of the Black aristocracy, but never really understood it,' Chip said. 'Not my area.' He waved a vague hand to indicate his lack of understanding of the niceties of Italy's social system. 'So how does that help us get information about Teresa's crucifix?'

'He has other networks. He works in the Library so he knows about art. I trust him, Charles; I have to. He knows more about people than anyone else in Rome.'

'I hope we can trust him too.'

'You can. Here's his address.' Aldo pulled out a gold ballpoint pen and a business card. He scribbled down the details. 'Get there by nine; he dines late.'

Chip did a little telephone research on his new acquaintances before they left his flat for dinner with Pietro. A couple of phone calls later, he offered Helen a glass of wine and some information.

'This guy Pietro's an odd one, Helen. He's a close friend of Aldo's, of course; a member of the 'Black' aristocracy. He has a title – Prince or something – his title came from the Church, although his university degrees came from Rome and London. Interesting guy.'

'Never mind his ancestry – can he really help?'

Helen was impatient. She knew that Teresa would have been fascinated by the idea of an aristocrat being involved in their quest for information. But anyone who could help would satisfy Helen.

And she was right. Chip rang Teresa at the meatworks, where Antony and she were, according to Teresa, playing 'sort of chess'.

'A real aristocrat, Chip? Does he talk like an English aristocrat?'

Helen reached out to take the phone, but Chip made a silent apology and stopped her.

'So we're having dinner with him tonight. Helen will ring you afterwards. OK?'

With only the briefest farewell, Chip hung up.

'Time to take you shopping,' he said.

Not unwillingly, Helen went with Chip to a nearby department store where she looked at an overwhelming number of dresses, skirts, tops and jackets in her size. With Chip's amused commentary, she tried on several things before settling for a rather smart suit and a matching blouse.

'There,' she said. 'This will do.'

And Chip agreed that it would.

She bought tights and a pair of sensible shoes: not all that easy to find in Rome, but she found them.

Pietro lived in a grand house with a marble-floored entrance. Helen couldn't decide if he owned the whole house – after all, he was nobility – or just the comfortable quarters to which he led them.

A silent manservant, smooth and supple in black pants and a tight-fitting tank top, brought them drinks and exchanged a smile with Chip as he left.

They talked about nothings: Rome's gossip, the weather, even a movie Chip and Pietro had seen.

Dinner came soon enough. A clear soup, pheasant (or so Helen decided) and a delicious creamy dessert. Then coffee and almond tuiles. The manservant brought the food and cleared away afterwards. He never spoke but his occasional glances at Chip were very meaningful. Or so Helen decided, as she shifted rather uncomfortably on her stiff and ornate chair.

'So can you help us?' she said, as the last dish was taken away.

'It is difficult,' Pietro said, sipping his liqueur slowly. 'Perhaps too difficult.'

CHAPTER 8

'IT IS, AS I SAY, DIFFICULT,' PIETRO SAID, sipping his liqueur slowly.

'This isn't just some fancy, you know,' Helen said. 'I have a genuine interest in finding out something which it seems is difficult to access. Perhaps you can tell me why that is so?'

She looked back at the two silent men, deliberately cool. She sipped her wine, and waited.

Pietro nodded slowly, agitating his wine glass in time with the nods.

Helen felt herself growing increasingly irritated. To have flown so far – on what she insisted on thinking of as 'borrowed' money – only to be met by this nonsensical barrier. Men; always a performance.

'Look – '

Chip raised a restraining hand. As she subsided, he patted her hand a couple of times, gently, almost imperceptibly. All right, she thought, I'll wait – but it is ridiculous.

After a few moments of silence, Pietro cleared his throat.

Here comes the momentous statement, Helen thought, just like my father. A cough, an intake of breath, a pursed mouth and then the proclamation. What nonsense.

Pietro leaned forward in his seat. 'It is very difficult.'

This time Chip had to leave his hand on Helen's.

'The information is unavailable? It's a secret? You don't know the answer?' Helen's voice was sharper than she intended.

'You could say,' Pietro said, 'that there is a stone wall around the answer to any questions; nobody will say anything about the third crucifix. Not a single word. I have been trying to penetrate that wall since we spoke earlier today.'

'But why?' Helen looked from one to the other; neither of the men seemed inclined to answer. Maybe Chip understood some of the Vatican reserve, but she certainly didn't.

'Is this usual? I mean, is it just Vatican caution?' Chip said, sounding ready to understand.

'There must be a reason for this – reticence,' Pietro said, 'but I could not learn what it is. However, I was able to go further than initially seemed possible. I found a breach, you could say, in the brick wall.'

'Someone told you about the crucifixes?' Helen was on the edge of her seat now.

'Was it the man who came with you today?' Even as he asked, Chip raised a hand, shook his head and made a gesture of erasing the question. It was not answered.

'I do not have the authority to tell you the answers to your question, Dr Lytton, but I shall do so. In the interests of science.'

It didn't sound like a convincing reason, but Helen was not going to argue.

'At first, I could not even get confirmation that Di Fiore made three of the crucifixes, although the experts in the Library seemed to be sure of that. Then I found a source who would talk to me. In confidence.'

With a great sense of theatre, Pietro paused, took a sip – two sips – of wine.

'Di Fiore had indeed made three crucifixes for Pope Paul the Third, just as he had made other items of religious significance for the same Holy Father.'

'Ah.' The sigh was Helen's.

182

'One of them the Pope gave to St Ignatius Loyola – you know about him?'

'Yes, the Jesuits. Go on.'

'The second was given to one of his followers, St Francis Xavier, when he was sent off to do missionary work. Yes?'

'Yes, I knew that too. The third?'

'Well now, that's the mysterious one, isn't it?'

Again the pause for judicious sipping of wine. Helen struggled to contain her irritation.

'Yes, so what happened to it?' This time, it was Chip who broke the silence.

'The third crucifix,' said Pietro, leaning even further forward in his chair, 'was delivered to the Pope along with the other two. We know that Saint Ignatius Loyola retained the first one, and the second one's history is known. So, it is believed – nobody's sure – it's believed that His Holiness gave the third one to another Jesuit missionary. But we cannot be sure; there seem to be no records. It is a mystery wrapped in an enigma, you might say.'

'A third missionary.' Helen's mind spun back to the blackened face of the man in the cave.

'We shall never know the truth.' Pietro signalled the manservant to approach the table. The servant, watched with hooded eyes by Pietro, poured more wine from the carafe and handed it round before retiring out of hearing from the group.

'How much is known about it for sure?' Chip said.

As the story of what might possibly have happened unfolded, Helen hardly dared to breathe.

'The Jesuits consisted of a small group of men,' said Pietro, 'chosen by Ignatius Loyola for the qualities of intellect and faith which have always marked the Society of Jesus. Despite their close relationship, the men were to be scattered as far and as wide as the Pope of the time deemed it expedient. The Jesuits would later produce diplomats, scientists, entrepreneurial men of all sorts, but their first tasks were to get out and be missionaries.'

'When was this?' Helen was doing a quick calculation.

'The Society was founded in 1540.'

'Four hundred and sixty years ago, more or less.' It matched Antony's calculations.

'Yes, about that. Some of the places the first Jesuits were sent to were very dangerous; the men might very well be killed. In obedience to the Pope and to their Society, they accepted all the risks and went willingly. Francis Xavier was sent first to India. He spent the last ten or so years of his life travelling: India, Indochina, Japan. He took with him the crucifix given to him by the Pope. It was the sole personal possession allowed him by the Society, which eschewed proprietorship of goods.'

'They still do,' interrupted Chip. 'I know one quite well. Do you know they still have a common pile of clean handkerchiefs in the seminary, the place where they go to study? Did you ever hear the like?'

'Charles – ' Helen's voice sounded a warning.

'Right. Interesting, though.'

'Saint Ignatius kept his crucifix and it was returned to the Vatican on his death, as was that owned by Saint Francis Xavier.'

Quietly, without interrupting, Helen drew the two photographs from her handbag and put them in the middle of the table. Pietro picked them up, looked at them carefully. He ran a finger across them, smiled at Helen and nodded.

'It is believed that the third crucifix was given personally by the Pope to another Jesuit missionary; the third man to be sent to a place of great danger. This man is barely mentioned in the history of the Society but it is believed – there was a traditional belief – that he was sent to the Spice Islands. To south-east Asia.'

For a moment, Helen and Chip were too startled to speak.

'Doesn't that mean Indonesia?' Helen spoke quietly. 'Just north of Australia?'

'My goodness, yes.' Chip reached across the table and grasped Helen's hand. 'My goodness.'

'Do you know his name, Pietro?' Helen held her breath. 'This third missionary?'

'Well, bear in mind that it's all speculation. I mean, apparently his name isn't in the records, not accurately anyway. Or if it is the Jesuits are keeping very quiet about it. There's some slight evidence in Britain about him, but nothing for certain.'

'In Britain!' Helen was surprised.

'His name – if it's right and if he even existed – was John or James Craven. He came from the County of York to Rome and then settled in France where the Jesuits were just getting going.'

'But why isn't his name known for sure? I mean, people don't just disappear – if he existed, surely – '

'His name is unverified; his place of birth is hazy, his manner of death unknown. If he did exist, then it is likely that he was the recipient of the third crucifix and that he was sent secretly to the Spice Islands on the Pope's behalf. That is all I know – all I could find out. A mystery, my dear, a mystery.'

Pietro smoothed his hands together, in a gesture that looked to Helen as though he was wiping away his part in the conspiracy to track down the elusive priest.

'It's a bit like the Unknown Soldier thing,' said Chip. 'No name but lots of honour.'

'But why isn't he in the records?' Helen said. 'I would have thought – I mean isn't history important to you?'

'Indeed it is.' Pietro had finished his wine. He loosened his collar. 'Odd, Doctor Lytton; it's very odd.'

There was a sonorous clangour which Helen understood to be the doorbell. The manservant glided out to answer it.

They waited in silence. Helen assumed each of them was mulling over the information in their own way.

The manservant returned, ushering in Bishop Imbrogno.

'Aldo, welcome.' Pietro seemed to have been expecting his visitor and waved a finger for the manservant to bring the bishop a glass of liqueur, which he did.

Chip greeted his friend with a hug, and Helen shook his hand.

'I thought we should brief Aldo about this mystery, Dr Lytton, Charles. He has a continuing interest in how it unfolds.'

Helen was not at all sure that she understood the nature of Aldo's 'continuing interest' but she listened carefully as Pietro told again the speculations and possibilities about the 'third Jesuit missionary'.

Aldo said nothing, just pursed his lips now and then, nodded, and looked occasionally rather surprised.

'Perhaps, do you think – ' Pietro spoke hesitantly, but with a degree of suppressed excitement that caught Helen's attention. 'Well, maybe he was doing some secret work for the Pope? Something to do with the government?'

'In the Spice Islands?' The bishop shook his head. 'It seems unlikely. What could the Spice Islands possibly contribute to the knowledge that resided in Rome?'

Aldo made an expansive gesture, that seemed to take in the world of wealth and universal power that was the Church. He smiled in a way that Helen found irritatingly superior.

She stirred slightly in her chair. 'Well, I suppose nobody ever has total control of everything – money, ideas, influence, power – ' She didn't complete the thought. It sounded weak. Chip looked as unimpressed as the others.

With a gesture to his manservant, Pietro stood up. 'I would like you to know, Doctor Lytton, that I have found out what I could with considerable difficulty. Certain people were very curious about my wish to get this information. I fear I must decline to be involved any further. If you find out anything, or need to know anything more, then I suggest your friend's brother either makes a formal request for help, or seeks it through the bishop.'

It sounded like a prepared speech. Helen nodded. Chip and Helen went to the door, ushered by the assiduous manservant, and followed by the bishop. With a benign, almost laconic, dip of his head, Pietro shook their hands as they left.

They stood together outside the large house for a few moments.

'Looks like you've found the real thing, Helen.' Chip included Aldo in the conversation. So much, Helen thought, for trying to keep the matter confidential. Still, Bishop Imbrogno had been helpful.

'If it is that priest's crucifix, I wonder how it got to Australia?' Helen meant how did 'that priest' get there, but she was only too aware that the revelation about the body would have frightening repercussions.

'Yes, it's an odd place for it to turn up.' The bishop sounded very casual, as though he had little interest in the story now. 'Maybe some millionaire bought it – maybe it was stolen from him? Who knows. Where exactly did you find it, Doctor Lytton? Does its – provenance – suggest anything about how it reached your country?'

His voice was too smooth, too laid back. Helen was not fooled now. This man was avid for information, as avid as she was. His slightly averted eyes, lit by the bright street lamps, could not hide his eagerness for her to talk.

'Nobody has said the thing has been found, Bishop. I came across a reference to it; that is all.'

'A reference – and a photograph?'

The bishop's voice was silky, but there was a note of asperity, almost viperish, as he spoke. Even Chip noticed it and looked up in surprise at his friend.

'I guess we'll never know for sure, eh Helen?' Chip led the way to his car; Aldo's was parked nearby, on the other side of the road.

'There is one other detail I gleaned from Pietro's research.' The bishop watched as Chip unlocked his car. His voice was without emphasis. He did not explain how he had gathered this extra information. 'The third crucifix was not quite as perfect as the others. It was found to be damaged slightly when it was given to Ignatius Loyola. A minor thing – quite minor.'

Helen lifted a hand to her face as the realisation hit her that the crucifix they had found was indeed damaged; that it had pricked Peter's finger where a thorn was broken off.

'Somebody recorded the incident,' said the bishop. 'Apparently Saint Ignatius made a humorous remark about a flawed gift for a flawed man – and the incident was noticed although it was a trivial matter.'

'They recorded a joke but not who was given the crucifix?' Helen shook her head. 'That sounds unlikely.'

Aldo buttoned his jacket high around his scarf.

'My dear Doctor Lytton. Nothing that happens in the Vatican should surprise you. Nothing surprises me.'

With a smile and a gracious handshake for Helen, he crossed the road, unlocked his car and got in. He gave them a wave through the window, and drove off.

'Well. There you are.' Chip opened the passenger's car door and helped Helen get in.

'I must get back to the others.' Helen had no wish to prolong her stay in Rome. Now that they had a name for the body – an identity – there were decisions to be made, and quickly.

Chip insisted that she stay for at least a couple of days, to rest and recuperate as he put it. Even seasoned travellers would suffer if they zapped from one continent to another and back again, he said. She must have a little time to look around.

'Maybe you could go to the Vatican Library,' he said, trying to persuade her. 'Maybe you could see some of the Jesuit documents.'

So Helen agreed to stay for two nights.

Chip's phone calls to the Vatican Library were surprisingly unsuccessful; nobody was free to speak with Helen, nobody could give her any special help.

'You can ask at the counter about your interests but it is not possible that you will receive the necessary accreditation as a scholar; the formalities take about three weeks. If not four,' she was told by an official when Chip handed her the phone.

And so it was. The man at the information desk was polite but firm: she could not see any of the records of the Jesuits. Nor were they available in photocopied form. Nor were they reproduced in books. Nothing.

Chip rang the Society of Jesus but got an equally polite knockback from them. The records were available to approved scholars only. And they were Jesuits, not Australian scientists.

During her two days of rejection and frustration, Helen saw very little of Chip, somewhat to her surprise. For a man who said he had time to spare, he seemed to have other demands to satisfy.

On the last day, Chip booked her return flight and took Helen to the airport. She gave him a hug and thanked him for his help and company.

'Without you, we would be no further forward with this puzzle,' she said.

'Let me know how it goes.'

'It's odd, isn't it, Chip. I mean, John or James Craven – he sounds real enough and yet the Vatican people are so reluctant to say anything about him.'

'Maybe he never existed, Helen.'

'We have the crucifix, though.'

'Yes, well, maybe there's another explanation. Are you going to sell it? To the Vatican? To a museum?'

Helen had given no thought at all to the ultimate destination of the crucifix. She looked at Chip, knowing she must have a somewhat astonished expression on her face.

Chip laughed. 'Hey, I didn't mean to put any pressure on you!'

'No, that's all right. We'll have to think about it, won't we.'

'I guess you will.'

'I wonder if he existed, Chip. I wonder what John/James Craven was like.'

'Well, it looks like we'll have to go on wondering.'

'Will you ring Teresa, Chip, and ask her to pick me up in Perth?'

On the flight home, Helen spent most of her time thinking about the man so long dead, the man whose body she had touched. The man whose existence was shrouded in secrecy and mystery. The third Jesuit missionary. John or James Craven from the County of York.

CHAPTER 9

ROME 1540

I T WAS GOING TO BE A HOT DAY. There was already that haze in the air. The stink of the streets seemed stronger and people passed by in a flurry of heat like a tiny whirlwind. Only the pigeons seemed affected by the threat of another scorcher; they puffed and pouted their way across the path of early risers, seeking shade on cool building steps, deep shaded windowsills, under the vendors' carts.

John Craven was in no hurry; he liked the heat and was happy to spend this early hour walking the streets of Rome. Soon enough he would return to the Casa del Gesu, for the start of another day's work.

'Rome is such an exciting place to be!' John's companion, Pierre, looked around, inhaling great gulps of air, shaking his head with wonder. 'So much is changing, John. The world is beginning to be – ' He waved his arms around, embracing the street, the buildings, the statues, his friend, 'the way it should be.' He nodded, satisfied.

They turned the corner into the Piazza Altieri. The noise grew louder, the scents stronger, the stinks more personal. Four of the Pope's guards marched past them, brilliant in their new uniforms whose tags and slashes fluttered as they marched. The tips of their pikes, held vertical to prevent accidents, were glittering triangles against the blue sky.

'Peacocks!' Pierre said under his breath. He and John wore black.

The piazza was already noisy with the daily bustle of commerce, buying and selling, hawkers crying their wares, buyers arguing about quality, prices, quantities. Everywhere there was laughter and loud greetings. Arguments broke out here and there, and were quickly resolved. People hurried through the square on their way to meetings, to work, to care for their children and the old ones, avoiding the donkeys that pulled carts laden with the brilliant reds and greens and yellows of peppers, the vivid, mouth-wateringly sharp colours of lemons and oranges, the crisp and leafy mass of dew-sprinkled vegetables. The smells of fresh food sharpened the air.

John and Pierre were part of the pageant, caught up in the stirring of the city. Small groups of men stood here and there exchanging gossip and ideas, their clothes a cacophony of colour as loud and assertive as their conversations. A mother hurried by with her children clutching her skirts, wailing for toy windmills on sale at a painted cart outside a painted villa. The windmills added a small flurry to the piazza as they flirted in a current of air.

Two young women looked with brazen interest at John and Pierre as they strolled past. Everywhere there was activity. The Piazza was not a place for quiet contemplation.

The brilliance of the sun made the brittle stone of the buildings glitter. John shielded his eyes as he looked towards the far north-west corner of the Piazza, where a cluster of people were listening intently to a small man, wearing black like Pierre and John, who stood on a box which gave him the height he needed to be seen by those at the back.

As John and Pierre approached, the man saw them. He stepped down, picked up the box and hurried over to meet them. The audience moved away into the larger crowd.

The Pilgrim had chosen this noisy Piazza carefully, in preference to the quieter environs most groups like his preferred. He had explained often to his friends that from his rooms overlooking the Piazza, he could watch the many civic and Papal processions, the soldiers marching to and from their work, the busy, exciting life of Rome. He could feel part of it. He was part of it.

'John, Pierre, I was waiting for you. We must hurry; come along.'

He handed the box to Pierre and strode off in front of them, limping slightly.

'Why the hurry, Pilgrim?' John caught up with him.

'We've been sent for. He's waiting. We have half an hour.'

'The Pope? Is this it, Pilgrim? Has he decided to give approval?'

'I don't know, John. Yes, I think so. He could hardly say no. I think it's all right. We'll see. Pierre, do hurry up.'

With a swish of his cassock, Ignatius of Loyola hurried into the house where he and his ten followers lived. It was too small, but it served their purpose for now. Even the most sceptical accepted that.

Pierre and John followed him. Pierre struggled with the box, and dropped it gratefully in the porch.

'Getting exciting, eh? Better than waiting around in Venice,' Pierre said. He breathed heavily as they hurried up the stairs.

'Oh, I didn't mind that.' John had enjoyed living in Venice until this year, and in Paris while he studied at the University. But he still missed his home in Yorkshire and sometimes wondered if his parents missed him as much. Certainly his life was more interesting than it had been in the Old House, watching his father prosper as a wool merchant. There John had wondered where his own life would lead, on what journey, what pilgrimage.

'Do be quick!' Ignatius paused on the landing, looking down at the two men. He turned away and they could hear him knocking on doors, rousing the others, telling them to put on their best clothes and be ready to leave the house in the time it takes to say ten Hail Marys. 'Ten and no more!'

And so it was. Refreshed, clean and tidy, the small group of men walked quickly across the Piazza to the Palazzo Venezia, the summer residence of Pope Paul the Third.

At the Palazzo, the massive wooden doors were open, no doubt to let in such cool air as could be lured from the Piazza. There wouldn't be much going in today, John thought. Two guards held their pikes at the ready as Ignatius led his men inside.

There was, as always, dust in the air. The sun struck long beams through the brilliantly coloured glass in the high windows and caught up swirls of dust that made the light shimmer. Long fingers of light – purple, crimson, brilliant yellow – sought out the silk and satin draperies, firing them with movement, swaying them into undulations of colour.

John loved coming here. This Pope knew about painting, music, poetry. Pictures and tapestries decorated the walls, graceful and dignified statues – some painted, some hung with precious jewels – stood in every niche, leather-bound and gilt-clasped books were stacked on shelves and tables around the hall. These were gifts from kings, emperors, the diplomats and wealthy faithful who shared the Pope's tastes, or at least knew and could afford them, so Ignatius told his followers, who were awed by the signs of immense wealth.

If the street outside had been bright with colour, the Palazzo Venezia was ablaze with it. Here the taste for gold, for silver, for purple, orange, crimson, brilliance in every shade, left no stone wall bare of seductive decoration. Heavily embroidered flags soared overhead, symbolising the spiritual and temporal power of the Pope. Brightly coloured birds cawed and screeched in a huge gilded cage built along one side of the corridor.

There was a pungent smell of oil paint; stronger even than the smell of the birds. Yet another great artist was working somewhere nearby on work commissioned by the Pope. John had seen him hurrying by one day, his robe spattered with paint.

On the long journey from the entrance to the salon where they were to be received, Ignatius and his followers moved like a scurry of black ants. A fanciful image, perhaps, but it amused John to think of it.

As they grew closer, they were embraced by an intoxicating drift of exotic incense. For a few moments, John could hardly breathe. Huge containers of sweetly perfumed flowers decorated the side altars and saints' statues on their way – full blossoms of red and white roses artfully mixed with Madonna lilies for the Virgin, flowering almonds and sprays of olives, orchids, and the sweet heady scents of country flowers that bore Our Lady's name.

John had been here several times but he could never take in enough of this wonder – such a contrast to the stark simplicity of his lodging.

They reached the reception hall. A magnificent guard opened the door wide. A rich Turkey carpet, dark red with deep blue and gold flowers woven into it, led to a small half-circle of unoccupied chairs flanking an empty throne. His Holiness the Pope stood with his companion cardinals and bishops in friendly conversation. Their robes, in every shade of scarlet, vermilion, orange, purple and green contrasted and clashed as they gesticulated and turned to each other in animated conversation. Secretaries and attendants, more discreetly clad, were standing alertly against the walls.

As Ignatius approached, the Pope walked several steps along the carpet to greet him.

'Ignatius, dear Pilgrim, I have a gift for you.' The Pope gesticulated with a slight move of his arm and attendants ushered the visitors to the gilded chairs, which had seats of vermilion brocade. The eleven chairs were set in a row, facing the assembled members of the Papal hierarchy and household. Ignatius was led by the hand of the Pope to a seat at the right hand side of the throne.

John and Pierre exchanged a quick smile as they took the seats indicated to them. For a few moments, the hum of animated voices continued as the Pope engaged Ignatius in conversation. One of the cardinals talked pleasantly about the weather to some of Ignatius's group.

Then the Pope, barely pausing in his remarks, held out a hand. Silence fell as a scroll tied with a scarlet ribbon was immediately placed in his hand by a secretary. The cardinal moved away to rejoin the other dignitaries.

'Here it is, my son.'

Ignatius took the scroll reverently.

The Pope's voice rose to a declamation. 'This is the Papal Bull of Approval of the Society founded by our good friend Ignatius of Loyola; the *Regimini militansis ecclesiae*. It is our hope that the Companions of Jesus will continue their work of feeding the poor of Rome, teaching, working in hospitals, and preaching the Gospel.'

There was a clatter of polite applause. The Pope raised his hand as it ceased.

'However, we have been moved by the plea that some of these good men shall also make their own pilgrimages.' He nodded and smiled in the direction of Ignatius. 'As we know, "The Pilgrim" is how Ignatius likes to be addressed.'

The Pope's voice rose again to a declamatory tone. John Craven held his breath. 'Under obedience to their superior, we believe this to be a useful direction for them to take. There has been much disruption in the Church. It is our wish that the teaching of the Church be spread as far and as wide as possible to counter the intrusions of the Protestants.'

The Pope blessed the document which Ignatius held up for his men – the Companions – to see. John and the others rose and applauded vigorously. The assembled court also applauded, although with more restraint.

Pierre turned in the direction of the door.

The Pope held up a hand. 'Wait a moment, young man. I know you must be in a hurry to go about your business – God's business – but I have something else to say.'

Pierre blushed and sat down. John gave him a grin. The skirling of black robes on the men eager to depart and celebrate settled again as they became still.

For several minutes the Pope spoke about the expectations he had of the Order, the kind of work he expected them to do, and his confidence that Ignatius of Loyola would accomplish much.

'You are,' he said, 'the best educated group of priests and religious in Italy. Every one of you has had the blessing of a good university education, yet all of you have chosen God's work, chastity, poverty and a vow of obedience to your superior. Feeding the poor is indeed God's work, but men of ability can accomplish more by taking their knowledge and understanding of the world to the world. The Protestants must be countered, and you will have an important part to play in that war.'

He took a sip of water from a decorated glass offered by an attendant. As he handed it back, the attendant took it reverently and stepped backwards from the Pope to hold the glass ready for the next summons.

Another attendant responded to a raised finger and brought to the Pope a box. It was a simple box, made from oak, with hammered iron corners. The Pope opened it.

'Ignatius, you are sending men today to countries most of us will never see, nor ever hear about. How many are leaving?'

'Two, Holiness.'

The Pope nodded. His heavily ringed hand reached into the box and he brought out a crucifix. John leaned forward. He could see that the crucifix was made of gilded silver, fabricated in such a way and with such infinite skill that the figure of Christ seemed to writhe in agony as the sun touched his body. The wooden support of the cross was of oak, like the box. The crucifix hung from a simple leather thong.

John, although accustomed to seeing beautiful things in the church, marvelled at it.

The Pope summoned Ignatius to rise from his chair and then kneel in front of him. He placed the crucifix around The Pilgrim's neck. The gold glittered in a spiral of dust. Ignatius kissed the crucifix, kissed the Pope's ring and tucked the crucifix into the belt which fastened his robe.

'This was made by the finest goldsmith in Christendom, Pilgrim. Keep it always as a token of our regard for you.'

'It will never leave me.' Ignatius stood up and took a step back.

The Pope took another crucifix from the oaken box. 'Who is going from Rome today?'

'Francis Xavier, Holiness.' Ignatius pointed out the first voyager. Again the Pope moved a finger very slightly and Francis went to him and knelt for his blessing.

'Where are you taking the Word of God, my son?'

'To India.'

'India.' The Pope spoke the word as if in wonder. He held up the second crucifix and placed it around Francis' neck. Francis kissed it, then kissed the Pope's ring, and took his place again in the semicircle of Companions.

'And the other traveller?'

'John Craven, Holiness.'

John was stunned. He had not expected to be sent away so soon.

'Your Englishman, yes?'

'Yes, Holiness.'

'And where is he going? To England? To match his wits against the excommunicated King Henry?'

'I have thought for him to go to the East Indies, your Holiness. He will travel with Francis for part of the way and then find a boat to take him further.'

The Pope summoned John to kneel at his feet and placed the third crucifix around his neck. John kissed it, kissed the Pope's ring and began to tuck the crucifix into his belt.

With a start, he caught his finger on a sharp edge on the crucifix. He tried to hide his reaction but the Pope saw him flinch.

'What is it, son?'

'The cross, your Holiness. It cut me.'

An attendant moved forward and gave John a linen cloth to staunch the small amount of blood the pricking metal had caused to flow.

'We must pray that you suffer no more for the Lord than that, my son.' The Pope gentled John to his feet.

Ignatius raised an eyebrow in John's direction; are you all right? he seemed to ask. John, embarrassed by his startled reaction to the minor injury, nodded.

'A flawed crucifix for a flawed man, Holiness,' Ignatius said, with a smile.

'Are we not all flawed?' The Pope spread his arms, including all his audience in the quip.

John barely heard the words. He thought about his mission, his pilgrimage. The Indies! He spoke English, Latin, French, Greek – would they be useful in the Indies?

The Pope rose. Immediately his entourage moved forward to assist him. Ignatius and the Companions rose too. The Pope bestowed his blessing on them and their mission, and turned to leave.

He turned back, briefly, to Ignatius. 'Make sure these educated men of yours send you letters, Ignatius. We want to know what they see in these countries.'

'I will make sure they do,' said Ignatius.

The group watched the Pope process from the salon, a white focus for the flattery of colour and pomp around him. They turned to leave.

CHAPTER 10

WHEN HELEN DISEMBARKED IN PERTH AT 5.00 AM she was tired, but not sleepy. The trip had passed quickly enough and when she had been awake, there had been plenty to think about. The Alitalia plane emptied slowly. As soon as the First Class and Business Class passengers were gone, Helen was among the first group to pass through the formalities of arrival. She had no luggage to collect. Her backpack, although fuller than when she left, had still fitted in the overhead compartment.

Teresa was waiting: Helen spotted her with some relief. She stood in a huddle of people who were watching with varying degrees of excitement the queue of happy travellers streaming through the glass doors and along the open corridor.

Helen pushed her way politely past an Italian woman shrieking in the arms of an older Italian woman who was also shrieking.

'They seem glad to see each other,' Helen said, smiling, as Teresa reached out a hand for her backpack. 'No, it's all right. I can carry it.'

'Any luck?'

'Oh yes. Both good and bad.'

'All I want to hear is the good news, Helen. I'm glad you're back.'

The queue of arrivals thickened as it neared the exit. There were a few men waiting near the final barrier, holding boards up with names on them. One by one, some of the early arrivals joined the board-holders and went off with them. As they reached one of the last raised boards, the holder turned slightly and Helen read her name scrawled in black Texta on the board.

'What's this about?'

They approached the man. He lowered the board. 'Lytton? Mrs Lytton?'

'Is something wrong?' Helen was suddenly anxious about Jack.

'No, no, nothing like that. Your friend is waiting for you in the VIP Lounge. If you'll follow me – '

The man tucked his board under his arm and used a hand to slice a polite path through the crowd. On the next floor, he pointed across the corridor to an unmarked door and left them.

'That's it? Through there, do you think?' Helen hesitated. Teresa walked over to the door and opened it.

Chip stood up. He half-raised a hand in greeting, changed it to a feeble wave, and gave Helen an apologetic smile.

Teresa and Chip greeted each other with affectionate hugs and thumps on the back as Helen stood just inside the door, waiting. There had to be an explanation for this, but she couldn't imagine what it might be.

'But why are you here?' Teresa said. 'I mean, you didn't come back with Helen, did you? She didn't say – ' Teresa looked at Helen, who shook her head.

'You didn't say anything about this,' Helen said.

'I didn't know myself – not until you had left.' Chip walked quickly over to Helen, his shoulders raised in apology, his head titled slightly in a visible wish to reassure her. Helen was not reassured. She waited.

'Let me explain, Helen. I was sent.' He gave her a boyish grin, the sort of disarming tactic boys use with their mothers. It didn't work.

'You might have told me,' she said.

'I truly didn't know. I told my boss – well, his boss – ' His voice faltered.

'We can talk on the way back to Lakeview,' Teresa said. 'Let's get going, huh?'

'No, I want to talk to Helen first.'

'You can do that on the plane.'

'No, please.'

Chip's voice was not loud, but it was so firm that Teresa stopped moving around and sat down in one of the large, comfortable chairs that faced the window.

'All right, Chip, I'm listening.' Helen sat down.

'Were you in First Class?' Teresa said.

'No, I came on another plane. I got here a while ago.'

'Another plane? What other plane?'

'An Air Force plane.' Chip moved away from the window and sat down, facing the women. He sat on the edge of the seat, looking worried; earnest.

Before Teresa could speak, and Helen could see she was more likely to explode, there was a knock on the door. After a few moments in which nobody spoke, Chip got up and opened the door. A man in uniform glanced around the room, giving a friendly nod and smile to the women.

'Ye gods! He's in the Air Force – our Air Force!' Teresa's loud aside drew a bigger smile from the military man, who spoke to Chip briefly.

'We'll be available whenever you're ready, Mr Vandenburg,' he said. He gave a kind of wave to the women as he left. Chip closed the door and turned back towards his sister and Helen. He ran a hand through his hair, clearly wondering where to start his explanation. Helen did not feel inclined to give him time to decide just where that start would happen.

'You were saying,' she said.

'Hey!' Teresa was on her feet.

'It's OK, Teresa, Helen. It was convenient, that's all.' Again the ruffled hair.

'Convenient? You came here in an Air Force plane because it was convenient?' Teresa spoke for Helen, who nodded.

'Yes, an embassy thing. You know. Happens all the time. Friendly arrangements.' Chip flapped his hands from his sides a couple of times and sat down.

Another discreet knock on the door and a woman came in immediately, with a tray. On it were three cups and saucers, a milk jug, sugar bowl, and a large jug of coffee. There was also a small plate with chocolate biscuits. She put the tray down as the three protagonists in the drama (Helen was not enjoying the theatricality of the moment but she recognised it as such) sat in silence. When the woman left, the coffee was ignored. Chip helped himself to a biscuit.

He crumbled the biscuit onto a paper napkin.

'I guess this isn't my scene, Teresa. I'm an economist, dammit.'

'I know that.'

'Your visit dropped me in at the deep end, Helen. I'm sorry about all this.' Again the flapping hand.

'The deep end of what?' Helen gave no quarter. She wanted Chip to explain. He got up, went over to the window, looked out at a plane moving slowly across the tarmac.

'I wish I knew. Your visit – '

'You said that.' Teresa reached for the coffee and poured a cup.

'No, but – to tell you the truth I'm pretty darn worried about this, Helen.'

'I can see that, Chip. Why?'

'I don't like being out of my depth.'

'Sit down, Chip, and start explaining. Right?' Teresa poured two more cups of coffee. She slid one over to Helen, who ignored it, and handed one to Chip as he sat down.

Helen felt it was quite important that she say nothing and give him time now to find the start of whatever he had to say.

'The fact is,' Chip started, and the words started to come in a rush. 'The fact is that one of the senior people in the Embassy hauled me in for a briefing. I had told my chief about talking with one of the Vatican people – we have to do that; tell them, I mean – and I gave him a rough idea about why. And about Helen's visit.'

He hadn't yet met Helen's gaze. Nor did he seem to look at Teresa. Helen waited.

'Mind you, I didn't tell him about your real interest, Helen. Just that there was some sort of connection with Australia and an interest in art history. I said you were curious about a missing crucifix made by Di Fiore back in the fifteenth century. Nothing wrong with that, is there?'

This time he did look at Helen and there was a note of asperity in his voice.

Helen wasn't sure that Chip should have said all that. She shook her head slowly; for the moment she would allow him the comfort of thinking that he had not revealed too much.

'I figure he sent for me because of one of my contacts.' Chip paused, looked at Helen, who blinked her understanding. 'Well, one of them must have said something to his chief and somebody higher up got worried.'

'Somebody said something to somebody? Hey, come on, Chip. And anyway, what's the problem?' Teresa emptied her coffee cup and poured another coffee. 'Hey, this is good.'

206

'I don't know. Well, I'm not sure. I do know that I have been counselled to say what I have to say and report back to the top man. I am supposed to tell him everything I learn here.'

Helen stirred in her seat. 'I don't understand – why is your boss so concerned?'

'I gather there's some sort of minor diplomatic crisis looming and he hopes to avert it. I wish to Heaven he'd sent Gus – my Chief. I'm not equipped for this sort of thing.'

Chip got up, restlessly, and wandered over to the window again.

For a few moments they watched a plane taxi across to one of the departure runways, vanishing over the slightly elevated horizon on the edge of the airport.

'A diplomatic crisis?' Helen wondered what to say. Teresa was looking to her for a cue; she must be curious to know if Chip had been told about the body. But Helen was under some restraint. Chip did not know about the body and she could not tell him about it now, not with that threat to tell the Embassy everything.

She dipped a biscuit into her coffee and took a bite.

'We'd better get you back to Lakeview,' she said, 'and let the others help to sort out this mess.' She drank her coffee quickly. 'I just hope I haven't caused everybody a whole lot of grief.'

They stood up.

Teresa gathered up her handbag and flight satchel. 'Let's be on our way then.'

'When we get back, we'll see what the others say.' Helen hoped her voice sounded as if she had a plan.

'We have to keep the Embassy side of things quiet, mind,' Chip said. 'I'm supposed to be discreet, hold a watching brief, and mind my manners.'

Chip made an ironic joke out of his speech but Helen knew he was struggling.

'Yeah, I see that,' Teresa said.

'I don't see how you can do that, Chip.' Helen spoke forcefully. 'The people up there know as much about our discovery as I do. Anything that makes the issue clearer has to be spelled out for them as much as for me.'

Again Chip ran a hand through his hair.

'Yeah, I guess you're right.'

'The truth never hurt anybody,' Teresa said. The others looked at her and said nothing.

'Well, Mom used to say so,' Teresa took a last sip of coffee.

Chip picked up his briefcase. Teresa led them out of the room and gave a dismissive wave, part amusement and part irritation, in the direction of the Air Force pilot who was waiting some distance away. He waved back, deprecatingly, and grinned. Chip went over after a brief 'Excuse me', and said a few words to the man before rejoining the others, who had not slowed down.

'I told him it might take a couple of days,' he said.

'This whole damn thing has turned into one big mystery, Chip. I can't see any answers, but maybe our collective wisdom can find a way out of the maze. Let's hope so.' Helen was far from confident.

There were still a considerable number of people in the airport, some huddled together in affectionate greeting, some struggling with their luggage, others using the telephones.

Outside the building a straggle of passengers waited for taxis. Helen, Teresa and Chip, quiet and preoccupied, joined the queue.

'Hang on a tick!' With a gesture, Helen directed Chip's attention to a short, plump man getting into the first taxi in the rank. 'That looks like – no, it can't be. He'd have said.'

Teresa had moved between Chip and the taxi, which was taking off rapidly. 'Who? What? Where? God, you make me sound like *West Side Story!*'

Teresa and Chip were looking in the right direction, but the taxi had turned the corner and other taxis were pulling up into the rank.

'It looked like your bishop.' Helen shook her head. 'I must be more tired than I realised. First you, Chip – and now I'm imagining everybody else is coming to harass me. Everybody looks like a bishop when you travel by Alitalia.'

'Not the women surely,' Teresa said.

'Not the women. *West Side Story* – what do you mean?'

Chip helped them into a taxi as Teresa started to hum a song from the musical.

At Jandakot airport, Teresa filed her flight plan in the office and they walked over to her plane, which was refuelled and ready to go. There were several other planes around, most of them privately-owned like Teresa's, and a few charter planes. It was a busy airport, as Teresa explained to Chip, servicing a state where private planes were not at all uncommon. The weather, as Teresa had expected, was fine and there would be nothing to slow them down. Within a few minutes, they took off, heading north.

Helen was grateful for the noise the plane made; she wanted all the time they had for thinking about this latest turn of events. She glanced from time to time at Chip; he too seemed preoccupied with his thoughts. Perhaps she should feel guilty about drawing Chip into this situation – but it was too late for him to back away now.

When they reached Lakeview House, Chip was given a drink – iced tea was his choice, to Barry's disgust – and he chose to sit on an upright dining chair rather than in one of the comfortable easy chairs. Introductions were over quickly. Nobody seemed surprised that Chip had, apparently, travelled with Helen from Rome. They didn't explain.

Helen had a small glass of whisky, which perked her up.

'Did you get the information we need, Helen? Did you sort it out?' Jack fussed around his wife, offering with a raised eyebrow to refill her glass, an offer she declined by putting her hand over the glass.

'Some of it. Lots to tell. But I want to hear from Chip first. He didn't go into details on the way up.'

Although Helen and Chip were both tired nobody suggested postponing the discussion until later.

Helen thought Chip looked desperately tired, more than she was, but declined to mention it. She wanted to hear what he had to say. Sleep could wait for both of them.

'He looks like a lawyer about to read the last Will and Testament,' Jack said quietly to Antony. Neither smiled.

Helen heard the remark. She had found Chip relaxed and pleasant in Rome, but he was much less at ease now. For a moment, she felt a disturbing tremor in the back of her neck.

'Why are you here, Chip? Is it because of Helen?' Antony was blunt, to the point. He wanted answers, Helen could see that. So did she; they all wanted answers.

'Yes. The Embassy sent me.'

Chip opened his briefcase and took out a book. It had a library label on the spine.

'You were sent?' Jack wriggled uncomfortably on his chair.

'Yes. The boss heard what I had to say about Helen's need for information and then he did his thing – talked around, contacted people. When he got back to me, he said to get my ass over here. So I did. He told me a whole lot of stuff first, though. About your quest, Helen.'

'My quest?' Helen thought the word made the mystery even more important. Again that edgy feeling at the back of her neck drew her hand to smooth it away.

Chip ran his fingers along the spine of the book he was holding.

'It's in there? The whole story?' Helen said.

'No, this is something I've been reading on the way across from Europe. I was told to do the research, get the background.'

'Well, that seems a good idea,' Helen said. She and Antony looked at each other, raising their eyebrows slightly, approving the methodical way, the scientific way, in which it seemed that information had been gathered.

'I'm afraid you're in for a bit of history; church history.'

Chip looked around. He seemed embarrassed. 'Look, this isn't my thing, you know? I don't have any religion, not what you'd call religion – '

'Chip, get on with it!' Teresa snapped.

'OK. This book. Well, it was written by an English monk or something fifty years ago. Something like that.' Chip started to scan the title page of the book, visibly trying to recall and establish its credentials. He turned a couple of pages, in unsuccessful pursuit of more information.

'So a monk wrote it. And?'

'Teresa, please.'

'OK, OK. The crucifix – remember?'

'I'll get to it. But I have to put you in the picture first. My boss said that without this kind of briefing, the information you want won't have the right impact.'

'Oh for goodness' sake.' Helen poured herself a glass of iced tea.

'Well, he gave me the book and said I should read it on the way out here.'

'You said that.' Helen caught a slice of lemon with her teeth and chewed it, her mouth pursing around its bitterness.

'Well, I don't want to bore you – '

'I must say, Chip, you're not doing a bad job of it.'

'No, but listen, Teresa. Gee, if I'd had the time to sort out what bits matter and what bits don't I'd have shut up long ago. But you try reading this sort of thing overnight and see what you can do.'

'Chip – '

'OK. Just recognise my difficulties, hey? Right, well the Catholic world in the Middle Ages was divided into two fields of thought, right?'

'The Middle Ages?'

'Please!'

'If you say so.'

'There were, on my left, the exponents of Gallicanism; and on my right, the Ultramontanes.'

He held up a hand as somebody giggled. 'No, this isn't irrelevant. Listen. The Gallicanists said the Pope should not claim to have power in the non-religious affairs of countries – like deposing kings if he felt like it, stuff like that. The Ultras said he could and should have that power. It was a power thing, you know?'

'So?' This time Antony was urging the story along.

'Well, the fight went on for a long time.'

'Like your story – ' Chip glared the grin off Teresa's face.

'A big Vatican meeting in 1869 was supposed to settle the arguments, at least about what power a Pope has. But it turned out that the Vatican Council was more concerned with deciding whether or not the Pope can make mistakes. Whether or not he's infallible.'

'Where on earth is all this leading?' It was Helen's turn to be impatient.

'Quite simply – '

'Well, that'll help,' Antony mumbled. Chip gave him an annoyed glance.

'Quite simply, it means this. There were a lot of Jesuits sculling around in the background of the Vatican Council, manipulating things.'

'They always did – and probably do. I remember that from school,' Barry said. 'I went to a Marist school and they didn't trust the Jesuits at all.'

'I suppose we all know that the Jesuits were into that sort of thing. It crops up all the time in history books.' Jack looked around and got confirmation from the others.

'Yeah, well, it looks as if they had the ear of one cardinal in particular. An English one. And he had the ear of the Pope, Pius the Ninth.'

'It sounds like the sort of thing you'd expect,' Antony said. He sounded fascinated. 'I mean, Parliament here is full of people bending each other's ears about special interests.'

Helen thought how easy it was to catch the attention of someone like him, a scientist, used to sorting out facts. If only she could sort out the facts that were troubling her.

'I guess it's that way in the US Congress too; pork-barrelling and stuff. But listen. This Englishman, Cardinal Manning, was the only convert to Catholicism there; at the Council meeting. The only one of the top guys who had been a Protestant first. That set him apart a bit.'

'Converts always sneer at us cradle Catholics; they reckon we got in just by being born, not by being smart.' Barry went off, saying he'd fetch a couple of sixpacks of beer.

'This Cardinal was a formidable power behind the scenes. And he was pushing real hard for the Pope to be called infallible. The others reckoned that saying so would make it impossible to attract back into the Church any Protestants who had an inclination that way. No, the Gallicanites reckoned infallibility was not only wrong, but wrongheaded. Right?'

There was a bemused silence.

Barry returned and offered the beer around.

'So this Cardinal was an Ultramarine,' Jack offered brightly, to show that he had been following the discourse. Helen smiled at him.

'Ultramontaine, yes. And it seems from this book, which is based on some gossipy notes written by an English bishop who took part in the Vatican Council, that Cardinal Manning was knee deep in skulduggery, intrigue, cronyism – and he was a real talent at lobbying to boot. And guess who was in cahoots with him?'

'The Jesuits?' This from Antony, by now visibly, and totally, fascinated by the story.

'Well, that's my reading of it.'

'And your boss's?'

'Well actually, Antony, it was his idea. He'd been briefed, of course. I don't know how. He rang around a few guys; vanished for hours, came back and – briefed me with all this. He has contacts at all sorts of levels. Knows his way around the Church too; he went to Georgetown University in Washington. Got his degree in Diplomacy there.'

'A degree in Diplomacy? Good gracious.' Jack was appalled, rather to Helen's amusement.

'Well, yes. The only place you can get one, I think. It's a Jesuit University.'

'Ah, I see.' Jack nodded. Helen wondered if he really did understand the connection. Anyway, it seemed that Chip was on the brink of explaining that there was a connection to her mystery behind all of this.

'Did he check his idea out with anyone who might know if it was right?' Antony said.

'Well, I guess he did. And he made me do some legwork, too.'

'Is that why you left me to my own devices?' Helen said.

'Yes, Helen – sorry about that. Most people we could get to were reluctant to talk much about it; I mean, why should they? My boss isn't a churchman, not an expert on these things, and I have no street cred at all. But we were allowed to gather a few basic bits of insider info.'

'Such as what?' Antony leant further forward in his chair.

'And how on earth does it help us?' Helen had lost interest in the possible influence of the Jesuits at the Vatican Council and could not understand what possible relevance it had to their problem.

'Well, this is where you come in, Helen. I have it on what I might call very good authority that the English Cardinal was shown some correspondence, long before the Vatican Council. And it was from these letters that he formed his very strong view that the infallibility of the Pope was an OK thing to have.'

'I would have thought it was an argument about what God wanted,' Antony said.

'You don't listen, Antony.'

Helen looked around. Despite the sparring, Helen thought they were all somewhat amused by Chip's impatience. He was clearly not happy with both his potted history and his

215

audience's inability to follow him closely enough down the labyrinthine tunnels.

'I'm talking here,' Chip said 'about the political arguments, not the religious ones. There were those who said it wasn't a prudent thing to do, politically speaking. The Brits would play merry hell if they got a whiff of the Pope trying to say he could boot their kings out like his predecessor tried with Henry the Eighth, and the French, for instance, would be just the same. They might have won the argument too if it hadn't been for this Englishman. He was something else. He won. He told the guy who wrote these notes,' Chip waved the library book around for a moment 'that he had studied societies where the absolute ruler ruled absolutely and in his view it was absolutely the best way to go.'

'Dictatorship!' Jack sounded shocked.

'Not democracy, for sure. But the Catholic Church has never claimed to be a democratic society, has it, Barry?'

'I don't know. We do as we're told, is that what you mean? We're supposed to, anyway.'

'Not quite that, but you get my drift.'

'I still don't see – '

'Helen, think! This correspondence, the stuff that clinched the argument, this was a series of letters about how some small society struggling against the odds had managed to survive for centuries in harsh circumstances because of a traditional belief that the top guy never makes a mistake when he tells them what to do.'

'I'm thinking.'

'Well, the Cardinal got the correspondence from the Jesuits. All very secret, and I guess they had their own agenda. I don't know why they wanted the infallibility thing so much but they had a weapon which served their purpose very well.'

'Explain it then; I don't get it.' Antony was issuing a challenge.

'This Cardinal's a smart man, right? He has come over to Rome from the Church of England for all sorts of reasons but getting a powerful seat at the Pope's court must have been one of them, OK? He must have read the history of the church; he knows how badly it was run and how some of the old controversies seem hellbent on destroying its power. He's not a modest man; and Jesuits know how to flatter.'

'I'll buy that, but how – '

'They offer him some correspondence, written in English very likely. Maybe not, but maybe so. These letters describe a society such as the Cardinal wants: absolute power whenever the Pope speaks absolutely.'

'Huh?'

'Oh, there's something about he's only infallible when he's talking about faith and morals. If he says, as the present one does, that homosexuality is a sin, he's not being infallible because he didn't announce the fact that he was speaking infallibly at the time he said it. So he allows that he might be wrong. Thank God for that, or I'd be out of a job.'

'Really? Are you – ' Jack went a little pink, and stopped abruptly.

'Come on now, just think! The letters which persuade the Cardinal that he – and the Jesuits – can see without any doubt at all just how invaluable the principle of infallibility is. These letters came – from a missionary! An English Jesuit missionary!'

Helen put down the cool glass of iced tea, gently, carefully, in the middle of the coffee table.

'You mean – there's a connection between the third crucifix and this missionary? This Jesuit missionary is John Craven?'

'Who?' Antony asked, his voice loud.

'Of course!' Chip slapped the book shut and put it down on the coffee table. 'He wrote back to his bosses yards of letters; they all did, they had to. Part of the job description.'

'And this priest wrote from Australia? About the Arundijilaba?' David spoke for the first time.

'Yes! He probably saw them as a kind of a microcosm of any group of people struggling against the odds. Maybe he exaggerated the size of the tribe; I don't know. Maybe he claimed there were thousands of – how do you say it? – Arundithingies around. But at the head of them was this guy – '

'My grandfather's grandfather.'

'Yes, yes! Well, a lot further back than that. This guy whose word was absolute law. And it worked, didn't it? The tribe – the nation – survived. Nobody got killed for arguing because nobody argued. This man had absolute power.'

'And it didn't absolutely corrupt him?' Antony asked.

'No, it didn't.' David's voice was strong. 'I would have heard. It would have been in the stories.' David was confident about it.

'So there's a connection if you like. A Jesuit missionary reports back to his HQ in Europe that this is a great way to run a country. His bosses keep the correspondence in a neat and tidy bundle until the opportunity arises. Which it does, in the form of this English cardinal. "Hey, they say, we've got some interesting stuff for you to read, written by another Englishman like you." And he reads it, gets the point and gets stuck in at the Vatican Council.'

'Still, he wasn't the only one to vote for it, surely?' Antony said.

'More than half the bishops either were against it or didn't vote. And this Cardinal Manning swayed everyone else with his arguments. They say he really won the case for the Pope.'

'Why didn't the people who were against him being called infallible go on arguing after the Council?'

'They couldn't, could they? The Pope said it was now a fact, so they couldn't argue. Even the strongest opponents came out and said they accepted the decision; and they did. Not another peep was heard out of them.'

'So you're saying – '

'Well, the people I talked to say – and those people my boss talked to – ' Chip made an expansive, all-inclusive gesture.

Antony interrupted him. 'That the letters sent from here – from Australia – are the main cause of the Pope being declared infallible?' He sounded stunned.

'Well, yes. Looks that way.'

'So that's why the whole affair has been kept such a secret!'

'And why my boss and the people he's talked to in the Vatican are scared out of their wits about it all.' Chip nodded. It made sense to him, too.

There was a silence that seemed to go on for many minutes. Helen was unable to handle the flood of thoughts; her memories of the visit to Rome produced a momentary vision of long-ago priests and bishops, purple and crimson robes, white-haired and black-haired men hurrying across to St. Peter's, anxious to hear about the missionary in 'south-east Asia' – Australia.

The sudden jarring of the telephone made Helen jump. Barry reached across the table and picked up the handset.

'Yeah?'

Barry looked briefly puzzled, then smiled into the phone. 'Yes, that's right.' He glanced at Helen. 'OK, Tom; I'll get the Hoover out. No problem.'

With a few brief civilities, the conversation ended and Barry hung up.

'Another bloke's on his way,' he said.

'The Hoover?' Teresa said.

'No, it's Tom – got a hire plane on the way. Said I'd make sure the strip's clear. Hoover it, see?' Teresa smiled and made a circle with a thumb and forefinger.

'You've another guest coming, Barry?' Jack sounded less than interested, Helen thought. They were all still taking in Chip's story.

'Someone looking for you, Helen. An Italian bloke – Imbolo, something like that.'

'My God – it's Imbrogno? Was that the name, Barry? Imbrogno?' Chip's voice was too high. He sounded scared, Helen thought, as her own fears escalated.

Barry shrugged in possible agreement to the name as Chip rose from his chair abruptly, sending it flying across the verandah. Helen rose more slowly to her feet.

'Chip?' She spoke quietly, firmly.

'Yes. Yes, it has to be him. What did the – airport guy – say he wanted?'

Barry shrugged again. 'He didn't say much. Just to get the strip ready – '

'Yes, we got that.' Chip was impatient and spoke too loudly.

'And this bloke called – ?'

'Imbrogno, yes.'

220

'This Italian bloke asked him to check if Helen's here – Dr Lytton – or if she had been here. So I said yes.'

'An Italian, Chip? Is this who I think it is?' Helen was still on her feet.

'Yes. Aldo Imbrogno. It must be him. How the hell did he find you?'

By now the other people on the verandah were visibly disturbed. Before Jack could put his question, Helen placed her hand on his arm. Jack sat down again, his eyes fixed on Chip's face.

'I lodged a flight plan,' Teresa said. 'Could he have seen you – us – at the airport?'

Helen nodded. 'You remember, Teresa? I said I thought I saw someone who looked like the bishop – '

'A bishop!' Antony's voice was harsh, incredulous. 'How is he connected with – ' He made a wide, sweeping gesture taking in the meatworks and everything that had happened there. 'All this?'

'I met him in Rome. He gave us some information – not much and not enough. Why is he here, Chip? Why has he followed me?'

'I don't know. I don't know. Did he mention me, Barry? The guy from the airport just now; did he mention me?'

Barry shook his head, looking bewildered by the passionate outbursts around the table.

'When will he get here?' Helen had calmed down. Now was the time, she thought, for concise, rational thought. Never mind why he's here, let's concentrate on what we must do.

'He's leaving when it gets cooler. Be here around ten tonight.'

'Did he tell your friend – Tom, was it? – how long he plans to be here? Is he flying straight back?'

'No, he couldn't do that. Tom would chalk up too many flying hours if they did a return trip right off. Usual thing when people come up to fix the generator, do a bit of business, stuff like that: stay overnight; no sweat. Lots of room.'

'A bishop.' Jack said the word with a note of trepidation which Helen picked up. 'Why, Chip? Why is a bishop coming here to see Helen? Where did you meet him, Helen? What is this all about?'

It was Helen's turn to look confused. What the hell did it mean? She started to speak but gave up – she couldn't imagine why Aldo was on his way to the meatworks. Or why he had left Rome so quickly, and on the same plane as her.

'I think he is probably travelling privately,' said Chip. 'You know, it doesn't sound to me like an official thing.'

'Not like yours, eh, Chip? Flights in the Air Force plane and that,' said Teresa.

'Air Force plane? What's going on here?' Jack was really agitated now; Helen watched carefully as Jack took a sip of water, then another, looking hot and somewhat breathless.

She leaned over and patted his forearm again, reassuringly. 'It's fine, Jack. Nothing to worry about. I met him in Rome and he was nice enough. Calm down, dear.'

'I think we should all calm down.' Antony made a broad gesture, opening his arms and stretching, relaxing. 'We can't work this out until the blasted man gets here, so let's just wait, shall we?'

'What about telling Chip? He doesn't know, does he?' David indicated with his shoulder in the direction of the cooling shed. Chip raised an eyebrow.

'That can wait too,' Helen said decisively. Chip looked from her to Antony, to David, and shrugged. Helen could see he was resigned to another mystery.

By unspoken consensus, the group seemed to accept the suggestion and Teresa went off with Barry to organise some food. Chip poured himself another drink, saw Helen's eye on him and poured one for her too. Antony went across the room, delivered Helen's drink to her and went back to the table to pour one, a long one, for himself and another for Jack.

David was still sitting on the verandah steps, where he had been quietly listening but not joining in the confusion about the imminent arrival of another player in the drama.

Lunch was sandwiches and tinned fruit. Helen could not have said what sort of sandwiches they were, nor what kind of tinned fruit. When she wondered about it, she glanced around and was sure that everyone was similarly distracted. After lunch, both Helen and Chip headed off to catch up on some sleep.

CHAPTER 11

THE SUN WAS LOW ON THE HORIZON BY NINE O'CLOCK. The red of the sandy soil had darkened and myriad stars were becoming visible; soon they would fill the sky, seeming to leave no room for the moon, for satellites, shooting stars, planes. The moon rose, heavy and dolorous, casting its cooling, pewter light across the landscape. This was the time of day when kangaroos came out to forage in the sparse grass around the meatworks, when bird calls were brief and sounded far away, when the trees around Lakeview House were moved restlessly by an occasional breeze. This was the time of day Helen loved; when she felt free of pressure.

But not tonight.

Helen, Jack and Antony had talked themselves out by now. They sat together on the verandah and looked into the distance, each with their thoughts about the day's discoveries and what was to come. Or so Helen assumed; her mind was full of the problems and both her companions seemed equally troubled.

A game of chess further along the verandah was keeping Barry and David quiet, with Chip and Teresa offering suggestions about moves, suggestions which Barry was inclined to accept much to the amused irritation of David, who protested loudly at every successful gambit.

A sudden susurration in the trees caused Helen to raise her head abruptly; the evening song of the magpies stopped. The two kangaroos fossicking along the other side of the fence paused in their eating and looked at each other, not yet alarmed but cautious. One of them sat back using its tail to hold it upright. Its ears were pricked, its face turned up towards the stars.

'I think it's here,' said Teresa. She went down the steps from the verandah and walked a few metres away so that she could look up into the sky beyond the roof of the house.

'Can you see it?' Antony joined her and searched the sky, his hand shading his eyes from the sinking sun.

'Hush. Listen; can you hear it?' Teresa turned slightly. She pointed to a distant light.

'It's just a star, isn't it?'

The pinpoint of light moved slowly until it passed beyond the roofline and was visible to those still on the verandah. As it approached, the light became twin lights, headlights.

'Tom's arriving.' Barry made the unnecessary announcement. 'Best get the kettle on; he'll be ready for a cuppa.' He switched on the lights which flooded the area around the house and the outbuildings and went indoors.

Helen was tired. Tired but excited. Nervous: she wasn't sure just what she felt but the imminent arrival of Aldo – the bishop – was the last visit she wanted. There was such a lot to do, so many decisions to make. Just how much the bishop needed to be told was crucial. And Chip, too, he was still in the dark about the finding of the body.

'What time is it, Jack?' she said.

'Almost ten.'

'What shall we tell him, do you think?'

'Best wait and see what he has to say for himself, barging in on us like this.'

'Tell him nothing, I reckon.' In the changing light, David's face seemed blacker and his eyes shone with what Helen thought was either excitement or anger.

The travelling lights became brighter as the sound of the engines grew louder. A small tick in the sky became a shape, a plane, and suddenly it seemed to be almost there. The plane landed on the 'Hoovered' strip and came to a silent stop just beyond the fence.

Barry came out of the house and walked briskly across to the open gate.

'G'day Tom! Got the kettle on, mate!'

Two men had emerged from the small plane, one with an easy jump from the pilot's seat, the other with a more careful reach for solid ground. Tom wore old blue jeans and a bright yellow and green check shirt. His passenger wore a black suit and carried an Alitalia travel bag.

As they drew closer to the house, Helen and Jack left the verandah and went forward to meet them. They stopped some distance away while Barry gave Tom a hug.

'Good to see you, you old bastard!' Tom said.

'You're looking worse every time, you bugger! Come in and rest your old bones.'

Aldo Imbrogno waited, smiling without apparent concern that his arrival was uninvited and possibly unwelcome. He kept his attention on Barry, politely, like a guest should.

After a bit of mutual thumping, Barry turned to the bishop.

'Guess you're this Italian bloke, eh?'

'Yes. I am Aldo Imbrogno, Bishop Aldo Imbrogno. I hope my visit is not too much of a problem for you, Mr – ?'

'Barry, your Grace. Call me Barry. You're very welcome. I'm not what you'd call a practising member of the flock but I am one in a way. Come in and make yourself at home.'

'What's come over Barry?' said Jack with such disgust in his voice that Helen's nervousness collapsed into laughter.

The sound of her voice caused Aldo to turn in her direction. He smiled broadly and walked over to where she stood with Jack, her arm defensively tucked into the crook of her husband's elbow. Aldo held out his hand to her; she took it and gave a quick and far from firm handshake.

'How nice to see you again, Dr Lytton. And so soon.'

He spoke as if this were a chance meeting at a social event, rather than an encounter he must have planned and had travelled many thousands of kilometres to achieve.

'What a surprise, Aldo. This is Jack Lytton, my husband.'

As they shook hands, the bishop still smiled broadly. Jack's response was chilly, his handshake minimal.

Barry led Tom off into the house and as the others went up the steps onto the verandah, Antony and David stood up to meet them. There was no sign of Chip, Helen noticed.

'This is Antony, and this is David,' said Helen. She saw no reason to explain either of them nor their presence at Lakeview House.

The greetings were guarded, except for Bishop Imbrogno's practised and excessive civility.

'You must be tired,' Jack said. He might just as well have packed the bishop off to bed with a good book, Helen thought. She was still struggling with amusement at Jack's visible antagonism.

'Yes, Mr Lytton, I am tired. It is a long way from Rome.'

'One wonders why one has made such a journey then.'

This was a little too obvious, even for Aldo. His smile faded somewhat, as he sat down in the seat Antony indicated.

'I came on private business, Dr Lytton. Private business, you understand?'

She didn't but it seemed politic to nod. A small and uncertain nod, but it might encourage the man to explain himself.

The bishop looked around. 'You must be an aboriginal,' he said brightly, conversationally.

'Yes I must,' said David. He joined Helen in a grin that nearly became audible.

'Quite so.' Aldo seemed content to sit there, smiling, being affable and silent.

Barry came out of the house, carrying a tray.

'Cup of tea, your Grace?' For the bishop, Barry had found a Wedgwood cup and saucer. There was a silver milk jug and matching sugar basin on the tray which bore a tray cloth gracefully embroidered with native flowers. As Helen's smile broadened again, Barry looked a little embarrassed.

Now it was Teresa's turn to be inducted into the polite ambience of the visiting cleric.

'And you, my dear – ?'

'Teresa.'

'A good Catholic name – are you one of my flock? A Catholic?'

'No.'

Aldo nodded. His eyes, Helen noticed, were less affable than his words. He was darting cold glances at the people assembled on the verandah, as though he were weighing them all in the scales of some monstrous judiciary.

'Dr and Mr Lytton, Antony – ?' His unasked question was not answered. 'David, who is an aborigine, Teresa, who is not a Catholic, and Barry who is a poor version of one. And why are we all gathered here in this extraordinarily remote part of this extraordinarily remote country, I wonder?'

228

His comment – he hardly seemed to expect an answer – seemed inordinately foolish to Helen. The blasted man had invited himself here; she saw no reason at all to respond to his unsubtle questions.

'We know why we are here, Aldo. What we don't know is why you followed me here. Perhaps you could tell us that now.'

Antony made a small sound which Helen took to be agreeing with her. She glanced at him, and he nodded firmly.

'We are here on private business, too, Bishop,' Antony said.

'Are all these people in your confidence, Dr Lytton?' Aldo looked around, still with an unassailable air of being there by invitation and right.

'Yes.'

'The pilot?'

'He's watching a video and going off to his bed. Tired out, the old bugger is.' Barry sat down.

'Ah. Well, let me explain.'

Without looking for an invitation, the bishop stood up and moved to a more comfortable chair alongside the small wicker table where Tom had placed the tray. After a glance around, Helen sat down next to Jack, facing the bishop across the table. David leant against one of the verandah posts, watching. Antony took a seat a little further away, with Teresa sitting on the arm of his chair.

First, Aldo finished his tea. Helen remembered the way he had kept her waiting in Rome, taking small sips from his wine glass. She determined not to show her impatience with his performance.

While he sipped and smiled, she looked out into the night. The kangaroos and birds had left. The sun had almost disappeared, leaving a moon so bright that she would have been able to read by its vivid light. There was a soft soughing in the air, a gentle movement of warm air. The scent of wild flowers, brown boronia mostly, drifted across in gentle waves from the patch of garden. A blissful night, she thought. *Sleep well, John Craven, may flights of angels* – she brought herself abruptly to full awareness. She must be much more tired than she had realised.

'Well, if my host will permit me?' Aldo glanced at Barry, who beamed with pleasure.

'Of course, your Grace. Whatever you say.'

Reassured by this apparent invitation, Aldo took off his jacket and leant back in the chair. He looked completely at ease. In the moonlight, his clerical collar seemed to gleam as though it were made of silver. He reached up a small, manicured hand and removed the collar, stretching his neck as he did so.

'I felt it my duty to have a talk with you, Dr Lytton, about your interest in the third crucifix. You understand?'

So now it was said.

Aldo glanced quickly around as though to confirm that everyone present knew about the crucifix.

'My interest?'

'My dear, your young friend from the American Embassy filled me in about your quest. Filled me in almost completely, I might say. Charming young man.'

'He's my brother,' Teresa said. She looked with distaste at the rotund shape of the bishop. 'Do you know him well?'

Helen thought she understood the reason for Teresa's question.

'Not well. We are mere acquaintances.'

'Good.'

His sharp eyes spat an unspoken retort, which Helen saw. She spoke before he could respond. 'I find that hard to believe, Aldo, that Chip told you more about my visit; it was private and confidential.'

'Confidential, yes. But he told me because he understood my concern.'

The bishop took another sip of tea, looking around, offering confidence and benevolence to his doubting audience.

'I told you nothing, Aldo.'

Chip came from his concealment in the shadows of the doorway onto the verandah. The bishop put his cup down in the saucer with a rattle and stared at Chip with astonishment. Almost immediately, his face changed into a mask of polite indifference.

Helen held her breath.

'I did not know you were coming to Australia, Chip.'

'You didn't say you were coming either. So what am I supposed to have told you?'

Aldo gathered his wits about him as best he could. Helen watched with near contempt as he smoothed his hair and pulled his shirt collar a little away from his neck. He was clearly disconcerted and struggling to find a way to begin his explanation, Helen thought. She was pleased to see him so disturbed.

Chip didn't wait for the bishop to find the words.

'It seems to me, Aldo, that you have poked your nose in where it is not wanted. I suggest you stop being so polite and pretending that you are welcome here. As soon as the pilot can leave – which I gather will be tomorrow – I suggest you get on the plane with him and head off back to where you came from. There is nothing for you here.'

The bishop sat in silence for a moment, as the others watched, waited. Then he leaned forward and slammed both his hands down on the table.

'I know you have found the third crucifix and I want it.'

Helen felt a tremor of fear.

'Chip is right; you'd better go.' Jack's voice was tight.

'No; wait.' It was Antony who spoke. 'If we did find something, why do you want it? What makes you think we would give it you?'

'Of all people.' Helen was not sure what she meant by that, but she really disliked this pretentious man. Her father was just such a man, always assuming his right to know everything, be better than everyone, be more clever than Helen could ever be. She pulled herself back into the conversation.

The bishop spoke with flat certainty. 'The third crucifix belongs to the Church. I am here to collect it.'

'You said you were here on private business,' Antony said.

'Yes. Private business. I have not been sent on this mission. I come at my own instigation.'

In the silence that followed, Barry shook his head, gathered up the cups, the silver milk jug and sugar basin. He put them on the tray and took them indoors. 'You sort it out,' he said, with disgust.

'There is much to be sorted out,' said Helen.

'If there is a third crucifix, it certainly doesn't belong to your church, or to you,' Jack spoke with certainty and not a little asperity in his voice. 'It belongs to – '

Helen interrupted, with a note of warning in her voice which she knew Jack would hear. 'If it exists, it belongs to science, Aldo.'

'I think we should concede its existence, Helen,' Antony said. 'He's come too far for it to be a guess. He knows. We must have given that fact away somehow.'

Although she wished she did not have to agree with Antony, Helen knew he was right. She looked around the group and saw only tired agreement with the proposition.

'All right. It exists. But it doesn't belong to anyone – anyone but us, that is. Or the original owner.'

'The original – ?' Aldo laughed. 'The original thief, you mean? An Australian tourist who found it in an antique shop in Florence or Paris or London and brought it here to gloat over? The Catholic Church has a much greater claim to it, believe me. Much greater.'

'Show it to him, Helen.' For some reason that Helen could not fathom, Antony seemed eager to display their find. She nodded. Jack went into the house and came back with the soap box. He put it down, gently, on the table. Antony, whose eyes hardly left the face of the sweating bishop, lifted the lid.

By now the group had pulled their chairs closer into a loose circle around the table. They watched the bishop reach out and lift the cotton wool from the face of the crucifix. They watched as his face transformed from that of a greedy, pompous man into one of awe and wonder. Even Teresa was moved by the transformation.

'It's pretty sensational, huh, Bishop,' she said.

'Sensational,' he said in a whisper.

'Don't touch it,' Jack said quickly as the bishop seemed about to do so. 'It'll prick your finger.'

The bishop drew back his finger abruptly. He looked up at Jack. 'It will prick my finger?'

'Yes. There's a sharp bit on it; just at the side there, see, where the thorn is a bit damaged, I think.'

' "A flawed crucifix for a flawed man",' Aldo said.

Helen thought she saw tears in the man's eyes. Italians, she thought. So sentimental. Still, it is beautiful. Be sensible; pragmatic. Get this man away from here.

'Flawed?' said Jack. 'Oh, not really. Just a tiny bit of damage, I think. I didn't notice it, though, when I dug it out.'

'Dug it out?' Aldo seized on the phrase. 'You dug it out? Where? Where did you find it? Was it buried here – in Australia? How did it get here? Who stole it and brought it here?'

Antony held up a hand.

'Please! Nobody stole it. At least, we don't think so.' He stopped, and Helen realised that Antony had been on the point of saying that they had found the body of the original owner.

Antony caught her eye and tightened his lips.

'What I mean is – '

'We will show you tomorrow where we found it,' Helen said.

Aldo nodded, apparently satisfied. For now.

She could see no alternative to this. They would let the bishop see the cave. They would not mention the body. The bishop would leave, persuaded that he could not have the crucifix and everyone would be satisfied.

Even as she had the thought, Helen knew it was ridiculous.

There was no more discussion. The silence became oppressive, and within a few minutes Barry's guests were yawning. Aldo admitted to being tired and went away sooner than the others, escorted by Barry offering extra pillows, a jug of iced water and an alarm clock. Jack went to bed before Helen; she wanted to stay for a while on the verandah. Soon she was the only one left.

Helen sat on, thinking, worrying. What on earth did all that religious nonsense have to do with her? Infallibility? What nonsense; nobody was infallible, not even her father. She smiled at the unexpected thought.

The moon was very bright. Helen wondered how often the dead priest had watched that same moon.

As she prepared for bed and slid in beside Jack, who had already fallen asleep, Helen wondered how their dilemma would be resolved. She wondered if in fact it could be resolved. Her last wakeful thoughts were something to do with the awful legacy of the British colonial powers and the cultural injuries inflicted by missionaries less than a hundred years ago. She thought about Truganini, the last woman, the last member, of her aboriginal tribe to survive the white man's arrival in Tasmania.

So many of the British colonials had been missionaries 'doing it all for God'.

She slept fitfully.

By seven o'clock, the stars were invisible again. The sun was high in the sky and the full and glorious cacophony of birdsong rang like bells in the air around the house.

It was going to be another very hot day. Already, on the edge of the horizon, David had seen the shimmer of dust that foretold the sudden gusts of wind that spiralled into willy willies. He pointed the signs out to Helen and Jack as they came into the kitchen to collect breakfast.

Chip was already there, sharing his cereals with Teresa. She had decided not to have any but took the occasional sultana from Chip's bowl.

'I don't like that man going into our cave,' said David.

'I don't think any of us like the idea,' said Helen. 'I am hoping that when he has seen it, he'll be satisfied and just go away.'

'Do you think he will, Chip? Teresa took another sultana. 'I mean, you know him, don't you? Will he settle for having been there and done that?'

'I don't know.' Chip slapped Teresa's hand affectionately away from his bowl. 'I hope so. If he is here privately, then that means he hasn't told anyone back in the Vatican about it. He won't be worried about failing to get what he came for. He might just go home.'

'But you don't think so,' said Antony, coming into the kitchen after an early walk. Helen noticed that his Adidas trainers were more red than white now.

'Maybe. Maybe not. I don't know.'

'But why would he come here "privately"? What's in it for him?' Jack looked puzzled.

'Power – promotion – who knows?' Chip finished his cereals.

'Well, we'd better be off to the cave. Who's coming?' Helen put her dishes in the sink. Jack was already filling it with hot water.

'I think it should be you and Antony who go,' said Jack. 'I'll stay and clean up. Just let you scientists go. Makes it formal, sort of.'

The others agreed.

Aldo Imbrogno had showered and dressed. He looked as neat and polished as he had in Rome when he joined the group in the kitchen. Barry offered him breakfast. It was made clear by Helen and Antony that Aldo needed to hurry as they wanted to get this visit over. Aldo had a slice of toast, already made and cold, and drank a cup of coffee quickly. Helen recognised that this must be a real concession; he probably always drank coffee slowly and appreciatively.

'It's only Nescafé, your Grace. I hope it's all right?' Barry sounded obsequious again.

'It's entirely adequate,' Aldo said. 'Yes, entirely so.'

So that explained the haste, Helen thought. He loathed the stuff.

Antony glanced down at the smart black Italian loafers on the bishop's feet. 'I think you might find those shoes too – fragile – for this expedition, Bishop. Did you bring any real shoes with you?'

Apart from a half-blink of his hooded eyes, Aldo did not let this implicit insult show if it had hit its mark. Helen was almost enjoying the sparring.

'These are what one needs to wear in a great city like Rome, dear boy. Farmers may need other footwear. I appreciate that.'

'Chalk one up for the Church,' Teresa said in a mutter. She handed another dish to Jack, who dropped it carefully into the suds.

'I can find something for you, your Grace.' Barry turned on his eagerness to help. 'I keep all sorts of gear for the meat workers. I can get something from the cooling shed – ' He looked up nervously as he seemed to sense the tensing of spines as he spoke. 'I mean, I can find something for you to wear. Your suit might get dirty too.'

His voice tailed off and after a brief pause, he scurried out of the kitchen.

'Thank you, Barry my boy,' the bishop called after him.

While they waited, Aldo took off his jacket and clerical collar. Helen wondered why he had bothered to put them on.

Probably to remind us of his exalted status, she thought, not at all impressed.

Smiling politely, immersed in his role of the happy guest, Aldo looked around seeming unaware that no smiles were returned. 'This is quite exciting, I think. Shall we be going a long distance? To the town, perhaps?'

Antony rolled his eyes upwards. 'Come on, Bishop. This is the outback. We wouldn't be here if the crucifix was found a few hundred kilometres away, now would we?'

'So it's nearby? The hiding place?' The bishop's voice was casual, conversational.

Before Antony could answer, or Helen interpose another distracting comment, Barry returned. He offered Aldo a choice of Wellington boots and three sizes of white overalls.

Helen started to laugh. Aldo, clearly relieved by the lightening of the atmosphere in the kitchen, turned to her, inviting an explanation.

'Isn't this what happens when you get a new Pope?' she said. Aren't there three sizes of that white thing he wears, so that whoever is chosen will fit into one of them?'

The tension collapsed with a gale of laughter, in which Aldo joined.

'Well, I'm hardly going to look like a Pope in this, am I?' he said, struggling into overalls that were wide enough but made for a much taller man. The smallest boots were a couple of sizes too large for his small and pampered feet. Helen sneered a little as she saw his black silk socks disappear into the boots. Grinning hugely, Barry helped the bishop to pull a pair of thick grey socks over the silk ones, and helped Aldo to tuck the excess fabric of the overall legs down into the boots.

When he was dressed, the Bishop took a few mincing steps up and down the kitchen, much like a parody of a model on a catwalk. 'Hardly Versace, eh?'

Chip stopped laughing and went quickly out of the kitchen, letting the door slam behind him. The joking stopped.

'Right, let's be on our way,' said Antony. 'Aldo, Helen and I are going with you. David will take us there in the four-wheel drive and wait outside. It can be dangerous; do as you're told immediately. Right?'

'But of course.'

Aldo stumbled down the verandah steps and walked with difficulty to the LandCruiser. As he struggled to get into it, nobody laughed.

The sun was rising still; the heat was not far away.

David gunned the engine and the group set off. Back on the verandah, Teresa and Chip stood arm in arm and watched them go.

Helen looked back, recognising the doubt on Chip's face, the distaste for Aldo on Teresa's.

Chip went into the house, leaving Teresa to watch until the plume of dust obscured the house from Helen as she looked back and the LandCruiser headed for the horizon.

By the time they reached the site of the cave, Aldo complained that he was hot and exhausted. The overalls were uncomfortable, he said, and the red dust seemed to have got into every nook and cranny of his body.

David and Helen were in light khaki shorts and shirts, which helped to keep them cool. Antony's canvas pants and thin shirt were equally efficient.

When David pulled up, they got out and looked around.

'It's up there, Bishop. Think you can manage?'

Without waiting for an answer, Antony picked up a lamp from the back of the LandCruiser and strode towards the hill where the cave was hidden from below. He started to scramble up the scree.

'I'll wait here then,' said David. It sounded to Helen as if David hoped he might be invited to go along with them.

'Yes, we shan't be long,' she said.

Aldo struggled gamely up the loose scree on the hill, using his hands to help him. Almost on hands and knees, he made the difficult ascent. Helen did not offer to help him, and Antony watched from the entrance to the cave without comment.

When the bishop had puffed and panted his way to Antony's side, Helen made her way up behind him.

'Mind your step.' Antony spoke over his shoulder as he led the way into the cave, flooding it with light from the lantern.

As they approached the edge of the bog, Helen put a restraining hand on Aldo's arm.

'Stop here. It may not be safe to go any further forward.'

There was silence as Antony swept the area with light. The trench they had dug seemed to Helen deeper, longer, than when they had excavated it.

'The colour of the soil hasn't changed, did you notice that?' she said.

'Yes, proves your point about how old it is. I wonder if – '

'No, please, tell me.' Aldo's voice was pitched higher than before. 'Please, is this where you found the crucifix? Buried here – in that hole?'

'Yes,' Helen said, curtly.

They stood in silence, looking into the trench.

'Why did you come in here? Do you explore caves? Is this your work – and yours too, Antony?'

'There was a willy-willy – a kind of mini-tornado – and it blew away the earth that hid the entrance.' Antony's response was equally cool.

'And you just happened to be here?'

'Yes. We just happened to be here.'

'Amazing.'

Aldo knelt down on the firm ground at the edge of the semi-circle and leant forward to touch the black area beyond.

'Why is it different? Do you know?'

'Scientists are never sure about anything, Bishop. Unlike people in your discipline.'

'You must tell me everything.' Aldo stood up. The light of the torch came to rest on his face, lighting it from beneath as children do to create the impression of diabolic features. In Aldo's case, his plumply cushioned face looked more angelic in the harsh light than demonic.

'There is nothing else to tell.' Helen spoke flatly, and turned to leave the cave, followed by Antony.

The bishop followed them, stumbling over the entrance and beginning to skid carefully down the scree to the dusty ground, where David waited, watching them. As the scientists reached him, David still had an eye on the bishop, who was slowly making his descent, a bare couple of metres from the cave.

'There's a willy-willy on its way.' David pointed to a distant swirl in the sky. 'Better get in the LandCruiser; we'll take off and try to outrun it. Won't be much of a thing anyway, I reckon.'

There was a scurry of rocks sliding down the scree, disturbed by Aldo's feet. He seemed to be stuck where he was, not yet halfway down.

'Is that one of your tornadoes?' He sounded frightened.

Antony winked at Helen as he called back. 'You'd better take shelter in the cave, bishop. Could be dangerous. Be over in a few minutes, mind you.'

Aldo scrambled back up to the entrance and into the cave. His voice echoed as he called out: 'I'll wait here then!'

'That's what I said, bishop. You do that.'

Antony helped Helen into the back of the LandCruiser and climbed in beside David.

'Better wait for the old fool, I suppose,' David said. He made sure that all the windows were tightly closed.

The willy-willy moved slowly towards them, deviating several times but its general direction had them fair and square in its course. Suddenly, it reached the clearing. Helen remembered the last time a willy-willy had struck the area. Hadn't someone said 'lightning never strikes twice in the same place'? Surely that applied to willy-willies too?

Not frightened, of course, but disliking the likelihood of an onslaught of viciously fast, spinning grains of sharpened rock fragments, she huddled down in her seat.

'Wish we had something to cover us with,' said Antony.

'Shouldn't be much of a thing,' David said, relaxed and only faintly interested in watching the developing spiral of sand.

At the last moment, the willy-willy picked up speed and hurtled across the ground towards the hill. It seemed almost attracted to the hole in the side of its target, the cave. For a few moments, it blew wildly across the face of the adit, seeming to reach inside. Helen was relieved that she wasn't there to take the brunt of the assault. It would have been an uncomfortable couple of minutes for the bishop, especially as he had no previous experience of the 'mini-tornado'.

There was a sudden loud crack; the willy-willy veered away in a confusion of clouds of dust.

As they looked up at the cave, there seemed to be a difference. David muttered a curse and switched on the engine. He flicked the windscreen wipers on and water flowed through to clean the screen.

They looked again.

The cave had changed.

Its profile now had a lean to it, a sag right on the top.

'My God, the roof's gone!'

David jumped out of the LandCruiser and ran up the hill with Antony at his shoulder. Helen followed as rapidly as she could.

The entrance to the cave was completely shut off.

'Bloody willy-willy dislodged something! Are you all right in there? Bishop Aldo!' David shoved a couple of times more and put an ear to the crack between two newly fallen rocks.

'Is he all right? Can you hear him?' Helen scrambled up alongside David, grabbing his shirt to keep her balance.

He took her hand and hauled her up to his side. 'Can't hear a bloody thing,' he said.

Antony started to pull at the rocks blocking the entrance.

'Keep shouting; we've got to know just where he is,' said Antony.

'No, don't shout!' Helen grabbed Antony's arm. 'If you shout you may bring more rocks down on him. He may be all right; maybe he's stunned. But don't shout.'

'Let's just get him out,' said David, as he hauled one heavy rock away.

'It would solve all our problems if he never gets out, though, wouldn't it.' Helen was startled to hear her own voice.

David and Antony stopped briefly to look at her, then turned back and continued to pull at the rock fall.

After ten minutes or so, Antony asked David to go back to Lakeview House and get Barry to come with something to work with. 'A crowbar, or something. And be quick!'

'I'll go with him,' Helen said. 'Get the First Aid stuff.' Helen had her ear to the wall of rocks. It seemed – just for a moment – that she might have heard something.

'Antony! Stop – be still! I think I heard him!'

They listened in silence for moments, a minute. Two minutes.

The cave was as silent as a grave.

Again.

David and Helen left in a swirl of dust.

CHAPTER 12

THE LANDCRUISER SCREECHED TO A STOP on the loose sand at the foot of the verandah steps. David, dusty and sweating from the drive, got out and ran up onto the verandah, where Chip and Teresa were sitting, sipping iced tea. Jack put down the book he was reading and stood up. Helen stumbled up the steps after David and waved at Jack as she hurried past him into the house.

'It's the bishop!' she said. 'In the cave!'

She passed Barry on his way out to see what the commotion was about and heard David's loud explanation.

'Got a willy-willy! The cave's fallen in! Fucking bishop's inside it!'

'Can you get at him? Is he OK?' Chip started to follow David into the house.

'Don't know. When we left we couldn't hear him. Need something to lever the rocks with – a crowbar or something?'

'Some bigger stuff?' Helen heard Barry's shout as Helen grabbed the First Aid box from her room; he was already moving in the direction of the cooling shed, clattering down the steps from the verandah.

'No time!' David called. He stopped and leant against a verandah post, his chest heaving, watching Barry.

Helen sat down on the edge of a chair, the First Aid box on her lap.

'Get me a drink, will you, Teresa?' David said.

Teresa looked at Helen. 'Yes, please. Me, too.'

Teresa went into the house and came back with two glasses of water. David drank his quickly, while Helen took a long sip and watched for Barry's return.

'I think you should wait here,' said Jack.

'They'll need me.' Helen indicated the box.

David finished his drink and went down the steps to meet Barry, who arrived huffing and puffing after running back from the shed. Barry had heard Helen's comment.

'No need for you to go, Helen. Could be nasty. I've done First Aid stuff here often enough.'

He took the box from her, looked inside. 'Not bad; I've got more stuff in the shed but this'll do for now.'

He gave David the two crowbars and a massive tyre lever. 'Come on David, I'll drive back.'

Without argument, David climbed into the passenger seat of the LandCruiser.

'Shall I come too?' Chip said. 'Do you need extra muscle?'

'No, not enough room. We may need to stretch him out. You stay here.'

'What about me?' said Jack.

'You too.' Barry was totally in charge.

'Thanks for the drink.' David raised a hand to Teresa, who was watching, tense and worried, with the two glasses in her hand.

Barry got into in the driving seat, and slammed the door. He switched the engine on. He let out a yell and opened the door.

'Bugger! Needs fuel!'

He let in the brake and raced the LandCruiser over to the fuel store.

'Should I contact the Flying Doctor Service?' Teresa said, anxiously looking at Helen who sat as patiently and as still as she could. Teresa waved her hands about vaguely, obviously concerned and frustrated that she had no role in the rescue.

Helen felt the same way.

'No, we just wait,' Jack said. 'Maybe everything will be all right. There's no need to worry any more as yet.' Jack calmed Teresa with his voice. Helen watched him exercise his skill. He could always calm her down too.

'You're right, Jack. Just wait. It's all we can do,' Helen said.

'Good thing Barry has all those tools.' Chip took a couple of steps forward so that he could see the LandCruiser, stationary outside the shed where the diesel was stored.

'Well, he'll need things like that for his work here,' Jack said.

The inconsequential conversation seemed to calm everyone down, Helen thought. 'But why is it taking so long?' She suddenly erupted, her patience gone.

They looked in the direction of the fuel store but Helen's attention moved further along, to the cooling shed.

She jumped up, almost toppling her chair, which Jack managed to catch.

'My God! He's left the door open!'

With instant understanding and a single leap, Teresa cleared the steps and ran full tilt towards the cooling shed. Helen watched, knowing that she couldn't run as fast as Teresa. Chip went down the steps and watched his sister's insane rush across the compound, puzzled and anxious.

'What's up with her?'

Jack suddenly understood. 'Oh dear, not in this heat! It's nothing, Chip – leave it to Teresa. Come and sit down with me.'

'No, she's really upset.'

As Chip set off in pursuit of Teresa; so did Helen, hurrying at first and then breaking into a run. Teresa was out of sight now, inside the cooling shed. They followed her through the open door. Teresa was standing quite still, her hands on her face with anxiety. She was over by the row of sinks, at the table supporting the long, black mound.

'Close the bloody door!' Teresa said, over her shoulder.

'It's closed. We shut it when we came in,' Helen said. She joined Teresa at the table. Chip followed her, stopping a couple of paces back, as Helen told him to do with a peremptory wave of her hand.

Helen touched the mound as Chip watched. She prodded it carefully, felt it with the palm of her hand. She drew back a handful of peat, and was still.

She looked around at Chip, suddenly aware that this was the first time he had been in the cooling shed. Chip moved cautiously towards her as though invited, but as though there was something about her stillness that made him want not to startle her, not to make a noise. Helen understood his uncertainty and turned back to her testing of the peat.

Teresa was at her side, equally still, equally absorbed.

As Chip came closer, Helen heard his sudden intake of breath.

'What the hell is that? Is it for real? Is it a carving or something?'

'It's a man, Chip.' Teresa said.

'A dead man!' Chip's voice was not loud but his astonishment made Helen turn to look at him.

'My God! It's real? A real man?'

'As real as you are are,' Helen said.

For a moment, no one spoke. Helen made a decision. 'This is where we found the crucifix, Chip. He had it with him.'

It was as though he didn't hear or understand what Helen had said. Chip's attention was fully focussed on the face of the dead priest.

'God, he's – well, almost beautiful, isn't he, the poor bastard. What happened to him? Is he a local guy? One of David's relations? Why is he here?'

'He's very old, not someone who died just recently. Antony knows about these things. It's four hundred years since he died, thereabouts.'

'Four hundred – ? Oh come on, Helen, that's a bit rich.'

'Maybe, but it's true.' She carefully replaced the peat shroud over the man's face, as Chip watched. She moved behind the table to look at the dial of the thermostat on the wall over the sink.

'I'm glad I spotted the door, Teresa,' she said. 'I was so afraid that the air might have got in. It's pretty hot out there.'

She glanced at Chip who, with a sudden frown, turned away from the body.

'Four hundred years – ? Hey, Teresa, did Helen know about – him – when she came to Italy?'

'Yes, of course. She found the body first. The crucifix was around his neck when they started examining him.'

He spun around to confront the two women, who were walking towards the door, ready to leave the body in peace again.

'Where the heck is Barry? Surely he's filled up the tank by now?' Helen looked towards the fuel store as she opened the shed door. The LandCruiser was still there.

If she had hoped to pacify Chip, she knew instantly that she had failed.

Chip grabbed Teresa' arm. 'So you knew about all this and didn't tell me? You had me stick my neck out for you when there was a dead body waiting in the background like something in a murder mystery? Who do you think I am,

Helen – Raymond Chandler? Was I supposed to get involved in your mystery and find the bad guys?'

By now, Chip's anger was boiling over. For a moment, Helen thought he might grab her, too. He turned sharply and strode off towards the house.

'Oh God, now we've something else to worry about,' said Teresa. She hurried after her brother.

Helen carefully secured the door and followed them. Chip was too far ahead of her to catch up, but she heard his attack on Jack as she reached the verandah.

'I suppose you knew all about that thing, too?' Jack stood up, visibly uncertain how to handle Chip's explosion.

'Yes, I knew. And you would have been told about it but for the arrival of your friend.'

'My friend!'

'Weren't you curious about where we'd found the crucifix?' said Teresa, who had arrived at the verandah almost at the same moment as Chip and was helping herself to a glass of iced tea. Helen had wondered about that, too.

'Curious? No, not really. You said it was in a cave. I'm no troglodyte.'

'Well, if you'd asked, maybe Helen would have told you.' Teresa laughed. Perhaps, Helen thought, she was trying too hard to relieve Chip's anger but it was clearly too much like making fun of him. Chip looked furious as he stormed off into the house.

Barry drove up at last, beeped the horn once, twice. Helen went down the steps to join David and Barry in the LandCruiser. After the scene with Chip, she wanted to make herself scarce.

'Chip knows about the body. I'm coming with you,' she said.

When they arrived at the foot of the hill, Antony waved to them to hurry.

'He's alive – I can hear him!'

'Are you sure?' Helen called out as she got out of the LandCruiser.

'He's OK,' said Antony. 'He's frightened, but he's unhurt. Just shaken.'

Barry scrambled up the scree with David. They pushed Antony aside, rather assertively, and looked at the fallen rocks. Helen decided that it was better if she and Antony got out of the way, so she waited as Antony slid down to the solid ground again, where they stood and watched.

After a couple of exchanges of ideas, Barry jammed a crowbar into a crack between two rocks and started to heave.

'If you can hear me, your Grace, get back away from here! I'm going to dislodge a bloody big rock and we don't want to hurt you.'

There was a faint voice from the cave. Helen and Antony smiled faintly at each other. The bishop was alive and responding.

Barry gave David another crowbar and they started to use both of them in the same crevice between two huge rocks. Slowly, the gap widened until one rock suddenly broke free and rumbled down the side of the hill, coming to a stop a couple of metres from Helen's feet.

The gap was wider now. But not wide enough to let anyone through.

'At least he'll be able to see,' said Helen. 'It won't be as frightening now there's some light in there.'

There was a sudden scream, which caused a small avalanche of loose rocks to slide down the hill.

'What's happened?' Antony headed back up the hill, but David raised a hand to stop him. There was an unexpected grin on David's face. Even Barry, sweating under the strain of working on the leverage needed to shift another rock, had a smile on his face.

'What was that scream?' Helen was frightened.

'The bishop. There's a snake in there.' David twisted his body to take a different angle on the crowbar.

'A snake?' Suddenly, Helen remembered the day she found the cave. She remembered the snake that had terrified her for a few moments. A King Brown snake. One of the deadliest snakes in Australia.

'It might be a venomous one! I saw a Brown snake here the day I found him!'

Barry stared at her for a moment and then bent to speak clearly through the widened crack between the rocks.

'Stand very still! Don't move, got it? Can you hear me? No, don't answer; keep absolutely still! Don't move a fucking inch, your Grace!'

The two men stopped their work, waited, listened. Down below, Helen and Antony waited too, their eyes and ears straining to know what was happening above them.

There was a faint moan from inside the cave.

'Stand still and shut up, your fucking Grace!'

The voice spoke again. Barry and David straightened up and laughed.

'It's gone,' David said to the others, waiting at the foot of the scree. 'Slid off behind a another rock at the back.'

'Nearly got this bugger!' Barry gave one more desperate heave on the crowbar and the massive rock moved slowly, reluctantly, to the edge of the platform outside the cave and tumbled, slid, rolled down to the ground below.

The rescuers cheered as the dusty shape of the Bishop appeared. He moved slowly, but upright and quite calm. As he crossed the entrance, he turned back and shook his head.

'I shan't do that again in a hurry,' he said. He made the sign of the cross as he turned away.

David helped Aldo down to Helen and Antony. Barry followed, brushing some of the dust off his shorts and tanktop.

'Can the cave be gone into again?' Helen said. 'I mean, it's of considerable interest to me.'

'Should be all right. Bit trickier to see from here, that's all.' Barry looked back up the hill. 'It's OK inside though.'

'Good.'

The small party dusted themselves off and piled into the LandCruiser. David drove.

'Better get home quickly. They'll be worried,' said Helen.

As indeed they were.

Chip was still in a fury when they got out of the LandCruiser.

He marched up to Helen and waved his arms about, for a moment too angry to speak.

'He's all right, Chip. Aldo's all right.'

'The hell with him! It's the other guy I want to know about!'

Aldo looked hurt when Chip seemed to dismiss his ordeal and went into the house, muttering about getting cleaned up. Helen, who saw the bishop's expression, sighed.

'I'll go and have a shower,' Antony said.

'No, I want some answers!' Chip gave Antony a shove. Not a forceful one, but Antony seemed to change his mind about the shower and sat down in one of the verandah chairs. Helen was glad that he was there.

'Why wasn't I told, Helen? Why the fuck wasn't I told about that guy in there?'

Helen wanted desperately to sit down, have a drink, and recover her wits after the last couple of hours. There was to be no respite. Barry went off with the LandCruiser, but Teresa joined Helen, looking determined.

'I did what seemed best, Chip,' Helen said. 'I hope that makes a difference?'

'No, it damn well doesn't! Do you realise that I put my job on the line and you didn't think it necessary to mention that you have a four-hundred-year-old corpse sitting – lying – here? Is that what you thought? It wasn't relevant?

'We were working in the dark, too,' Antony said. 'We didn't expect to find a body.'

As Helen and the others turned to listen to Antony, someone else had joined them.

Bishop Imbrogno stood in the doorway, his face and hands pink and wet. He was rubbing his hands slowly on a towel. 'A body?'

'Oh shit.' Antony stood up and moved closer to Helen, defensively.

'Let's all sit down.' Jack was in a managing mode again and the group slowly took its cue from him. Aldo stayed where he was, quiet, patient, a man very much accustomed to being informed fully and politely about events going on around him. Helen knew only too well how effective that could be.

Antony sat down by Helen's side. Chip and Teresa sat on the steps but Chip ostentatiously moved away from her when she attempted to link her arm through his.

'A body?' Aldo discarded the towel and spoke again, quietly, firmly. He pulled a chair into a central position and sat down.

'When we found the crucifix, it was around the neck of a dead man.' Helen spoke equally quietly, with relief in her voice. Now there were no secrets to guard.

'The thief?' Aldo said.

'Perhaps,' said Antony. 'But more likely the original owner. The body has lain there for four hundred odd years.'

There was silence. Aldo looked down at his hands, which he spread so that he could look more carefully at them. Helen thought he seemed unaware of what he was doing. He looked up at her.

'How do you know that?'

'We have scientific proof.'

Aldo nodded. Accepted what was said. 'I wish to see him.'

Helen took a deep breath and got up. She led the bishop down the steps and across the yard to the cooling shed. She closed the door behind them and led Aldo to the recumbent body. She gently lifted the covering peat from his face and stood aside.

Neither of them spoke until the bishop and Helen rejoined the group on the verandah.

'I want a clean white sheet,' Aldo said, 'to cover him. Do you have candles?' Barry nodded. 'Then arrange them, two at his head and two at his feet.

Still nobody spoke.

'I shall take him home to Italy. Barry, you have someone who drives a refrigerated truck?'

Barry nodded.

'Then contact him, say as little as possible. He must be here quickly. I shall contact Alitalia and say I am bringing home a dead tourist – '

Antony and Teresa exchanged a quick and rueful smile.

'The formalities can be arranged easily by the Vatican. Is he safe – fit to travel?' Antony nodded.

'Good. Then that is all arranged.'

'No, wait a minute, Aldo. It is not arranged!' With a quick and irritated gesture, Helen stood up. 'That body does not belong to you – it belongs to science. You involved yourself in identifying it, that's all. Nobody asked you to come here and nobody is going to hand over my discovery to you. Right? You understand that?'

Aldo, now a less foolish figure than he had seemed, took a seat. Helen sat down too.

'That body, dear lady, seems to be that of a priest of the Holy Catholic Church. Now do you understand? He must come home with me to Rome, to the Vatican, where he can be accorded all the honour due to him.'

'You mean stuck on exhibition in the bloody Vatican,' said Chip. 'It's not yours, Aldo, like Helen said. It's hers. She found it.'

'Finders keepers?' Antony's voice was barely audible, but when he looked up it was with something like awe on his face. 'You can't claim him now, Helen, not now.'

David spoke up. 'Put him on show in a church? Is that what you want?' David sounded angry too. 'And what would you scientists do with him, eh? Eh? Put him on show in some Australian museum? With a label on him: *Priest found in Western Australia by Doctor Helen Lytton.* Is that what you want to do, Helen?'

She shook her head. 'I don't know. Truly, I don't know.'

Antony slapped his hands on his knees. 'I get it! Now I understand! Taking this man back to Rome will be the making of you, won't it, Aldo? That's why you came here "on private business" – to get the crucifix and make your grab for a cardinal's hat! I've seen this played out so often in the University; ambition, Aldo, that's what it is, isn't it? Not religious fervour. Take a piece of historical jewellery home and swap it for a cardinal's robes. Now you can add a long-dead man to the trophies. God, you make me sick.'

As the others watched, the bishop slowly subsided in his chair, shaking his head.

'No, it won't do,' Helen said. 'This must stop. Whatever we decide, I have made my decision. I found the body; I was right. I can say "I told you so" to anyone who ever doubted that I could succeed in anything I take on.'

'Good on yer,' said Jack.

Helen glared at the little Italian who reminded her in his pomposity, and in his certainty, of her father.

'I have made my point. I found what I was looking for. I am free of the need to prove anything. Take it, Aldo; do what you like with it.'

'What about publishing, Helen? You will make your name with this discovery if you publish.' Antony was unpersuaded.

'I shan't publish anything, Antony. It's over. Over.' In her mind's eye, her father shrank to a small, a very small image, and vanished. 'Yes, it's over.'

'If you take the body,' said Antony, addressing the bishop, 'you must guarantee absolute silence about its provenance – where it was found. Can you do that? Otherwise there will be an intolerable fuss here.'

'I can assure you of my discretion,' said Aldo.

'No problem there,' said Chip. 'Aldo is used to keeping secrets, aren't you, Aldo?' They exchanged a long and serious, silent exchange.

'If anything does come out about it, then I shan't hesitate to reveal all I know about you,' said Chip. 'Everything. Understood?'

'Understood,' said the bishop.

Jack was puzzled. 'What do you know, Chip, that can harm the bishop?'

'He knows. We move in the same circles in Rome,' said Chip. He enforced his threat by holding Aldo's attention as he spoke. Helen could see just how powerful the threat was.

'Good gracious!' Jack had understood, Helen realised. Now he'd have something to think about.

'I must say – well, the Church will have its own good reasons to keep the whole business of this man secret, won't it?' said Chip.

'How do you mean?'

'Well, look, they're not going to want everyone to know that the Pope's authority came from a small group of aboriginal people who organised themselves well, are they?'

'What are you talking about?' The bishop looked disconcerted. He looked from Chip to Helen, to Antony, in search of clarification.

'This man,' Chip suddenly sounded authoritative as he pointed across to the cooling shed, 'had more influence on your Church than he had on the local people, Aldo. That won't go down too well in the Vatican, will it?'

In the silence that followed, Helen realised for the first time that there was still a great deal that Bishop Imbrogno was in the darkness about. 'I think we had better talk to Aldo in private, Chip,' she said. She stood up and led the way inside. Chip and the bishop followed her.

'Anyone for a drink?' Barry asked. Nobody looked at him, or answered.

When Helen and Chip returned, half an hour later, they were both smiling.

'Aldo's suffering from shock,' Helen said.

'Or acute cowardice, having to take back to Rome the news we have given him. Shock-horror stuff for the Vatican, I reckon,' said Chip. 'He's not exactly going back the great hero. He won't be trying on a cardinal's hat for size.'

'Either way, he's having a lie down,' said Helen.

Now that the future of the dead priest had been resolved, Helen felt easier and happier than she had since its discovery.

Teresa and Chip were talking comfortably with each other, she was glad to see, and Antony seemed reconciled to the loss of scientific kudos for his part in the discovery. Perhaps it had been too much for all of them; too much they didn't understand.

Only David seemed less satisfied. He had left the verandah and was standing over by the fence, his hands holding onto the spaces in the cyclone wire, looking for all the world, she thought, as though he were a prisoner in his own country.

CHAPTER 13

PATIENCE WAS A DIFFICULT ART TO PRACTISE, Helen decided. After a lifetime, or so it seemed, of sitting at a machine watching satellite photographs unravel a few mysteries, she found herself with a need for a greater degree of patience than she had ever felt before.

While the bishop slept far into the morning, Lakeview House moved to its own rhythm. Barry and David fiddled with the ute. Jack planned what they should eat and helped organise lunch; Teresa did some of it but the men tended to expect to be in charge of barbecues and so it was today.

'I'll be glad when it's all over.' Teresa came out and sat with Helen and Chip, looking towards the cooling shed, as Helen had found herself doing too.

'Yes. Won't take long, I think. Once the bishop's up and about. Soon be over.'

'Will he get his promotion, do you reckon?' Teresa's voice was amused.

'Maybe,' said Chip. 'Depends on how quiet they can keep everything, I suppose.'

Antony came out and passed the others with a quiet 'Hi there' as he went down the steps and wandered off in no particular direction. Maybe just walking for the sake of stretching his legs, Helen thought. Nice man. Hope he isn't too disappointed.

'I thought things between you and Antony were heading somewhere,' she said to Teresa. Hope he isn't going to be disappointed.' Even as she said the words, Helen realised how unlike her it was to intrude into anyone's private life. And in Teresa's brother's company, at that. 'I'm sorry – '

'No, don't be.' Teresa stretched her arms above her head, her attention and Helen's now diverted to the tall and lanky frame of the scientist striding along the perimeter of the compound.

'I didn't mean to be nosy,' Helen said.

'You aren't being. I like him. A lot, as a matter of fact. But I like Ian too. More maybe.'

'You do seem to be avoiding Antony. Is that necessary?'

'I reckon it will make the point, eh?'

Teresa stood up as Antony turned and headed back towards the house. 'I'll go and have a shower, I think.'

Antony wore, to Helen's embarrassment, a very sad expression when Teresa passed him without speaking. It was as though Antony had been watching her move around but didn't know how to approach her. Whatever Antony had hoped for, it clearly wasn't going to happen.

A pattern of early morning use of the bathrooms had long been established; everybody was considerate, towels were taken to the laundry and suds were mopped up in the showers. Conversations this morning were about almost any-thing except the imminent solution to the problem which occupied most of their minds.

Only Barry seemed to feel free of the burden. Helen thought he was one of those people who decided to leave decision-making to others, on the grounds that they knew best. They would let him know if they wanted him to do anything.

Jack was already taking a nap on the verandah, his face hidden under Helen's straw hat. Even Chip seemed close to drifting off to sleep.

Teresa was being a bit tiresome about Antony, Helen thought. When she had seen Antony coming back, surely Teresa need not have turned on her heel and gone straight back inside the house? Despite the rebuff, Antony sat down with Helen and they soon become involved again in a discussion about a common interest in the movement of surface soil, loess, around the world. Chip was asleep very soon after they started.

At eleven o'clock, with still no sign of Bishop Imbrogno, Teresa came out and sat down at a distance from the others. Within a couple of minutes she was engrossed in a new murder story as she sipped iced tea. Barry and David were sitting in the red dirt behind the ute, where they sheltered from the sun and drank icy cold beer.

'I think I'll check out – things – in the cooling shed, Helen,' Antony said.

This had become a ritual every morning and afternoon. She noticed that Antony seemed averse to calling it 'the body' now. As he stood up, she got up too; maybe moving around in the sun wouldn't be quite as oppressive as it seemed. They walked slowly across the yard. Antony unlocked the door and they both stood for a moment, enjoying the chill of the air as it challenged the heat flowing through the open door.

'Funny smell in here, have you noticed?' Antony was casual about it, but Helen sensed a note of alarm.

'Oh Antony, it – he isn't, well, going off, is he? Oh Christ, not that!' Her voice was a whisper. She didn't want Barry and David to hear and they were only a few metres away with the ute.

'No, it's not that kind of smell. Sorry, didn't mean to alarm you.' Antony switched on the light above the cutting table where the peat-clad body lay. He bent over, and gently lifted the loose peat away from the face.

'What kind of a smell, then?'

'Oh, I don't know exactly. We've noticed it before. Sweet, yes it's sweet. Can't put a name to it. Seems to be coming from – this, though.'

'Not soap? Not something Barry uses for disinfectant?' Helen looked around to see if there were any open containers by the sink. There was nothing.

'No, it's different from that. Pleasant, though. You can't smell it?'

'No, but I don't have a very well-developed sense of smell. Is it a worry?'

'Oh no. Not at all. It's just a little odd.'

'Probably something in the peat, do you reckon?'

'Maybe so, but I can't pin it down. Still, the vegetation up here's different, I suppose.'

They looked at the face of the long-dead man. Helen marvelled again at how the man seemed to be asleep, at peace with himself.

'Does he look like a priest to you?' she said.

Antony smiled. 'I don't really know what a priest is supposed to look like, do you?'

'No. Chapel people tended to look pretty severe, I remember.' A brief memory raced across her mind: her father going to the Chapel at the corner of the street and bringing home the minister to help him upbraid her for telling lies. She had been to the pictures with a friend on a night when she was supposed to stay home and help her mother. Forty-five years later, the humiliation stung and tears filled the corners of her eyes.

Antony had seen her reaction and he abruptly turned away. He must think I find the body moving, Helen decided; and I do, it's a fact. A fact. I must concentrate on the facts, she thought.

263

'Maybe that smell is making my hay fever come back,' she said, aware that she spoke unconvincingly. Antony said nothing.

They covered the body again, locked the door behind them and walked through the heat back to the verandah.

'Hey, I've got an idea!' Teresa's voice was bright and cheerful.

It made Helen realise just how oppressed everyone had sounded the night before, weighed down by the responsibility of making a good decision.

'Let's try to forget about – Himself – and just sit around and tell tall stories, and sing a little, and – I don't know, enjoy the space the sleepy old bishop is giving us? OK? Come on, let's loosen up a little!'

David caught on quickly to the idea. He went indoors and brought out a radio. He turned the dial until he found some country and western music. Heigh-ho-ing and whooping, Teresa grabbed David's arm and spun him around in what looked to Helen more like something choreographed for the Whirling Dervishes – but then she could barely dance a quickstep at the best of times.

They started clapping to the rhythm of the song as David and Teresa danced along the verandah, her skirt flying and David's open shirt flapping as though it were on a clothes line in a strong wind.

The song stopped and somebody on the radio started talking.

After a few seconds, David lowered the sound, waiting for the next record to be played. Teresa plonked down on the verandah steps, hot and temporarily exhausted.

'Here, drink this.' Chip handed her a glass of iced tea.

Teresa sipped it, squeezing her lips together at the acidity of the slice of lemon which floated on top.

'Well, I don't think I can contribute much to the jollity, but I'll gladly give you my party piece,' said Jack. Helen watched him with affection as he settled himself into a chair and recited the full length of a Banjo Paterson poem, acting the parts with as many different voices as were called for.

The applause was genuine; especially from Barry, who immediately offered to entertain the others and did so by humming *The Sailor's Hornpipe* and doing a version of the traditional dance, flexing his ankles and twisting his legs around in rapid succession. It was rather comical but nobody laughed, until he finished and remarked, puffing with the exertion: 'Always put my wife in mind of an emu gone off its rocker.'

When the laughter subsided, Helen said: 'Is it long since your wife died?'

'Yeah. Too long. Nice woman; you'd have liked her. Had a bit of humour about her too. This place, you know? Lakeview House? Lake view? Her idea, that was.'

'An odd name for it, surely,' said Antony.

'Well, yes. She had a good laugh about it. Got the name from the old records. Seems it's a fair translation of its original name. Thought it a bit of a lark to keep the name – in English.'

'The original name?' Helen sat upright.

'It had an aboriginal name?' Now David looked interested.

'That's right. Seems it had a name that meant the same thing. "lake view". Can't see it myself.'

'But don't you see how significant that is!' Helen jumped up. 'For Heaven's sake, if it had that name, then there must have been a lake here – somewhere – some time! It proves my case! Doesn't it? Doesn't it?'

265

'It doesn't prove anything, Helen, but it's a nice point. Well worth mentioning when you write it up,' said Antony.

'If you write it up,' said Teresa. It was meant to be a joke, but the comment made Helen's excitement change to uncertainty and she sat down again.

'It's your turn now, Antony.' Teresa smiled at him. Helen could have sworn he turned pink under the tan which his work and the present conditions had created.

'I don't have much in the way of talent for this sort of thing, but my former wife – ' He glanced at Teresa, who immediately found something interesting to look at on her fingernails. 'Well, Angie said it was OK. My party piece, I suppose. She used to make me do it when we had her family over for dinner. God, I hated – Still, bear with me. Here goes.'

Quietly, but with increasing confidence, Antony began to sing.

Helen, who always claimed she wasn't musical, didn't know what it was but guessed it was by Mozart or Schubert. It was a pretty, delicate sort of song and he sang it in German. To her surprise, Antony's singing voice was quite unlike the voice he used normally; it seemed much higher, lighter, and altogether splendid.

When the song ended, Antony glanced around at the faces of his colleagues, and saw that they were moved. Helen watched his face change, and the blush deepened.

'My mother was German,' he said, as though to brush away his embarrassment.

'I already did my thing,' Teresa said. 'I dance like Ginger Rogers, right? And David makes a very good Fred Astaire.' The voice on the radio was still talking. Teresa switched it off.

'Don't look at me,' said Chip, laughing. 'All I can do is Judy Garland and Teresa'll kill me if I do it again.'

'Too right I will. Going over rainbows is definitely not for my family.'

For a moment, it seemed the entertainment was over.

'Tell us a story, David.' Teresa said.

'I thought I was Fred Astaire?' He grinned, but sat down and drank a deep swig of beer. 'All right then. Once upon a time, there were three bears – ' In the laughter that followed, those who were without drinks got them, and they settled down again, quietly.

'David?' Helen held out a hand, encouraging him.

'I've been thinking. About that story I was telling you – the one with the Great Lizard. You know, that man in there – ' He jerked a thumb in the direction of the cooling shed. 'He will have heard the story, too. Funny, that. Dead four hundred years and me not yet thirty and we both heard the same story. Funny that.'

'The story?' Helen nudged him with the words.

'I don't know that I remember it any better than last time. I wouldn't be able to look my uncle's uncle in the face, you know? He made me memorise that story and half a dozen – a dozen others until I knew them backwards. Then I went to school down in Perth and I can remember more of your kind of stuff,' this with a nod to Jack 'like Banjo Paterson poetry than the secret, sacred stories of the Arundijilaba. I am the "keeper of the stories" and I don't remember them.' He shook his head and fell silent.

'The keeper of the stories.' Antony repeated the phrase.

'Secret, sacred stories, David?' Teresa was clearly intrigued by the idea; her question relieved Helen of the need to ask.

'Yes, that I do remember. That's what they were. The Arundijilaba were special people, right? We were the only people. We were – I don't know – specially chosen by the Great Lizard.'

'Chosen for what?' Teresa should be careful not to press too far. Helen warned her with a glance, but there was no stopping Teresa now.

'Do you mean like the Jews?' she said.

'No, not like them. I don't think so. I don't really know what it meant. Chosen. Favoured. The Great Lizard chose us to give something special to.'

He was silent again.

'Tell us the story, then. The one you told before.'

David closed his eyes. As he spoke, the stumbling memories seemed to become more sure-footed; only the difficulty of language, it seemed to Helen, made him hesitate.

'There was this Great Lizard, see. The Great Lizard takes care of us. He lives alone in the place beyond the Arundi Mountains where nobody has ever been. He has a name but I can only speak it in a whisper. Say his name aloud and the river sinks down and the mountains drop back into the earth and the sky falls.

'He gives us the law and we have to do what he says. That way some day the Arundijilaba will live over the Lizard Mountain with him. If we do as he says he sends us enough to eat, and water to drink. There are animals and fruit and grains in plenty for food and our children grow strong. If we ask him, the Great Lizard lets us off when we don't follow the law right and part of that means that we don't get into fights with people who don't do what the law says either.

'Obey the law and the Great Lizard will take care of us.'

His voice by now had the lilting sing-song cadence of a child who repeats a lesson learned by rote. David stopped speaking, and opened his eyes. For a moment, nobody spoke.

'Amen.' Barry leant across the table and took another tin of beer.

The heat of the verandah seemed to Helen to intensify in the silence. She could hear nothing at all, except the sound of Barry drinking from the tin, and Jack sniffing slightly.

With a sudden shock, Teresa turned sharply towards Barry, nudging Helen with her elbow by accident as she did so. 'What did you say?'

Helen saw that Barry was startled. All eyes were turned to Teresa, who was sitting up, her face alert and excited.

'When?'

'Just now. You said – '

'Amen. I said Amen.'

'Why, Barry? Why did you say Amen?'

Barry shuffled his feet, embarrassed by the question and the attention.

'I don't know. It sounded like a prayer, I suppose. Haven't been to church for yonks but I reckon it must have sounded like a prayer. Anything wrong with that?' He sounded truculent now.

Teresa leapt to her feet, looked around at the others, wildly. Chip looked completely bewildered. Helen had a glimmer of understanding but no more than that. There was an elusive thought in her mind struggling to get out, but she wanted desperately to make it go away.

'For goodness' sake!' Teresa pleaded, her arms flung wide. 'Don't you see?'

Helen slowly stood up.

'It was a prayer, Barry,' Helen said, but her eyes were on Teresa, not Barry. And certainly not on David; she couldn't look at David.

'Yes! Yes! And not just any prayer – that prayer!' Teresa clung onto the verandah post, so excited she was almost laughing.

'What prayer? I don't understand.' Jack was upset; he had a totally baffled expression.

'The Lord's Prayer.' Helen said it. The thought had found words and the words had found speech. 'That's why Barry said 'Amen', because he's the only one of us who's had any contact since childhood – am I right? – with religion. What David's story sounded like to him was The Lord's Prayer.' She sat down, quickly.

'Well, I'll be buggered!' Barry was quite pleased to have spotted the resemblance, Helen thought, but did he see its significance? She doubted it.

Teresa looked to Helen for confirmation of her guess. Helen smiled faintly and shrugged her shoulders. I don't know what to say next, the gesture meant.

Antony had so far said nothing and had reacted much more cautiously than the women. He was still not convinced. He asked David to repeat his story, phrase by phrase, and Antony himself (with only a little prompting from Barry) said the words of the Lord's Prayer parallel with David's recitation, intersecting phrase with phrase. There seemed to be no discrepancies. When he had finished, he looked around the table.

'It's a pretty good match,' he said.

'No, it isn't! Where's that bit at the end?' Jack seemed keen to dispel the discomfort they were all showing. 'You know: "For thine is the Kingdom, the power and the glory. For ever and ever. Amen." ' For a second, Helen was relieved. Barry was shaking his head.

'No, that's a Protestant bit. We don't use it. It stops earlier for Catholics.'

'The body; the priest.' Chip's voice slowed, as his excitement gave place to what sounded like awe, and certainly speculation. 'Can it be?'

Helen knew they had to move carefully through this terrifying tangle of possibilities. Logic, that's what was called for. Logic. She looked to Antony for support; he returned her appeal with a firm nod.

Helen filled her glass with iced tea. When she spoke, it was with clarity and precision. She was aware of Jack's attention and his pride in the way she was taking control.

'What we are thinking is this, am I right? The story David has told us is a – what? A paraphrase? A retelling of the Lord's Prayer. Right? And yet this is one of the sacred stories David was asked to learn by heart, to carry as the living legacy of his people. It was important, vitally important for his people. Is that right, David?'

David looked scared. 'Yes, that's right.'

'It seems to us, then, likely that David's grandfather's grandfather – ' She looked at David for confirmation of the correct use of his lineage, and he sketchily smiled approval. 'might have learned the sacred story, the Lord's Prayer, from the priest who was here with them four hundred years ago.'

'No, you mustn't say that, Helen. We can't make any such assumptions. It's not – decent. It's not – '

'Not politically correct, Antony?' Chip said.

Teresa was sitting down now, all her exuberance gone. 'What are we saying here? I don't think I really want to know.'

Helen remembered something, a phantom wisp of a memory – something Barry had said. Something about something David had told them.

As the others sat struggling with this new concept, Helen tried to remember the incident. They had all been talking about David's tribal history, his Dreamtime, and Teresa – yes, it was something Teresa said. She had said -

'Teresa, do you remember when we were talking about David's beliefs and you said something about women?'

The memory slowly resurfaced in Teresa's mind. 'Oh, yeah, sure.'

'What exactly did you say?' Helen tried to keep the urgency out of her voice. She saw Jack sit up straighter; he could hear that this was important.

'Well,' Teresa said. 'He was talking about all those hierarchies – you know, men doing this, men doing that – and I said something about women having been of no significance. I think. Is that what you mean?'

'Yes!' Helen was visibly excited now. 'Yes, you did and what did David say? Do you remember, David? Oh, please remember?'

David didn't like this at all, Helen could tell, but it was too late now to cool down her passion for getting at this last bit of the truth.

'I told her some sort of scrap from another story. Maybe I shouldn't go into it.'

'You must, David. It's too late to back out now.' Helen spoke so firmly that David didn't argue.

'I told her that there was one woman who was important, or at least – ' As his hesitation grew, the attention of the others intensified. At last, David looked up at Helen and finished his statement. 'This one woman was important and so was one of her children.'

'Mary, Mother of God!' Barry's whisper was shocked. With those words said, Helen shook her head and subsided, afraid to go further now. But she had to go on.

Helen asked, in a voice so calm as to sound perfunctory, 'David, there's something else. Wasn't there something about that body, something you said your grandfather said, about three days? I can't quite recall what it was?'

David didn't move his eyes from Helen's face. 'I said that the teaching was that a man's body could stay out of the grave for three days, unless – '

'Unless?' David had hesitated again.

'Unless he could come back to life. And that was not an impossibility.'

'The Resurrection?' Barry leapt to his feet. 'What the hell is this? What are you saying? Is this some sort of mocking God you're doing? Or the Catholic church? I'm not a good Catholic, far from it, but look here, mate – ' This was hurled at Helen. 'I'm not having you lot taking the mickey out of the church. I won't have it, right?'

Jack mumbled a few 'Now, now's' and Barry sat down, grumbling noisily.

This time Antony took the lead. 'It's nothing like that, Barry. I'm afraid it's not you who should be worried, even offended.'

He looked at David, on whose face Helen could read cold comprehension. 'What we are all afraid of saying is that there seems a possibility that David's antecedents learned some of their beliefs from a Catholic priest. That some of his traditional stories are Catholic prayers.'

'You are saying that I have no Dreamtime, no aboriginal Dreamtime. That my Dreamtime, the Dreamtime of the

Arundijilaba, is nothing but a heap of missionary's prayers.' David seemed icy calm to Helen.

'David, listen to me. Bear with us, please; we're as embarrassed and puzzled by all this as we can be.' Antony spoke quietly. 'I hope it isn't true but if it is, and if we can establish the fact that it is true, then you must remember that all beliefs rub off on other beliefs.'

'What do you mean?'

'Well, look. When the Christian church got going in England, whenever that was, there were all sorts of things going on. People held all sorts of beliefs.' Antony waved a hand around, vaguely.

Jack came to his rescue. 'Roman gods, Druids and things, is that what you mean?'

Antony nodded vigorously, relieved to get a little help. 'Yes, that sort of thing. There were celebrations going on at different times of the year; all sorts of rituals. I can't remember the details but I remember my father was quite interested in them once. Something to do with spiritual healing, I think. Anyway, the point is that the early church didn't make people give up all those rituals. They were too clever for that. No, they adapted them; made them into church rituals and church celebrations.'

'That's why there are still differences in the way people do things in the very same church, David; I've read something about it. Catholics in South America, for instance, behave very differently from those here.' Jack smiled encouragingly, but David was still stone-faced.

'My mother, too. Now she was German. I mentioned that, I think?' Antony struggled to keep David's attention. 'She told me all sorts of things that the Church had adopted from pre-Christian times. I can't remember any of them offhand, blast it,

274

but there are plenty of them. Even Christmas itself was based, I think, on a pagan celebration. Not the birth of Christ, of course, just when it was celebrated and some of the details of the rituals.'

'It's a proven fact,' Jack said.

That was always enough for us, Helen thought.

'So if – and it is still "if" David – if this priest did bring a few prayers into your tribe's life – ' Antony tried, without much success, to diminish the probable impact of the priest's presence. 'If that happened, then it was your people who adapted his words to fit their own circumstances, do you see that? Their own belief system simply took on a few new ideas, rituals, that's all.' Antony sat back, exhausted.

David looked unconvinced. David was unconvinced. Helen thought what a dreadful shock it must be for anyone to be told that all their lifelong traditions, even if he had himself abandoned them, were brought in from the outside. And, in David's case, perhaps it was an even sharper sting that the Dreamtime had been corrupted by a white man.

'It's nothing to do with race, you know that, David,' she said. 'He could just as easily have been another aboriginal, from another tribe far away. He made himself important enough to be taken notice of, that's all. His ideas must have seemed good enough, must have seemed to fit in with your grandfather's grandfather's ideas. Maybe they sort of encapsulated them; maybe he already had a traditional belief in the same sort of God. Maybe your people were already 'special, chosen' by reason of what they had believed for generations.'

David looked at Helen, silently, for a long time. She hoped he could see that she was groping in the dark but trying to be honest, not attempting to push him into a safer course.

Finally he nodded. 'Maybe; maybe.'

As it was lunchtime, the discussion faded away into silence. Antony and Helen talked for a while, when everyone else had gone off to their rooms. There was still no sign of the bishop waking up. Frankly, Helen was glad he was not there. The latest revelations – if that was what they were – needed to be mulled over by the people involved in finding the body. They did not need the input just now from an 'interested party'; if at all.

Teresa wanted to get some rest, she said, without having lunch, so she had only a sandwich in her room. Jack made a quick meal – scrambled eggs on toast – for the others, although David ate hardly anything. He sat alone on the verandah steps at the other side of the house from where the others were.

Barry once or twice attempted to get a conversation going but gave up soon and retired to play video games with the visiting pilot, who was observing his usual custom and keeping himself to himself, as Barry explained it.

They didn't see the bishop again all day. Barry reported during the afternoon that Tom had torn himself away from the video games and had been to ask Aldo when he wanted to go back down south and the bishop had said he would make his arrangements 'in a few hours'.

In the early evening, Teresa and Jack organised a quiet barbecue meal. The bishop was awake now. He asked for a sandwich in his room, which Barry was happy to provide, along with the Wedgwood cup and saucer and a pot of tea.

After they had eaten, the air grew cool and the group moved indoors; all except David and Chip who went off through the gate, walking in the red glow of the desert evening. Chip seemed to be talking animatedly, David listening quietly. Helen watched them go.

The rest of the visitors sat in the living room, quiet at first, reluctant – or so it seemed to Helen – to start again a conversation which none of them wanted to have.

After a while, Chip and David rejoined the group. And still nobody spoke.

CHAPTER 14

S UDDENLY DAVID LAUGHED. 'I was bloody upset when I thought about this bloke writing my Dreamtime. But, you know, those letters he wrote home – the bloody Church owes something really important to the Arundijilaba!'

So Chip's quiet chat with David had accomplished something, Helen thought. At least David could see both sides of the equation.

Chip gently swirled his drink around in the glass – not the best thing to do with decent wine; Helen's father would have been shocked. Chip's face was locked in an expression she could not read: part puzzlement, part shock, and not a little excited. She wondered if all that added up to Chip being scared out of his wits.

'Did you notice the smell again, Helen?' Antony reached across her to fill his hand with a few peanuts from a dish Teresa had brought out.

'Yes, I did this time; can't put a name to it. Odd, though.'

'A smell?' Chip still swirled his drink but he looked up from his contemplation of the floorboards.

'The body; some kind of sweetish odour. Not due to anything I can pin down. I mean, in that place, he's as safe as houses. Safer.' Antony spoke with difficulty through some of the nuts. 'We check him out every so often, that's all.'

'The odour of sanctity,' Chip said. 'Oh God.' This time, the wine glass stopped. Chip's eyes were round with shock.

'What?' Helen asked, puzzled.

'It's the man in the Vatican – when he was telling me about the other crucifixes he got talking about St. Ignatius and

St. Francis Xavier and all the other saints. There's thousands of them.'

'Yes, I know.'

'I don't like this. I'm out of my depth here.' Chip's voice had risen a little. Teresa, who had gone in search of another drink, came back into the living room end of the house, clearly alerted by whatever it was in Chip's voice that was different.

'They have some of them in the Vatican. You know, dead ones.'

Helen felt she knew where Chip was going. 'That's not like our priest, though, Chip. Ours was in a bog for four hundred years.'

'I don't know about that sort of thing, Helen. I know only what I was told. He said that there are a couple of things that suggest some dead person is a saint, and one is that they give off a sweet smell. It was sweet in there, wasn't it? That smell? I noticed that; I thought it was soap or a room deodorant or something. The "sweet odour of sanctity", the Vatican guy said. I'm sorry, but he did say it.'

'Oh come on now.' Helen was shocked, but Antony seemed to be enthralled by the notion.

'And the body isn't corrupt.' Barry said. 'I remember that bit – the body of saints don't corrupt! Is our bloke corrupt, Helen? What does corrupt mean? Gone rotten, isn't it? Well, he isn't, is he?'

Barry was agitated, frightened. As the implications of what was being said sunk in, the group started talking all at once.

'No! We can't go on with this!' Teresa put down the wine bottle. 'Is this right, Helen? Are we seriously talking about that man – oh grief! – being a saint? The genuine article?'

'I don't know and I don't want to know!' Helen wanted to go away. She stood up but stopped when Antony spoke. Jack

279

made a couple of steps in her direction, as though to follow her, but changed his mind and sat down.

'I don't believe in saints,' Antony said firmly. 'Nor any other kind of mythical creature.'

'But let's face it, Antony, what we might have here,' said Teresa, summing up, 'is Saint John Craven?'

'I never thought it would be this complex a situation.' Chip was squeezing his hands as though he could mould some kind of answer with them.

'Wait.' Helen left the room briefly and returned carrying the crucifix in the box she had found for it. She gave the box to Chip, who very promptly put it down on the coffee table.

'Take it,' Helen said. 'Take it back to Rome, Chip. I don't want anything more to do with it.' She sat down.

'Maybe that's for the best,' Jack said slowly, turning back to the kitchen. Helen watched him go, knowing that he would be happier pottering around, mixing drinks or tidying up than struggling any longer with these awful problems.

'Look, I want to make my position clear.' Helen stood up and walked over to the window. 'I have no wish to find out anything else about the body. My belief about the existence of the bog is substantiated and that is all I care about. I have no knowledge of church things and absolutely no interest in them.'

Antony put the tips of his fingers together and rubbed his hands against his lips, thinking.

'I think we must sort out our priorities, Helen. All of us. Do you still intend to publish?'

Helen was startled. Her eagerness to be rid of the body, crucifix and all, had not allowed her to think again about the scientific aspects of the discovery she had made. She looked at Antony, trying to think clearly.

Jack carried a bottle of port to the coffee table. On his tray were clean glasses, more nuts, table napkins.

It seemed that everyone would wait for Helen's answer. She took a glass and filled it. She took a sip. Nobody spoke.

After a few moments, and another sip, Helen wiped her mouth with a table napkin.

'I am sixty-three years old. My career is over. I was right; the cave is there, the bog is there. I do not need to publish. It is enough to know I was right.'

Jack took her hand and squeezed it, affectionately. 'I have no interest whatsoever in what we found,' he said. I'll be happy to see this – adventure – end.'

'I'm damn sure I want it over.' Barry drank from his tin of beer. 'I'm a pretty bloody lousy Catholic and I don't understand much of all this but I do know if he's a bloody saint I want him off my property.'

There was a quiet cough from the door. Aldo Imbrogno stood there, scrubbed and shiny. 'You want me off your property, did you say, Barry? I am sorry to have been such a nuisance. I am ready now to make the arrangements for removing both myself and your other guest.'

The mood of the group lightened a little.

'That's not what I was saying at all,' said Barry, who looked as if he had been caught out in a lie. Helen thought he had been.

'We were talking about – ' Antony spoke, but Helen got in quicker.

'Other things, Aldo. Publication, amongst them.'

Antony nodded. He seemed effectively distracted from whatever he had been going to say. Helen felt relieved. Publication could be very important to him. To his career. Helen wondered if he were thinking about the acclaim he would have received for the delicate work of disinterring the body, for his quick thinking about its preservation. If he passed up on this opportunity, then he would not be able to refer to it in the future; it seemed that whatever decision they made today would bind them all for ever.

Antony put down his glass. 'I have no religious beliefs. If anything, I am anti-religious and pro-science. I don't want to be involved in some mad rush to make a Lourdes out of this place. I don't want to create an opportunity for any church to increase its membership. I won't publish.'

'Well, I think it's a darn shame.' Teresa had not taken any more wine. She stood apart from the others, looking agitated and unhappy. 'I mean, this is like Machu Picchu; it's like King Tut's tomb. Not everybody finds a buried saint, do they? And we just let him go, just like that?' She grabbed a handful of peanuts, held them for a moment and put them back in the dish. 'Well, I guess I didn't find him. It's not for me to say what we should do. I just think it's a pity not to get some credit for it. But I go along with whatever you all say.'

Aldo again coughed gently and politely.

'I think you may be going rather too far, Teresa, my dear. You said "a saint". Establishing that takes many years and much argument.'

'There's a smell in there,' Barry said. 'You know, the odour of sanctity?'

Aldo's brow furrowed. Helen couldn't decide whether the bishop looked more puzzled than excited, but certainly both emotions were there.

'The odour of sanctity, really? You have been reading a great deal into this fortuitous discovery, I think.'

The bishop smoothed his hand over his head, moved forward and pulled a chair into a central position amongst the group. 'Perhaps we can go and check this out?' He spoke to Antony.

'No, not now.' Antony was firm, dismissive. This was not the bishop's move.

'But the other priests were saints, weren't they?' Helen wished Chip would just shut up, let this difficult conversation cease. 'I mean, Ignatius Loyola, Francis Xavier?' And if this is John Craven – why wouldn't he be a saint?'

'And his body hasn't corrupted, has it?' Barry spoke with force.

The bishop raised a hand to stop them. Helen was surprised to see that his hand was trembling.

'No, no! Please! This kind of talk is dangerous. Stop!'

The voices stilled. Helen looked around. She took over. Time to be in charge again.

'I want the body to go back with you to Rome, Aldo,' she said. 'I have no objection to that as long as you can guarantee that there will be no publicity.'

Helen looked at David. He shook his head.

'Well, I guess you decide what to do with it.' Chip looked relieved, Helen thought. She could imagine him reporting back that there would, at least, be no trouble from the Australian end.

Helen was thinking clearly now. 'I believe we must send the crucifix back to Rome with Chip. I suggest we ask him to get – his boss – ?'

Chip seemed to anticipate what her next suggestion would be.

'The Australian Ambassador,' he said, and Helen thought she saw his eyes light up slightly at the thought of having to deal directly with such an exalted person.

'Yes, the Ambassador,' said Helen. 'Chip must ask him to arrange – not you, Aldo, the Australian government must do this – with whomever is interested – the return of the body to the Church. To Rome.'

'Let them decide if he's Saint John Craven SJ.' Jack's words shocked Helen.

'Oh don't think that for a moment, Jack! I won't have it!' Helen was surprised by how cross she was.

'I think I can undertake everything necessary now,' said Bishop Imbrogno. 'I can contact the authorities here – ' Helen looked up sharply and Aldo added, carefully, 'with the guidance of Chip, of course. Together we can arrange for the removal of – your discovery – within a few hours, I feel sure.'

The discussions went on for a while but eventually everyone seemed satisfied. It was agreed that Tom would fly Chip and the bishop back to Perth the next day. Teresa would carry Antony back to Perth, a prospect which seemed to embarrass her but please Antony.

Chip was to fly back to Rome in the Air Force plane, taking the crucifix with him. There, he would talk with his boss, Gus – and the Australian Ambassador – right away. Meanwhile, Aldo would make a few discreet telephone calls and arrange for the body to be put on an Alitalia flight to Rome, once Barry's truck driver had reached the airport with its valuable cargo, which would be crated by Barry under supervision by Antony. The Ambassador would be urged to have waiting the necessary clearance for the body to leave and to be received in secrecy in Rome. Travel arrangements – security, maintaining the appropriate temperature, and other protective measures – would be the responsibility of Antony and Chip together.

Helen asked Aldo and Chip to observe the strictest secrecy about the negotiations, at least as far as she and the other people in the group were concerned. Nobody wanted publicity, once a decision had been taken in Rome about just how the body of the dead priest would be dealt with.

The decision having been made and everyone seemingly satisfied by them, the group went off to their beds, all of them, to Helen's relief seemingly more lighthearted than they had been before.

Even David seemed to Helen to be a great deal less stressed.

The mood the next morning was cheerful, courteous and much relieved. The bishop got on the telephone and rang several contacts in Rome. There seemed to be no insuperable problems. The excitement and worry of the past few days was over.

Antony sat on the verandah with Helen and Jack after breakfast, drafting notes to show his father about what had been decided and why. He told them that he knew that Peter would agree absolutely that the decision to hand the body back to the church was the right one.

Both Teresa and Chip slept in longer than the others.

Helen listened for a while as Barry and David chatted about cars, and Harley Davidsons, and the local shortage of water. She watched Tom watering Barry's scrappy garden with a long, faded garden hose. He had been briefed about the journey that day and seemed glad to be getting back in the air.

Soon she and Jack started talking about having a real holiday, perhaps in Greece.

Jack and Antony went off to start thinking about how to build an appropriate crate.

As she sat on the verandah, waiting for the end of the phone calls, the discussions, the anxieties, the plans, Helen's eyes closed for a few moment while she reflected on the excitement and the anguish of the last few days. She came to when David spoke. He had taken Jack's chair next to her.

'I've been thinking,' he said. 'about my uncle's uncle, anxiously and patiently telling a small boy the stories of which he was to become the guardian for the Arundijilaba. Me. And I was thinking about my father, who wasted his life and his responsibilities by drinking too much.'

Helen said nothing. She understood that what David wanted was just this: for her to listen as he told another story.

'I didn't think about my mother much; but she was a kind of vague presence in my thoughts, as she has been in my life. I was very young when she packed me off to live with my uncle in Perth and start getting an education. Visits home during the holidays usually began with her tears of welcome and ended with more tears when I went back.

'By the time I started teacher training, she was dead of breast cancer. My uncle died a month later.'

Helen nodded. David looked at her; looked away again.

'The Arundijilaba were a special kind of family. I told you that. But by the time I was born, there were few of them left and almost none of them except the oldest men spoke their own language. It was not the coming of the British that destroyed the Arundijilaba; they never came to this part of the land and the opportunities their society offered for work, for money – and drink – were not much talked about up here. It was other tribes that finished the Arundijilaba. Some stories tell about jealousy, of greed. No special people are without enemies. They took Arundijilaba women for wives and taught them their languages and their ways. The young men of the tribe were encouraged to join with others, strangers, and move away to easier country despite the ownership links between the country and the Arundijilaba right here.'

He sat in silence for a while. Helen heard with him the distant birdsong, the rustle of dry and thirsty leaves, the empty invitation of the country.

'I am Arundijilaba,' David said, his voice quiet. 'This is my land and I am of this land.

'I've been thinking about the white man who brought his religion to the Arundijilaba and somehow added his prayers, his knowledge of God, to the old knowledge. And not without getting something in return; the ways of his grandfather's grandfather played an important part in the way his church decided to run its affairs. Now they run it in imitation of my grandfather's grandfather's way!'

David smiled. He took out a cigarette and lit it, drawing deeply on the smoke which scented the air.

'The odour of sanctity, eh? You know what, Helen, if this man, this priest, was anybody's saint, anybody's special man, he was the Arundijilaba's saint, our special man. He brought a new Dreamtime into the tribe, he was the man for whose presence the tribe was made "special" by the Great Lizard. Well, that's what I reckon.'

He tossed the cigarette away, and walked down the verandah steps to tread on the glowing butt, extinguishing it.

Lunch was a pleasant hour, filled with laughter and comradeship. Even the bishop was cheerful and full of bonhomie.

The problems were over now; resolution had been reached.

Antony said he and Helen must continue to keep an eye on the body until it was time to construct a crate and move the body into it.

'More important than that, my boy,' Aldo said. 'I will maintain vigil. Light candles. Say prayers for you all.'

'Yes, well, as long as you keep the door closed, right?' Antony had to leave it at that.

Barry was delighted that he would continue to play host to a prelate of the Church, at least for a little while longer. And to a possible saint. 'I might even think about going to church again sometime,' he told Helen.

At last the time came for departures. Chip loaded up Tom's plane with his things and Aldo's. Helen was amused to watch Aldo issuing unnecessary instructions on loading the aircraft carefully. He was as usual pompous and now he had a gleam in his eye that suggested to Helen that he was already rehearsing for his moments of glory in the Vatican.

Chip and Teresa exchanged promises to keep in touch. Chip said he would write to let Helen know exactly what was done with the body once it arrived in Rome and Helen said she would let everyone else have copies of Chip's letter.

When Tom rolled the aircraft out onto the strip, Barry looked up from the ute, where he was again tinkering, and waved goodbye to the bishop and Chip. Jack remarked to Helen that Barry was the least disturbed of them all by the 'goings-on'; maybe being a Catholic meant that he accepted the presence of a saint – if the body were that of a saint – more easily than the rest of them.

'You know what, Helen?' Antony said when Tom's plane was finally out of sight. 'I'm actually looking forward to getting back to Adelaide – to the halls of academe.' She knew what he meant – the quiet life.

Meanwhile, they could chat about scientific things; safe, scientific, provable things. How agreeable that will be, she thought.

She went over to the cooling shed, a little reluctantly, later that morning. She felt an urge to see again the face which had awed her with its indifference to death. She wanted to reassure herself that it was the face of a man, not the face of a myth. Because he had the key, Antony went with her. She sensed his reluctance, too, but thought it was probably because Antony was not so sanguine about giving up the opportunity for fame and peer approbation. Maybe she was wrong, she thought; maybe I'm doing him an injustice. When he opened the door, Helen immediately noticed that the sweet smell had dissipated. The peat on the boning table was disturbed, she could see that as soon as they stepped inside. With rising panic, Antony and Helen rushed to the table. The body was gone.

CHAPTER 15

Western Australia, 1553

IT TOOK MOST OF THE RELENTLESSLY HOT MORNING for John Craven to reach the cave. He rested briefly in the lee side of a boulder and watched the shadows move across the red and stony ground as the sun rose higher in the cloudless sky. He must reach shelter, or he would die.

His shoes, too thin for this country, had been scraped from his feet. There was blood on his hands. He prayed for strength to reach the cave.

When it was still dark, he had come to this corner of the world with Wurrla, the grandson of the grandfather of the Arundijilaba. He climbed part of the way up the hill, carelessly caught the skirt of his robe on a stone, and fell. He landed awkwardly, the bulk of his body landing on top of his left leg which was see-sawed across a sharp rock. The bone was broken, no doubt of that. Wurrla had set off back to the sleeping place, to get help.

They would come soon, before the sun had moved much further across the sky, speaking too quickly for John to understand their words. They would smile and touch him with healing hands and carry him back. His leg would be straightened, held fast by sticks and twine, as he had shown them, and coated with thick mud and feathers plucked from netted birds. The leg would heal.

The red kangaroo he and Wurrla had followed sat back on its haunches a few metres away. John glanced at the animal as he dragged himself up the hill. As tall as John, the kangaroo was curious, but it came no closer. While it watched, the animal scratched its chest and its back the way the Arundijilaba's yellow dogs scratched their bellies when the heat made them itch. Soon the kangaroo would leap away, to seek its own shelter from the day's heat.

This was Wurrla's cave. John lived with the Arundijilaba for many months before they gave permission for him to visit the cave and see where the water came from that nurtured the people and kept them alive when the distant waterhole ran dry. Wurrla was the keeper of the cave, and of its secret. No outsider was told about the cave, and no woman knew its whereabouts. Only Wurrla brought precious water to the camp when it was needed. The need was not frequent; the Arundijilaba stayed nearer the other, more accessible, water source and did not often come this far into the desert. The waterhole was a two days' walk from the camp but the water was fresher for being at a distance.

Wurrla and John sometimes visited the cave together; here John taught Wurrla the Church's prayers and talked about God's love for His people.

God be with me now!

John rolled into the mouth of the cave. A stab of pain made him scream. At the sound, the kangaroo sat up abruptly, then turned away, going about its own business of survival. John watched it go. He thanked God for helping him.

Under the robe, John was naked. Still too well clad for this awful climate but the Arundijilaba seemed to be in awe of him because of the black robe. It was useful; a symbol of his power. A sign of his being the bearer of new ideas. Of caring for their souls.

But here, in the cave, the robe was hot, cumbersome. John struggled to unfasten it. He slid first one arm out of the robe, then the other.

Standing up was difficult but at last he put his weight on his sound leg, and leant against the wall of the cave. He folded the sleeves inside the robe, carefully, so that it would make a more comfortable mattress than bare ground. He had slept on harder beds.

He took the book from the reed bag and placed it at his side. When the robe was smooth and flat, on the edge of the blackness, John slowly stretched his body onto it. For a moment he was still, waiting for the waves of pain to recede. Wash me in the blood of the Lamb, he said; Mary, Mother of God, pray for me.

He sank his bare arm into the bog, as deep as he could reach and pulled out enough water on his cupped fingers to suck a little and wipe his face clean. That felt fresher.

Oh God, take my pain and use it to help me through the hours of waiting.

Around John's neck hung the crucifix. As he turned his head, he could feel the sharp prick of the thorn. He wouldn't take the crucifix off, not now or ever. Even the grandfather's grandfather, the oldest of the oldest, had not persuaded him to remove it. John held it tight, the familiar shape and heft bringing calm to his aching body. The broken thorn would be his scourge; no need to whip his body today, to subjugate it to God's will. The pain, the thorn, were whips enough.

There was no blood on his leg, nothing more than scratches. The break would surely mend.

All he had to do now was wait.

He picked up the book, his copy of the York Use. John was glad to have permission to use this order of service for the Mass; one of the five approved Uses. He liked it better than the Sarum Use, which the Church seemed to prefer, because it reminded him of his schooldays in Yorkshire.

His arm felt too heavy to lift the book. There was no need; he knew the Office. Indeed, he also knew the Spiritual Exercises backwards, or so he used to tell his friends in the Society, scandalising the straitlaced Frenchmen.

He recited prayers, his eyes half-closed in dutiful repetition. His voice, quiet though it was, seemed to find an echo in the cave; it was a comfort, as though he had company. It sounded like that at school, when the boys learned the alphabet and tables by rote. Three times three is nine; Blessed art thou among women. Four times three is twelve; Blessed is the fruit of thy womb, Jesus. Many voices as one; so it is in the Society, where we say prayers together, recite the Office together.

John Craven slept. In his dream he saw the small Grammar School in Lidget Green, a bleak hamlet cut into shape by snow and bitter wind in a hollow of the Yorkshire moors. He could hear the grouse calling their doleful cry; the clatter of pheasant started from their nests on the ground by the rushing feet and shouts of small boys.

He could hear his groans as the pain in the broken leg seized him again.

School. Seven years old and at the start of the long journey, as his father called it, to manhood. Learn all you can, my son, his father had said, and you can reach the highest position in the land.

The *trivium*; grammar, rhetoric, dialectic. Not hard to learn.

And then the *quadrivium*; geometry, arithmetic, music, astronomy.

There was Latin now, and the art of composition in both prose and verse, a smattering of ancient history, geography. There was trouble for any boy who failed to keep up. Quite right, too, the man told the boy in his sleep: a flogging is good for the soul. The Church says so. The scourge of pain took his breath for a moment.

The priest slept for a few minutes, then woke, his mind full of his childhood. As the pain bit, he thought about the flagellation which he inflicted on himself every day for the good of his soul. Had it all been a waste, or did God have something still in mind for him? He should never question God's will. The Pilgrim spoke most severely about such presumption but lying here, in a cave in a strange country, it seemed that the future was bleak indeed. Until he died and joined those others in Heaven. Soon, he thought, soon, as the pain swept over him as he moved.

Sleep took him again, back to his uncle's house in Cawood, just out of York. There, at the age of fourteen, John had been told that the former Archbishop of York, now a Cardinal and the King's chief minister and Lord Chancellor of England, had agreed to help John, whose dead parents had once served the Cardinal, to find a place in his own old College, Magdalen, at Cambridge. The boy was to start his studies there next month.

'You must take full advantage of this kindness, John. He will expect much of you. No doubt you still intend to be a priest? Good, you were always a pious lad; the Archbishop – the Cardinal – is a kindly and wise man as well as a powerful one. He will see that you get on in the world.'

And so he had. Cardinal Wolsey was himself a man who had risen from humble origins and enjoyed using his power to help likely young men along.

When he was eighteen, John Craven had his degree in Divinity and wrote to the cardinal in the hope of employment as chaplain or secretary. Or perhaps, he said, there was a rector's position he could take? He knew he would have no obligation to perform any duties if he were given a parish; indeed, he need never visit the place; a curate would look after all that. Cardinal Wolsey saw no need to set foot in York simply because he had been given the diocese; he had never been to his house in Cawood. But the revenues of the diocese went to Wolsey; the revenues from a parish went to the rector.

Yes, given preferment by a powerful man, such as Wolsey, John Craven could hope to become a bishop himself before he was forty.

As it happened, the cardinal had another idea. And it was all to do with politics. John had no interest in politics; it always seemed to him that they got in the way of good government.

Nothing could be better governed than the Society of Jesus and that was largely because Ignatius Loyola was the General for life and brooked no politicking. Jesuits were ambitious for God, not for themselves.

The Archbishop sent a messenger to bring John from York to his Palace at Hampton Court.

As the messenger, Wilkin, and he travelled along the Great North Road, Wilkin enlightened the innocent John Craven about many aspects of life outside the Church and the university. Because he worked for the Cardinal, and had done so since His Eminence was a mere Archbishop, Wilkin's concept of the hierarchy was very different from John's, who thought a Bishop was a very exalted personage. He told many stories about life at a Bishop's palace, designed to amuse John Craven, who found them not at all funny.

Because he rode for a living up and down the few roads the country boasted, and carried messages between important people, Wilkin knew – or seemed to know – a great deal about the way the battle for people's souls was going. And much else.

John moved slightly as he remembered the stiffness in his back after a ride of thirty miles on the last day, the seventh he and the Cardinal's messenger had spent on horseback. The movement sent a wave of pain through his thigh and the sweat started to run on his forehead. Hail Mary, full of grace; the Lord is with thee. Blessed art thou...

According to Wilkin, the King was still trying to persuade His Holiness the Pope to let him divorce the Queen, Catherine of Aragon. Wilkin shook his head as he told the story. He thought it unlikely that the King, even with Cardinal Wolsey's help, would persuade the Pope, who didn't like it when Catholic princes stepped out of line.

He's a good King, of course, said Wilkin, judiciously. I mean, he's very popular.

John remembered how he had smiled at the messenger's presumption. It was true, though. King Henry was much admired at the university; he had brought scholars to England – Erasmus, Vives – and artists who had new and wonderful skills. The King had invited painters to come to England; they were soon showing their work to the nobility and offering to make pictures of them and their families. There were no paintings in the Great Hall of the Cardinal's house in York, only tapestries, but a Dutchman had painted a splendid likeness of John's uncle, which John liked better than any tapestry.

'He's quite an athlete, our King Harry.' Wilkin reined in his horse for a rest. 'You know of course that he rides in the tourneys? His jousting is the best in the land! What a man; what a King.'

'He goes to Mass five times a day,' John said.

'He does that, but he plays cards and gambles on them every night. He plays the lute and writes music – '

'For the church, I know.'

'And he can eat like a horse – or like me, for I'm very hungry. Shall we spend the night at this inn or try to ride into London?'

John wanted to reach Hampton Court Palace as soon as possible, so the two men, tired and dusty, rode as quickly as their weary horses would carry them. They reached the walls of London just as it grew dark. They rode through Bishopsgate and soon they were on their way to Hampton Court.

The heat in the cave was rising now. John stretched his arm and sought for water in the bog; it seemed further away this time, deeper.

The Palace was magnificent, as John's uncle had told him it was. The Cardinal had recently been persuaded to give the Palace to the King but he retained the right to occupy a magnificent suite of rooms. It was a vast building, with so many anterooms before he reached the room where the Cardinal awaited him that John feared getting lost, even though a footman accompanied him on the first part of the quick walk through the Palace. Twice a secretary joined them and twice the footman gave way to another.

At last John was in the presence of the Cardinal, and fell to his knees to kiss his ring. He was afraid that he would have fallen to his knees anyway, the journey had been so trying.

The extended hand was used to help John to his feet and Wolsey looked closely at the face of his new protégé.

'You have just arrived from Cawood, John?'

'Yes, Eminence. My uncle sends you greetings – and his thanks.'

'Yes, yes. You need rest, I think. And a bath. Are you hungry?'

'I need all of that, Eminence.'

The Cardinal laughed. He turned his head a little, with a quizzical look at John.

'Go and refresh yourself, then. We shall talk later.'

Another footman took John to his quarters. It seemed to the tired young priest as though he walked another thirty miles to reach them. He bathed; food and drink were brought to him, and a fresh set of clothes.

When he was brought again into the presence of Cardinal Wolsey, two days had passed.

John Craven was eager to hear what service he could perform for this powerful man. Would he be offered work in the Cardinal's household? He hoped so.

The Cardinal asked John if he spoke French and was not pleased that he spoke only English and Latin. Still, they would suffice.

It had been decided that John was to be sent, as a personal envoy, to Paris. He would continue his studies, which had already been arranged with the University, and he would write to the Cardinal in confidence about matters of interest to him. Were the students political? Was religion much talked about? Were the Protestants making ground and were there any English exiles fomenting trouble?

John was disappointed to be offered so dull a mission but he accepted the role, as he saw it, of a spy, with good grace. And University life had a strong appeal.

Paris was an exciting city, different from Cambridge but making just as many demands of an earnest student. He was soon engrossed in study and made sure to write interesting letters back to the Cardinal, even though their contents seemed innocuous. He doubted if the Cardinal read his letters, for they certainly lacked substance.

A year after John was sent to France, Cardinal Wolsey was charged with offences against the King and ordered to remove himself to his diocese in the North of England. His power at Court gone, Wolsey relied even more on the letters, the intelligence, sent to him by his agents in Europe.

In exile, Wolsey was seized again by the wish to build a huge mansion, and the King took this as an indication of continuing ambition. Wolsey was arrested and died on his way to London for trial.

There was no interruption to John's work, as the Bishop of London, Edmund Bonner, took over the Cardinal's interest in the letters home.

John Craven received one letter from the Bishop, in which he was told that he must continue the work. The Bishop said that he had been with Wolsey when the latter was arrested and that it was he who told the King, personally, about the last terrible days of Wolsey's life. Now Bonner had become a confidant of King Henry.

After five years, John Craven was still at the University, tutoring. Twice each year he made the long journey home, and longed for the day he would return for good. Then came the news which changed his life.

King Henry, tired after six years of waiting for the Pope to assist him in his marriage woes, had married his mistress, Anne Boleyn and repudiated the Papal supremacy over the Church of England. Bishop Bonner was sent to Rome to inform the Pope that nobody was going to tell the King of England what he may or may not do!

England's link with the Pope was terminated in 1533: John was 23 years old. At last the letters could stop.

But it was not safe for John to go home.

Two years later, John Craven joined a group of six priests from the University who had taken vows with their leader, Ignatius Loyola, a Spanish Basque, and formed a new religious Society, The Society of Jesus.

In 1537, the news from England was bad; Bishop Fisher, Sir Thomas More (whom John remembered as the scourge of Catholics in his day) and a group of Carthusian monks were executed for refusing to acknowledge Henry as the head of the church.

Anne Boleyn was executed and Henry married Jane Seymour. The King was still popular; an English priest John knew said that King Henry only persecuted unpopular minorities; he never challenged powerful and well-liked groups. Catholic or Protestant, Henry did away with assertive minorities.

The West Australian sun pushed the shadows deeper into the cave. John stirred slightly when the book fell from his fingers. He was beginning to feel cooler now. Perhaps the night would be cool enough for dreamless sleep.

By 1540, most of John Craven's brother Jesuits knew that they would soon start their work as missionaries. Francis Xavier would be the first to go; the General would undoubtedly miss him the most. Now it was John's day to go, to be sent away from Rome.

It had been a strange last meeting with the General. Ignatius Loyola was a strong man, a man with high ideals and a very disciplined sense of his own power. He had pledged obedience to the Pope personally; it was clear that John's mission was not of the General's choosing.

His Holiness the Pope was interested in the world beyond the familiar. His emissaries moved among princes, indeed were princes themselves. Church officials travelled with as much pomp as did the princes, and rightly so. The Pope, tired by endless squabbling and worse, had decided to take more notice of countries other than those which were at war with each other, or with the Church. Did he not represent God everywhere?

It was His Holiness's whim – remembering the word Ignatius had used, John smiled a little; two stiff-necked people must have argued for a while about the work John was to be sent to do.

The Pope had decided to send one of his Jesuits on a voyage. There was a Portuguese sailor who believed he had found an unknown land in the south; his maps were very persuasive. A Jesuit missionary was to go there, with the aid of the Portuguese, and see for himself. If there were such a land, and it had people, then it would be the Jesuit's mission to bring them to Christ.

Further, the Pope wanted Ignatius Loyola to require letters to be sent from this new land, describing what was found and what was accomplished. 'Our beloved brother in Christ, the late Cardinal Wolsey, told us about Father Craven, and what a good correspondent he had been.'

So Father Craven was to be sent to Portugal and thence to discover this new land.

Because the young priest was English, his work had to be kept secret. The English king was already planning to send ships around the world, looking for places to conquer, doubtless jealous of the success of the Portuguese Vasco da Gama and Magellan. If a new world were to be found, then a priest would conquer it for God, but if it were known that he was English that wretch King Henry of England would claim the place for himself.

Three days later, in the company of the other Jesuits, John Craven knelt to kiss the Pope's ring and was given the crucifix which he would wear until his death and beyond.

Captain de Mendoza, who had made the voyage before, happily accepted Father Craven as a travelling priest who would say Mass for him and his crew on the three caravels he was taking south.

When they reached the southern country, after a long and arduous voyage, Mendoza set about his task of making maps of the coastline. Father Craven said he would go ashore and try to make contact with the people they had seen watching them from among the mangroves. The Portuguese had encountered them before and found the people friendly enough.

John Craven thanked the Captain, gathered up his few possessions – clothes, a box of paper with ink and quills and a powder horn.

The crew put together a supply of food for him; and he left the ship. He took no weapons, saying that his crucifix would defend him.

That had been ten years ago now. Ten long years.

Sleep seemed to promise relief; John wished he could decide whether to allow himself the sleep he seemed to crave or whether he should pray more. He asked God to accept his intention of prayers as though they had been said.

The people he met were the Arundijilaba. They were curious about him and, as they were naked, they at first believed that his robe was part of his skin. Fur, perhaps. He soon realised that he needed its protection from the sun and took it off only when he was safe from the eyes of the Arundijilaba.

From the first month, John had written letters which he sent back to the General.

When his ink ran dry, Wurrla made a dye for him from leaves and berries, which ran as freely as ink and kept its colour as he wrote. When the paper ran out, Wurrla found someone who pounded retted leaves until a kind of crude paper was formed. The letters reflected the interests John had observed on Cardinal Wolsey's behalf: what people talked about, politics, religion.

There was much to report as John learned their language: the Arundijilaba talked about water, food, the spiritual needs of the people and their relationship with the land.

Because of his experience in the Society, and what he knew of politics in England, John Craven wrote about the way the Arundijilaba were organised, how decisions were made after long discussions but once the decisions were made, by the grandfather of the grandfather, then no man questioned them. This was obedience and John, a Jesuit, understood the power of obedience.

His letters were long and full of admiration.

Mendoza had many contacts around the southern land. Fishermen who traded with him were not infrequent visitors to the sea just north of where John had landed. Every few months the Arundijilaba watched out for the fishermen and John would hurry down to the beach to give them a letter to take back to Java. Sometimes there was a box for him; a new robe, shoes, books.

From Java, his letter was sent on its way with other traders until, some months later, it reached Rome.

Ignatius Loyola took delivery of John Craven's letters and handed them personally to the Pope. Ignatius always asked the Pope if the news in it justified Father Craven's stay in such a remote and seemingly little populated land and the Pope always said it was more than justified and would the General care for more wine.

The Pope judged it politic to return the letters to the Society for safekeeping once he had read them. Interesting, in a way. The young priest had a good sense of political niceties. Should go far. If the situation in England improved, which God willing it soon would, then Father Craven could be a useful man to send there. He would keep his name in mind.

Night came swiftly in the cave. John Craven slept fitfully, worried by dreams and the mocking laughter which seemed to fill them. By morning, he knew that his strength was waning.

John's thoughts went back to the Spiritual Exercises, devised by Ignatius as rigorous training for men going into danger. The Exercises had taught him to expect death, were he to go back to England. They taught him to contemplate martyrdom, to live in his imagination through the humiliations, the agonies of being arrested, tried for treason, tortured on the rack, executed by fire or decapitation, first having his entrails cut out of his living body. In time, the Exercises made death lose its horror, and a traitor's death could even be contemplated as the glorious way to martyrdom. To die for one's faith was the best possible death.

As he reached the end of the Exercises, he recited prayers until his voice ran out and then thought the rest of the words.

Amen; so be it. With a sigh, as his heart stopped, John Craven, SJ rolled over into the bog.

When Wurrla came to find his friend, he went into the cave alone, as custom required. He saw the body, already settling lower into the bog than when John had fallen in. Wurrla picked up the robe and laid it on the peat. With great care, he lifted John's body and placed it on the robe. The crucifix glittered in the sunlight. Wurrla thought about taking it away with him but remembered how John would never take it off. Wurrla touched it again, tracing the shape of the cross with his fingers.

He stepped back. Soon the body would sink out of sight. A good place to lie. The cave would be left unused now. The Arundijilaba would have to rely on the waterhole, or find another.

Wurrla picked up the book, as he had picked up the torn shoes outside, and took them home with him; relics of a friendship which had puzzled him. On the way back he started to recite again the words the priest had taught him; words that would make a difference, would lead him to the Dreamtime. That had been John's promise. The other men joined in, repeating the words which Wurrla had put into their own language.

The Great Lizard would take care of their friend now. He hoped he would see John Craven again.

CHAPTER 16

THE BODY WAS GONE.

'Oh my God!' Antony spun around, as though hoping to see the body somewhere else in the shed.

'It can't have – I don't believe this, Antony. Tell me it's all right; tell me what's happened.' Helen was shaking.

'I don't know. There has to be an explanation; a logical explanation.' Antony visibly struggled to gather his wits. Helen watched him slow himself down. 'One thing I'm sure of, Helen. This isn't some kind of resurrection.'

'It's been three days.'

'Even so.' His smile was thin but it had the effect intended: Helen calmed down too.

'It didn't weigh much. Did somebody take it away?' She could think of nobody who would do that. They had all agreed to return the body to Rome; who would do anything so foolish?

The steel door opened. David stood in the doorway, holding the door open. There was no longer a need to be concerned about maintaining the low temperature in the shed. As she looked at him, Helen knew the answer to the missing body was here.

'You took him?' Her voice was gentle.

'Yes, I took him.'

'For Heaven's sake, man, why?' Antony was not so gentle. He grabbed David's arms and seemed about to shove him back against the steel door.

'I'll tell you why, if you'll let go.' Antony dropped his hands, and looked embarrassed.

'David?' Helen watched David, who took a deep breath.

'It seemed to me – well, this man – ' David jerked his thumb in the direction of the desert outside the shed. 'Well, look, he might have been important to your church – '

'Not mine, I assure you.' Antony said it firmly.

'Well, to the Catholics, eh? But what was he to us, to me? This man brought something to my people, right? The Arundijilaba learned something from him just as he learned something from the Arundijilaba. He brought us, this one small group, some of our Dreamtime.'

'It's really quite a wonderful thought, David,' Helen said.

'So I reckon he deserved to be treated like an Arundijilaba, not something to send off like a bloody parcel to Italy.'

'What have you done with him?' Antony said.

David shifted his feet. He stood taller and looked as though he was prepared to be aggressive if necessary. Helen could see that he was not going to yield an inch on this.

'I did what we should have done when we found him.'

'You've put him back in the cave?' Helen was astounded.

'No, not the cave. Too many people know about that place now. I took him and put him somewhere my uncle's uncle showed me. It's a place I can't tell you about; it's sacred. I've buried him.'

Antony took a deep breath.

'He's as much an Arundijilaba as I am,' David said, simply. 'He has been given the full honour of an Arundijilaba burial. I recited those stories over him as I laid him down.'

'The Lord's Prayer.' Helen's voice was no louder than a sigh.

'Well, either way, I reckon it was the best thing to do.'

'I don't know, David. There's going to be a terrible fuss about this.' Antony shook his head but Helen thought he seemed more pleased than worried.

'Look, I don't know why he turned up now, but I reckon if there's a need for him to turn up again in another four hundred years, he'll do it, right?' David was visibly embarrassed by this sentiment and turned abruptly and left the shed. After a few strides, he turned and walked back.

'I was right, you know. I did the right thing. I had the responsibility. My middle name is Wurrla; my grandfather's name. I did what he would have done and he was always right.'

'I'll tell the others. Barry can switch the power off now,' Antony said.

'What shall we say? We have to contact Teresa and Chip, too. And quickly! Oh goodness, it's getting complicated again.' Helen bit her lip, suddenly very anxious.

'We'll tell them the body was corrupting; we had to – dispose of it. Right?' Antony spoke firmly, so firmly that Helen had to agree. David just nodded.

'And they'll have the crucifix. Teresa can say that's all we found. Chip won't want to be in any trouble about things; he'll go along with that.'

Antony and Helen exchanged a long questioning look. It seemed a good enough way to end the adventure to them.

She chose not to mention the priest's finger, wrapped in tissues, which she had retrieved in the cooling shed.

It was now in her pocket.